BASSINGTON

CONFIRMED BACHELORS BOOK 2

JENNY HAMBLY

DEDICATION

To Charlie,
Thank you for being my muse and the model for my cover!

CHAPTER 1

Lady Selena dismissed her maid and glanced in the mirror. She grimaced as her eyes swept over her dress of French figured gauze, worn over a slip of white satin. Wreaths of lilac decorated the deep flounce of blond lace, and the flowers were also blended into her chestnut curls. She took no pleasure in the pretty picture she presented. How could she enjoy something so frivolous when she yearned for news of Charles? She had received a letter from him only yesterday, but it had been sent five days earlier and she knew much had happened since then.

She opened her reticule and withdrew the missive. She smoothed out the creases before allowing her fingertips to trail over the loopy scrawl. There was no need for her to read it as she had every word by heart, but she did so anyway.

June 15, Brussels

Dear Selena,

I very much enjoyed your letter. Pass on my congratulations to Miles and Lady Allerdale when you next see them, will you? I told you he was smitten. I am very happy for him but could have wished he had not taken his bride to Brigham for his honeymoon quite so soon. However, if Carteret is watching over you in his stead, you are in very good hands. He would make a fine husband, you know. He is such a sensible fellow and very flush in the pocket. Not that that need weigh with you as fortunately circumstanced as you are, but it would make him acceptable to your father. I am sure you would be more comfortable in your own establishment far away from your dragon of a stepmother and her daughter. I met Albina before I came up to Town and it seemed to me, they were peas out of the same pod. She hardly said a word and seemed very cold.

Selena hastily blinked as a teardrop fell onto the paper, smudging the ink a little. She had been surprised and pleased in equal measure when Charles had asked her to write to him. A small kernel of hope had lodged itself deep within her, that perhaps he was, at last, beginning to regard her in a different light than just that of a little sister. His letter, however, suggested otherwise. He would hardly be encouraging her to marry another if he had discovered feelings of a more romantic nature for her in his heart.

Lord Carteret did indeed seek her out if he was attending the same event and took her for a drive regularly. He *was* sensible and so very gentlemanly that she could not help but like him, but there was a reserve in his manner that did not suggest he loved her. Neither did she wish him to. Her heart had always belonged to Charles. There could be no comparison between Lord Carteret's cool, grey gaze and Charles' warm, laughing blue eyes, just as there was no comparison between a still, wintry morning and a glorious summer's day.

She sighed. She would not feel sorry for herself. Even if Charles only loved her in a brotherly way, it was better than nothing. If only he was safe and well, she would be content. Her eyes scanned the last few lines of his letter.

Most of my time has been taken up with drills. Lord Uxbridge professed himself to be very satisfied with both the appearance and performance of the regiment at the last review. I have come into Brussels to stock up on provisions but must return to camp tonight. The spirits of the regiment are generally good, but I admit I hope things come to a head sooner than later. The weather is unsettled and the food sometimes scarce and of poor quality. However, I return with fresh bread, meat, and wine, so shall make a feast of it tonight. I will raise a glass to you.

Yours affectionately,
Charles

She carefully folded the letter again and slipped it back into her reticule. Although she did not in the least wish to go to Lady Bessinborough's ball, Selena picked up her shawl and made her way downstairs.

It seemed Charles had got his wish. For the last few days, there had been a ferment of confusion and debate as to what had happened across the channel, but one thing seemed certain; the battle between Wellington's and Napoleon's forces had commenced. Various rumours were circulating, some suggesting almost certain defeat, others claiming victory, but as no official communication had yet been received, all was conjecture. There was a general expectation that the much-anticipated despatch would arrive at any moment, however, and it was only the hope of receiving some news that tempted Selena out that evening.

As she came down the last flight of stairs, a querulous voice reached her ears.

"Hurry up, Selena," Lady Sheringham said. "Most girls in your position would be eager to attend a ball in Grosvenor Square, but you are always dragging your heels. It is extremely tiresome. We will be going home in another week and so you must make the most of what little time you have left."

"Yes, of course," Selena murmured, following her step-mama out of the door.

"Those gentle tones do not fool me any longer, Selena," Lady Sheringham said sharply once they were settled in the carriage. "You pretend to be meek and obliging, yet nothing I say to you seems to have the least effect. I do not understand why you are such a stubborn creature."

"I believe it is my nature," Selena said, a small smile edging her lips.

"Selena," Lady Sheringham said in exasperated tones. "I have spent a great deal of time and energy escorting you to numerous society parties, and you have had every opportunity to attach an eligible young man, yet to my knowledge, you have not received a single offer. Not even the fortune hunters have approached me."

"Perhaps they did not dare," Selena said dryly.

Lady Sheringham bristled with disapproval. "I was pleased when Lord Allerdale and his bride took you under their wing a little, but I see now that it was no very good thing. Your confidence may well have grown, but so it seems, has your insolence."

Selena sighed. It was a pity that humour was not one of Lady Sheringham's strengths.

"It was not my intention to be insolent," she said quietly. "And I told you and Papa at the outset that I did not wish to come to Town."

"Yes, that is all very well, but you are nearing twenty and it will be Albina's turn to make her come out next year. Do not expect a second season. It seems that Lord Carteret is the only gentleman who frequently seeks you out. I suggest you make a push to bring him to the point."

"Oh, no," she murmured. "I would not know how to go about it even if I wished to. Besides, we are merely friends. Charles asked Lord Allerdale to watch over me, and then when he went away, he asked Lord Carteret to do so."

"Really?" Lady Sheringham raised two haughty brows. "I think it very impertinent of Captain Bassington. Why he thought you needed someone other than myself to watch over you, I can't imagine. But let me tell you this, Selena, there is no such thing as friendship between men and women. Such a notion is preposterous! What have they in common?"

"Charles is my friend," she said softly.

"Oh, so that is it. I suspected as much when I saw the way you looked at him at Lady Brigham's ball. Well, I'm sorry, Selena, but he won't do. He is a younger son, and military men, unless they rise to the very highest ranks, have barely enough to feed themselves never mind anyone else. The disparity in your fortunes makes the match impossible. Besides, there is every likelihood that he won't come back at all."

Selena was used to her step-mama being plain spoken but this last comment took her breath away. The worry that had been gnawing at her for days turned from a constant dull ache to a sudden bubbling anger.

"I have no expectation of ever marrying Charles, but if he loved me, I would marry him in a heartbeat. Even if I were penniless, I would marry him." She leant forwards, her hazel eyes alight with a rare passion. "And he will come back!"

She slumped backwards and breathed deeply, trying to slow the rapid beating of her heart.

Lady Sheringham's hands tightened on her lap, but she said more gently, "I hope that he will. I am sorry that you have lost your heart to one who is neither suitable nor available to you, but you must not let it blind you to the admirable qualities of other gentlemen of your acquaintance. I would not wish you to form an alliance with someone you could not admire, but if you like and respect Lord Carteret, if he is as you say, a friend, then I think you should consider carefully before dismissing him as a suitor." She dropped her eyes and smoothed a crease from her gown. "You must marry someone, Selena, and there is a gentleness about him that suggests he would treat you kindly. I think your papa would approve of him."

There was a note of sincerity in these last words, and the last wisps of Selena's anger dissipated.

"Perhaps, I don't know," she said in some confusion. "I cannot think of anything until I know that Charles is safe."

"Then I hope that we will have news of him very soon."

By the time they had reached the head of the line waiting to be greeted by Lady Bessinborough, she had recovered her equanimity if not her spirits.

She went through the motions of dancing with any gentleman who requested the pleasure, but although she was no longer as shy as she had once been, her mind was too preoccupied to allow her more than the most mechanical of replies to their attempts to engage her in conversation.

She relaxed a little when she saw Lord Carteret approaching but felt a flutter of apprehension when she realised the next dance was to be a waltz. It appeared that Lord Carteret had observed her habits more closely than she realised, however, for when he reached her, he offered her a gentle smile and said, "I know that you do not like to waltz, Lady Selena, so perhaps you will oblige me by taking a turn about the room with me."

"Yes, thank you," she murmured, accepting the arm he offered her.

As they made their way around the periphery of the hot, stuffy ballroom, her ears strained to catch any snippets of news. She gasped and trembled a little as she heard a deep, booming voice say, "There can be no doubt about it. If we had the victory, why has Wellington taken so long to inform us of it? No, we must have suffered a heavy defeat."

"Do not believe everything you hear," Lord Carteret said softly.

Selena's eyes flew to his, and his calm, cool expression soothed her lacerated nerves. "I try not to. I have received a letter from Charles, and it took five days to reach me, after all. But I would have thought that a despatch from Wellington would have been granted a much higher priority, wouldn't you?"

"Undoubtedly," Lord Carteret agreed. "But even

if he has sent his most trustworthy aide with the news, many circumstances may have delayed him; the state of the roads, a lack of wind, illness, a buckled carriage wheel—"

"Yes, of course," she said quickly, a grateful smile curving her lips. "Thank you. Charles mentioned how sensible you were in his letter, and he is right."

Lord Carteret raised a brow. "He means I am dull, no doubt."

"Oh, no," Selena said, colour rushing into her cheeks. "He only meant to reassure me."

He quirked a brow. "And did he?"

"He had no need to do so," Selena assured him. "I have greatly appreciated your support, although I thought it a little unfair of Lord Allerdale to have asked you to watch over me."

"I would not have accepted the task if I had not wished to, Lady Selena."

She sent him an uncertain glance, unsure if this was an attempt at gallantry or not.

"And what else did Charles have to say?"

As she could hardly tell him that he had suggested that Lord Carteret would make a good husband, she said, "Oh, just that Lord Uxbridge had been pleased with his regiment and that he hoped that the battle would soon commence as conditions were not very comfortable."

"I am sure they are not," he said. "You are worried for him, but he has the devil's own luck, you know. Try not to tease yourself too much."

"If only we had some news," she said, blinking rapidly to dispel the tears that threatened.

"Come, you are hot and a little overwrought,"

Lord Carteret said, leading her towards one of the windows that looked over the square. "Let us brave the censure of all by opening a window."

As he thrust it up, the faint sound of cheering reached them. They looked at each other and then leaned out, breathing deeply of the cool, evening air. The cheers grew louder, and as they penetrated the room, other windows were opened by those close enough to hear.

Selena's eyes widened as a mob of people ran into the square. A post-chaise and four followed them, its progress hindered by the crowd that surrounded it. Two French eagle standards protruded from the carriage windows. It pulled up and a figure jumped down. He wore a military uniform that was far from pristine, the bright red of his coat being dulled by what appeared to be dried mud. He waved at the crowd before shaking hands with a group of gentlemen who were standing outside a residence a few doors down. These gentlemen quickly disappeared inside, and the cheers outside were suddenly replicated in the ballroom.

Lord Carteret eased Selena through the crowd that was now gathering about the windows, allowing others to take their place.

"It seems we have won," he said, a slow smile dawning. "That was Major Henry Percy, Wellington's aide-de-camp. He has gone into Lord Harrowby's residence. I believe Lords Liverpool and Bathurst are dining there this evening, as is Lord Brigham. I shall visit Lord Brigham in the morning and bring you any news he may have. It is not beyond the realms of possibility that he might have some word of Charles."

Only the presence of so many people prevented Selena from grasping his hands in gratitude. She did briefly squeeze his arm, however, and returned his smile.

"Thank you. You are so kind, so good."

"Nonsense," he said. "Remember Charles is also a friend of mine."

"Yes, of course," Selena said. "Lord Allerdale told me of some of the scrapes he and Charles found themselves in when they were younger. I believe you helped them out of more than one."

"I may have occasionally used my powers of persuasion to defuse an awkward situation, that is all," he said with a wry smile.

The ball came to an early close as so many guests hurried away to see what more they could discover, to inform their families of this latest development, or to celebrate in less refined surroundings. Selena was glad of it, although she did feel rather sorry for Lady Bess-inborough. She must have expended a great deal of time and money on her ball and now was left with only a handful of people to enjoy her lavish supper.

Lady Sheringham did not have a paper delivered, and so the following morning, quite unable to wait for Lord Carteret's arrival, Selena sent a footman to find one. He brought her an extraordinary edition of The Gazette. It brought her little comfort, for although the contents of the despatch were recorded and victory confirmed, one phrase outweighed all others for her: *our loss was great.*

Lady Sheringham found her seated in the drawing room, her gaze far away, the paper open on the table in front of her.

"Have you discovered anything of Captain Bassington?"

Selena shook her head. "No, only that there have been many casualties."

"I expect there have, but it will do you no good to sit there fretting," she said brusquely. "Come along, we have shopping to do. I wish to ensure that Albina has everything she will need for her come out next season before we return to Sheringham Court."

"I would rather stay at home if you do not mind." As Lady Sheringham's brows drew together, she added hastily, "I am expecting a visit from Lord Carteret. He thought he might be able to discover something of Charles."

"I see," Lady Sheringham said thoughtfully. "You should not receive him alone, but if you leave the door into the hall open and ask your maid to sit with you, I will allow it on this occasion. You see, I am not as heartless as you think."

Selena gave a relieved smile. "Thank you."

She did not think her stepmother heartless precisely, only tactless and lacking in sympathy. It had been an unpleasant surprise when her father had returned from a visit to Harrogate, where his doctor had sent him to take the waters after he had deemed him to be in low spirits, and informed her he was to marry Lady Tate, a widow residing in the spa town. Her mama had only been dead nine months. She had been pretty, gentle, and kind, and the new Lady Sheringham had seemed like a hurricane to her gentle breeze. Forthright, decisive, and determined, she had taken over the running of Sheringham Court without a blink, or it had to be said, any great consideration of how the changes she made might upset Selena.

They had upset her at first. It was true that the curtains in the principal rooms had been a trifle faded, and that some of the chairs had needed recovering, but she had not expected Lady Sheringham to change the colours so dramatically. Her mama had favoured light, floral decorations to combat the darkness of the many wood-panelled walls, but now deep ruby and olive green were the order of the day. Selena had felt as if she was trying to erase all traces of her predecessor.

But her father had found no fault with the changes. When she had told him that she preferred things as they had been before, he had patted her on the shoulder and said gruffly, "We must let her put her mark on the court, Selena, it is her home now. I need a wife and you need someone to guide you and bring you out. It is what my dear Amelia would have wanted. I know that Elizabeth is very different from your mama but give your stepmother and your new sister a chance."

She had done so. She thought Charles had been a little unfair in his assessment of both Albina and her stepmother. Albina was handsome rather than pretty, with a forthright, practical nature like her mother, and although only just turned seventeen, the tone of her mind was serious. They had little in common, but Albina was not unpleasant. And Lady Sheringham was not a dragon. She had suggested that Selena join Albina for her French lessons as she was not as fluent in the tongue as she liked but had done very little else to change her habits. It was only since they had come to Town that the burgeoning relationship between them had become so strained.

She glanced up as Lord Carteret was announced. Although she was desperate to hear if had discovered anything, she tempered her impatience and addressed the butler.

"Thank you, Markle. Would you ask Cardew to come down?"

"Of course, ma'am."

As soon as he had left the room, leaving the door ajar, she smiled at Lord Carteret.

"Please, sit down and tell me what you have discovered, if anything."

The newspaper still lay open on the table, and she hastily closed and folded it.

"You have read the despatch, then?" Lord Carteret said gently.

"Yes," she said, her tone sombre. "It seems our victory was hard won."

As her maid entered the room with some sewing in her hand and seated herself on a chair set against the wall, Lord Carteret gave a small smile.

"Very proper."

"Please," Selena said, observing the grave look in his eyes, "do not leave me in suspense. What news have you of Charles?"

He raised a hand and brushed at a few stray locks of hair that had fallen over his forehead. It was a gesture she had seen him make many times. Every-thing about him was always neat as a pin with the exception of his hair. He made no attempt to arrange it in one of the more fashionable styles but wore it a little long. She tensed as she realised that his habit of brushing aside the wayward locks usually occurred when he was considering something, and at the present moment, that something was how best to convey to her his news. At last, he spoke.

"His regiment performed most bravely. When Major Percy left Brussels, Charles was not numbered amongst the list of those killed in action."

Selena felt prickles of cold perspiration dampen her brow. "Thank heavens!"

"He is, however," Lord Carteret said gently, "amongst those counted as missing."

Selena felt sick as she registered these words. Surely missing suggested that he was either seriously wounded or dead and had not yet been found? Lord Carteret's voice seemed to come from far away.

"Fetch your mistress a glass of water."

She clenched her fists until her neatly trimmed nails bit into her palms, determined not to succumb to the faintness that threatened to overcome her. She would not give in to such weakness. Something must be done. Dead or alive, Charles must be found.

CHAPTER 2

C aptain Charles Bassington struggled to open
heavy eyelids. He was aware of a feeling of
extreme fatigue and after a few moments
decided it was not worth the effort. Instead, he
attempted to marshal thoughts that seemed shrouded
in fog. The annoying and persistent ringing in his ears
would not allow him to, however. He became aware of
a heavy weight pressing on his chest, but when he tried
to lift his arms to discover what was making it so difficult for him to breathe, he discovered they would not
obey his wishes. It seemed he could still frown
however, and he did so as he heard a voice above him.
It spoke in heavily accented French, and Charles could
not make out the words. The vague thought that he
was in considerable danger crossed his mind, although
he could not immediately recollect why this might be
the case. After a moment's struggle, he let the thought
go and once more sank into oblivion.

Although he did not know it, it was three days
before Charles again made the attempt to rouse

15

himself. A violent fit of coughing jolted him from the comfort of his insensibility. His eyes fluttered open and he winced as he felt a stab of pain in his chest. His vision was blurred, and as he saw a figure suddenly loom over him, he tensed. However, this unknown person merely laid a damp cloth across his forehead and bade him good day in a low, soothing voice.

He tried to answer but his throat was so parched that only a strangled sound emerged. His comforter seemed to understand his difficulty for he felt a cup pressed gently to his dry lips. He raised his head slightly and drank greedily.

"Thank you," he murmured, his eyes already closing again.

When next he awoke, he was surprised to find himself covered in blankets for he felt very cold. He was shivering and his breathing was laboured. As he attempted to draw in a deep breath, he again felt a stab of pain in his chest. With shaking hands and a great deal of effort, he managed to push the heavy blankets down a little and lift the neck of the rough nightshirt he wore. He was surprised to discover that his chest showed no sign of serious injury. Only some faint red marks disturbed his skin.

Charles had no recollection of how he came to be here, or indeed, where here was. A glance about the room shed no light on either of these knotty problems, but the rough brickwork of the walls and the single rustic chair that sat by the bed suggested he was in a cottage of some sort. One small, latticed window set high in the wall allowed him a glimpse of blue sky.

His head felt itchy, and the irritation persuaded him to make the supreme effort of lifting a hand to relieve it. His fingers encountered a thick bandage which prevented him from reaching the offending spot. He pressed gently against this obstruction and winced. The flesh beneath felt tender and bruised. He searched his memory for the cause of his injury, but his mind remained stubbornly blank.

His eyes snapped to the door as it opened, but he relaxed, and a faint grin curled his lips as a pretty girl with long, dark hair entered the room.

"Ah," he murmured, "now I understand. I have died and gone to heaven."

He attempted to sit up as she approached but he managed only to lift his head from the pillow. The girl shook her own and hurried to his side. She carried a cup from which steam and a bitter, pungent smell issued. When he looked at it doubtfully, she spoke to him. His French was rather rusty, but he understood that it was to help his fever. He nodded and she slipped her hand beneath his head and helped him raise it again. The potion tasted as disgusting as it smelled, but he was glad of its warmth.

He asked the girl for her name, and she smiled. "Magdalene Bruillet. And yours, monsieur?"

Sleep was already reclaiming him, but as his eyelids slowly shut, he murmured, "Do you know, I haven't a clue."

His fever continued unabated for many days, and he slipped in and out of consciousness. In his rare moments of lucidity, Magdalene would press him to drink something or swallow a few spoonfuls of soup. His breathing remained ragged and was accompanied by a wheezy rattle. On one occasion he awoke to discover a bearded figure standing next to him and his exposed chest covered in leeches. Charles had no very great opinion of leeches and although he knew it to be futile, tried to pull them off. Strong hands clamped about his wrists, and still in the height of his fever, he tried to struggle with the man who proclaimed himself a doctor, but he was unequal to the task. He soon slipped back into a troubled sleep dogged by nightmarish dreams. The battle played itself out again and again in his head, only, instead of routing the French, driving them from the field and giving chase, it was the English and their allies who were forced into a disorganised retreat, the French cutting them down unmercifully with shouts of *Vive l'Empereur.*

After one particularly bad night, he woke to find his covers half flung off. His body ached, and his head throbbed, but he had regained his senses. He remembered everything with more clarity than he could have wished, up until the moment he was thrown from his horse after a fleeing French soldier had turned and shot it.

Magdalene sat in the chair by his bed. She had slumped forwards so that her forearms rested on the mattress and her head lay upon them as if she were sleeping. Charles was dimly aware that she had rarely strayed from his side. He reached out a hand and slowly stroked her hair. She must only have been in a light doze for she suddenly sat up and started talking excitedly.

"Monsieur! Monsieur! Vous êtes en vie! Vous êtes en vie!"

He gave a weak chuckle and agreed that he was certainly alive. His nose wrinkled as he became aware of the stale smell of rank sweat. He stank and his sheets were damp. He told Magdalene as much and requested a bath. She laughed and reached into the pocket of her apron. She passed him a letter, telling him they had found it in his coat, and she hoped it would help him remember who he was, before running from the room.

After a few moments struggle, he managed to sit up. He opened the letter.

June 9, 1815

Dear Charles,

I hope this letter finds you well. You were quite right, Lord Allerdale did like Miss Edgcott. They were married a few days ago in a private ceremony in Berkeley Square. I was fortunate enough to attend the event as Eleanor has become my particular friend. Oh, Charlie, if you could have seen the way they looked at each other, you could not have failed to have been moved. I have never seen two people so much in love. Your mama was quite overcome and even shed a few tears!

He has taken Eleanor to Brigham for their honeymoon, and Lord and Lady Brigham will follow as soon as they hear the outcome of this horrid war. I know that you asked Lord Allerdale to keep an eye out for me and think it was very kind of you to have done so, but it was unnecessary, I assure you. I am not quite so helpless as you appear to think! I must admit, however, that I am glad of it for otherwise I would not have become so well acquainted with him or Eleanor.

Lord Allerdale appears to think me as in need of protection as you and has asked Lord Carteret to watch over me. I did not like it at first, but I have found him to be a very pleasant and easy companion so do not mean to complain.

Lady Bassington has returned home, and I very much hope that we shall soon. I think my step-mama has all but given up hope of me making a great match. It was a stupid idea. You know, I hope, that I have no such grand ambitions.

I miss Papa and am very much looking forward to seeing him again. That is all my news. Please write to me soon, Charlie. I worry for you. There is so much talk and speculation of the coming battle that it could not be otherwise.

Yours affectionately,

Selena

Although he had not needed the letter to remind him of who he was, it had grounded him back in reality, but before he had time to reflect on all that had occurred since he received it, the door opened and Magdalene came in carrying a tin bath. It was too small to lie in so he would need to stand. He only hoped he was capable of it. Magdalene sent him a swift smile and then disappeared, only to return with two buckets of steaming hot water and a large sponge. He grinned at her and asked if she intended to wash him. She giggled and waved the sponge at him.

"Would you like that, monsieur?"

"I think I would be able to bear it," he murmured.

She winked at him and then called, "Come, Grand-mère!"

A wizened matron of uncertain years came through the door, followed by two burly young men. Magdalene laughed again and left the room. Although it was not the scenario he had envisaged, Charles found himself very grateful for the two boys as, when he attempted to stand, his legs buckled. The painful jarring of his knees against the hard floor made him groan. They each took an arm and surprisingly gently, raised him to his feet. Once he was standing in the tub, they pulled his shirt over his head and the matron began to wash him, only giving up her sponge to one of the young men when she could reach no higher.

As they vigorously dried him with rough towels, Magdalene came back into the room, averting her gaze. She efficiently stripped the bed and made it up again with fresh linen. He found himself very grateful to crawl back into it when he had donned a clean nightshirt.

Magdalene presently brought him a bowl of gruel but he found he could not manage more than a few spoons.

"But, sir," she said earnestly, "now the fever is gone, you must build up your strength."

He obediently forced another spoon of the thick sludge down his throat. Magdalene smiled and nodded encouragingly.

He handed the bowl back to her. "I must thank you, Magdalene, for the very great care you have taken of me."

She shook her head and coloured. "Do not thank me," she said earnestly, rising from the chair. "It was the least I could do after Stefan… after Stefan…" Tears started to her eyes. "I am too ashamed to speak of it. I must go. Mayor Panquin wished to be immediately informed if, I mean when, you were better. He will tell you everything, I am certain."

Charles found it far too fatiguing to force his sluggish brain to search for the meaning behind her words and as it turned out, it was not at all necessary for him to do so. He received a visit from the mayor before the hour was out. He was a tall, spare man with a thin, curling moustache and a grave countenance. When he expressed his pleasure that Captain Bassington seemed to be making a recovery, Charles discovered that Monsieur Panquin had a good command of the English language, for which circumstance he found himself grateful. He had many questions to ask, and it would be much quicker and easier if he did not have to force his slow wits to constantly search for the right words.

He discovered that he was near the village of Braine-l'Alleud, which he knew to be no very great distance from where the battle had raged.

"We did win, didn't we?" Charles asked, the remnants of his nightmare not quite having faded from his mind.

"Most certainly," the mayor assured him. "But at a terrible cost to all concerned. I organised teams of men to go and bring back any who were injured the morning after the battle, and even now the church and barns about here are full of wounded men. Most of them French."

"Ah, so that is how I come to be here. How very fortunate I was to be discovered so soon. It was very kind of you to house me apart from men who have cause to resent my presence in their midst."

Monsieur Panquin looked a little uncomfortable. "That is not quite how things were. Most of the inhabitants hereabouts are honourable men, Captain Bassington, but I am afraid that a very few of our number disgraced themselves by going out on the night of the battle with less than honourable intentions."

Charles raised a brow. "Looting?"

"I am afraid so. Stefan Bruillet was amongst them. He is usually a harmless character but is slow-witted and very persuadable. You were discovered beneath another man they had searched. They thought you were dead and completely stripped you of all you wore. Stefan did not understand the seriousness of his actions you understand, so much so that the following morning he dressed himself in your things and paraded himself in front of his family as if it was a very good joke."

"I should be grateful that he left me my teeth, I suppose," Charles said dryly.

The mayor winced. "I am afraid that some scavengers will always flock to the scene of the battle. I assure you, however, that I do not condone such behaviour here. When Madame Bruillet realised what he had done, she made him change and brought him straight to me. Fortunately, he was able to lead us to you. I had no great expectation that you would be alive, but Madame Bruillet was most insistent that we check. I then sent him, and the other two young men involved to join the group of volunteers who have been tasked to clean up the battlefield. Under strict supervision, of course. I think you will find that the experience has been a quite sobering one for them."

"I should think it was," Charles said wearily. "I have never seen so many dead in such a small area in all my years as a soldier."

"Precisely," the mayor agreed. "Madame Bruillet wished her family to make some sort of reparation to you, and so they agreed to take you in and do what they could for you. As they were not entirely sure of the nature of your fever, it was agreed that only Magdalene would tend you. Besides, Madame Bruillet is a poor widow trying to scratch out a living on this small farm and could ill afford to even allow her daughter to attend you. It was only two days ago when Magdalene washed your things, that she found the letter in your inner pocket. Until then, we had no idea who you were. We immediately sent word to Brussels of your whereabouts and your condition at that time as I am sure there are those who will be concerned for you."

"Good God! I expect you have led them to believe I am at death's door!" Charles frowned. "I hope the news will go no further than my regiment."

The mayor shrugged. "I can offer you no information on that head, sir. Are you satisfied with the steps I have taken to punish Stefan Bruillet?"

"Yes, of course. The people hereabouts have suffered enough inconvenience as it is, what with thousands of soldiers trampling their crops, requisitioning their homes, and eating their livestock. Besides, if he is a half-wit, Stefan cannot be held entirely responsible for his actions."

The mayor's visit exhausted him, and he again fell into a sleep rendered fitful by the frequent bouts of coughing which assailed him. Perhaps it was Selena's letter that made him dream of her when she had been a child. There was a particularly old and twisted oak tree in the park of Sheringham Court and Selena stood in front of it, her eyes narrowed as they rested on her brother.

"I shall not go back to my governess, Gregory," she said, her chin jutting forward in a determined manner. "I do not wish to sew or read a fusty book. I wish to climb this tree."

"You'll never do it," her brother said impatiently.

"I wish you would not follow us about like a dashed dog!"

"Watch me!" she said, turning towards the grand tree and setting one small slippered foot on a gnarly protrusion.

"No! Dash it, Selena!" Gregory protested, torn between exasperation and amusement. "You'll break your neck, and I will be blamed for it."

But she had already found a handhold and pulled herself up. She was a skinny little thing, all arms and legs, and Charles watched with a lopsided smile as she scampered up the trunk to the lowest branch. This sturdy bough obligingly swept down towards the ground before curving up again. Not satisfied with this triumph, she carried on up into the leafy canopy until she disappeared from sight and only the rustling of leaves marked her progress.

"You have proved your point, Selena," Charles called up to her. "Come back down, little squirrel!"

"I wish I was a squirrel," she said haltingly. "For I feel a little dizzy when I look down. I had not realised I had come so far."

Charles and Gregory exchanged a look.

"The silly chit has frozen," Gregory said. "I'd best go after her."

"I will go," Charles said. "She's more likely to listen to me."

Gregory suddenly grinned. "Ain't that the truth! I do believe she'd follow you to the ends of the earth, Charlie."

"God forbid!" he said softly.

"If that's how you feel then you shouldn't

encourage her. Nothing but the harshest treatment will put her off, you know."

"It would be like kicking a puppy," Charles protested, beginning to climb.

He found her sitting on a branch, her arms hugging the trunk of the tree. He paused on the bough below her and offered her his hand, but she shook her head.

"I'll fall," she said in a small voice.

Charles regarded her wide eyes and trembling lip and said gently, "Do you think you could hold on to me as tightly as that tree, little squirrel?"

Selena nodded.

"Good girl!" He turned carefully and curled his hands around another branch. "Just put your arms about my neck, and then slip down and wrap your legs about my waist. It's not very ladylike, but I doubt you'll care for that!"

Selena giggled and did as she was bid. Charles descended the tree with her clinging to his back.

"I'm glad to see you looking more cheerful, sir."

Charles opened his eyes to see the doctor leaning over him. He realised he was smiling, but his lips thinned as he observed the jar of leeches in the doctor's hand.

"No," he said firmly.

"But, sir," the man said with a frown, "although your fever has broken, you are far from well. We must draw the poison from your lungs."

"No," he repeated. "What is it that ails me?"

The doctor sighed and contented himself with removing the bandage from Charles' head.

"You suffered a head injury," he murmured,

closely examining the side of his scalp, "but it is almost healed. I think we may leave the bandage off now."

"I was thrown from my horse."

"That you have regained your memory is a good sign, but your head is the least of my worries. You must have been soaked to the skin the night before the battle for there was quite a storm."

"We all were," Charles confirmed.

"Indeed, but then you were stripped of your raiment and lay out all night as naked as the day you were born. We had the devil of a time to get you warm, and then you were struck by fever. You, sir, are suffering from an inflammation of the lungs. I did not think you were going to survive it."

"I'm a hard man to kill," Charles said grinning.

"You are not out of the woods yet," the doctor said grimly. "It will take some time for you to recover, and there is every possibility that you may suffer a relapse if you will not allow me to try and draw out the infection."

"Well, I won't," Charles said stubbornly. "At least, not with those damned leeches. I will, however, swallow any concoction you deem necessary."

The doctor sighed. "That is something, I suppose. I shall make up my own recipe of lemon juice, honey, and syrup of poppies. I believe it will prove beneficial to you."

"It sounds delicious," Charles said cheerfully, glancing at the door as it opened. His eyes widened and he gave a sudden laugh as an immaculately dressed gentlemen strolled into the room.

"Carteret! What on earth are you doing here?"

Lord Carteret offered him the sweet smile that only his intimates were permitted to see.

"I have come to find you, of course. After an unprofitable and deeply unpleasant visit to all the hospitals in Brussels, I was informed you were here. I was told you were at death's door, and I must say, old fellow, you do look rather done in."

"He is still not many steps from it now, sir," complained the doctor. "But he refuses to take my advice."

Lord Carteret raised a brow. "Being difficult, Charles?"

"I am not being difficult. I have offered to drink whatever medicine the doctor sees fit to give me, only I will not have any more leeches suck my blood!"

Lord Carteret glanced at the jar that lay at a drunken angle on the bed. "I do not think that I blame you, Charles."

The doctor tutted, shook his head, and took his leeches and himself away.

"I am delighted to see you, of course," Charles said. "But what on earth made you come all this way?"

"You should rather say, who," Lord Carteret said gently. "Lady Selena was in Town when news of our victory arrived. With it came the less joyous news that you were missing. She became consumed with the idea that someone must search for you. Lord Brigham informed her that there was bound to be a lot of confusion in the immediate aftermath of the battle, but she would not be satisfied. When she avowed that if no one else would look for you, she would, I took the task upon myself. It seems she is quite devoted to you, Charles."

"She has been ever since she was a young girl," Charles said, a fond smile on his lips. "It has become a habit with her. But what a goose! You should not have listened to her!"

"Perhaps not," Lord Carteret said. "But I was at a loose end, and although I could not imagine that she really would come after you herself, I would not have liked to have wagered any money on the chance."

Selena had changed much over the last few years. He had been surprised to discover quite how reserved she had become when he had met her in Town, but it had not taken much effort on his part to draw out the girl he had once known. His dream had reminded him of the intrepid, stubborn little puss she had once been. What had Gregory said? *She'd follow you to the ends of the earth, Charlie.* He chuckled.

"No, neither would I. Have you any news of my regiment, Carteret?"

"They started for Paris soon after the battle."

"Napoleon escaped then?"

"Yes. He fled to Paris but was forced to abdicate."

"Damn it! I wish I could have been there." He spoke so forcefully that he again fell prey to his rattling cough.

"I think it will be some time before you can rejoin your regiment," Lord Carteret said dryly.

"Yes, so the good doctor informed me," Charles admitted.

"In which case, I think it would be better if I took you home, old fellow. I have been given permission to take you to Bassington Hall to recuperate when you are well enough to do so."

Magdalene just then came into the room, a steaming potion in her hand. She dropped a careful curtsy to Lord Carteret before offering Charlie the cup.

"Thank you, Magdalene," he said, gulping it down although it burnt his throat. "Now, fetch my uniform, will you? I'm going home!"

Magdalene looked shocked and turned pleading eyes upon Lord Carteret.

"Do not be so hasty, Charles," he said.

"If I must be ill, I would dashed well rather recover at home. I cannot see that sitting in a carriage will be much more fatiguing than laying here in this bed."

Lord Carteret eyed him thoughtfully. He had been acquainted with Charles for years and knew full well that behind his easy-going exterior lay an obstinate and determined nature. "I will take you nowhere until the doctor has had time to provide me with his potions and instructions on how often to administer them."

Charles sank back against his pillows. "Oh, very well. But I warn you, you will not hold me here long." He smiled ruefully. "I hope you have plenty of blunt, Carteret, for I haven't a penny about me. I dare say the journey will be dashed expensive, and on top of that, I wish to leave the Bruillets a generous sum. Magdalene has taken very good care of me."

He took her hand and kissed it. She clearly had not understood their conversation for she had been looking from one to the other, a confused expression in her eyes. But at this gesture, she smiled.

"You will stay?" she said.

"For today," Charles conceded.

She looked relieved, curtsied, and left the room.

A small smile twisted Lord Carteret's lips. "I see that even at death's door you are still breaking hearts. Of course, I have enough blunt. You should know me well enough, Charles, to know that I would never have left home without considering all outcomes. I would be a fool indeed if I had been run off my legs by the time I found you."

"You are the last man I would call a fool," Charles said. "Which is why I'm surprised you're here! But no one knows better than I how Selena can persuade someone to do her bidding when the mood takes her. I told her you would make a good husband, you know. But, on reflection, I don't think she would do for you, old fellow. Don't be fooled by the shy demeanour she displayed when she was in Town. She's a hoyden when she's on her own turf!"

CHAPTER 3

When Lady Sheringham understood that far from encouraging Lord Carteret, Selena had sent him on what she considered to be a wild goose chase to find Captain Bassington, she stared at her in stupefied amazement. Her incredulity gradually gave way to anger. A dutiful woman who respected her husband's wishes, she was determined to do her best to make him happy and knew that seeing his only daughter creditably established could not fail to do so.

She had not complained when he had informed her that he had no taste for politics or Town or usually made an inspection of his other properties at this time of year. Indeed, she had thought that Selena might prove to be more malleable without his presence and had not doubted her ability to find her a suitable husband. Selena was blessed with a good figure, a pretty face, and a fortune, after all. But it was now entirely clear to her that she had abjectly failed in this endeavour. That she could honestly tell her lord that she had tried her utmost for Selena, offered her little consolation.

"I wash my hands of you, Selena," she finally said. "That Lord Carteret would go on such an expedition merely at your request suggests that he holds you in very high esteem, but that you would make such a request cannot leave him in any doubt of your feelings for Captain Bassington. You have shot yourself in the foot and must take the consequences. We shall leave for Sheringham Court as soon as we are packed."

Travelling in easy stages, it took them nine days to reach Northumberland, Sheringham Court laying some three miles past Alnwick. Lady Sheringham was not one to labour a point, and so she made no more complaint about Selena's actions but maintained a dignified silence only broken by polite requests or occasional observations on the passing landscape. At any other time, her icy civility would have quite sunk Selena's spirits, but she was numb with worry for Charles and quite impervious to the chilly atmosphere that pervaded the carriage.

Her thoughts often strayed to Lord Carteret and she burned to know if he had discovered anything. She did not set much store by her stepmother's assertion that his willingness to search for Charles suggested that he held her in high esteem. Lord Carteret was also fond of Charles, and she had not failed to note the glow of excitement that had sparked in his usually cool eyes at the prospect. She suspected that he had been heartily bored of the round of social gaieties that marked the season, and that the prospect of an adventure had overcome his usual caution.

Charles' letter had finally dispelled her half-formed hopes that he would one day return her regard, at least in the way she wished him to. It had been like waking from a dream and she had been forced to consider her future. She was very fortunate that she was to inherit the fortune her great aunt had left her, but she could not see how it would benefit her. It seemed that fortune or not, marriage was the only way she could live a life away from Sheringham Court at any time in the near future. Did she want to? Did Lord Carteret like her enough to marry her? And if so, would she be a fool to refuse him? She asked herself these questions many times on the journey but always came up with the same answer. It was too soon. She was not so fickle that she could so easily transfer her hopes to another.

Her mood could not help but lift once they approached her home. Moorland and woods gave way to a sheltered valley and fertile farmland. As they passed through the gates of Sheringham Court and she saw the acres of park that had been her playground, a small smile lightened her wan countenance. Her eyes came to rest on an old oak tree that stood in splendid isolation in the middle of the park. She had been but ten years old when she had scaled its impressive heights only to become stuck in the uppermost branches. It had all been to impress Charles, of course. She would have done anything to impress Charles. Her descent from the tree had been far from impressive, however. He may have called her little squirrel, but as he had climbed down, she had clung to his back like a baby monkey to its mother.

A faint sigh escaped her as they turned a bend in the drive and she saw the pale stones of Sheringham

Court. From the front view, it looked modest in size, boasting only two main storeys and the attics, and having only three sets of windows on each side of the entrance porch. This was deceiving, however, as it was not until any visitor approached the gravel sweep in front of the building that one of the two side wings was revealed. A later addition, they were built in a grander style and were substantial.

As the carriage pulled up, it was not Trinklow, their butler, but Lord Sheringham who strode out to meet them, a warm smile of welcome on his lips. Selena threw open the carriage door, leapt down, and ran into his arms. She squeezed him as hard as she could and smiled as she heard his soft chuckle sound above her head.

"I thought you'd have acquired a little Town polish, m'dear," he said, gently putting her from him so he could take a good look at her.

"Whilst I am not as a rule in favour of overt displays of affection," Lady Sheringham said coolly, coming up to them, "if Selena had shown any of the gentlemen she met in Town a fraction of the warmth she has shown you, my lord, we might have brought some welcome news home with us. As it is, she has sent her only potential suitor across the channel to search for Captain Bassington."

Lord Sheringham pinched his daughter's cheek. "I know. Brigham wrote to Lady Bassington to inform her of it. You always were a silly puss where Charles was concerned, Selena. Still, he has run tame here since he was in short coats, so it is not surprising that you would worry for him as if he had been your own brother."

Lady Sheringham snorted and carried on into the house. Seeing her father frown, Selena said quickly, "I have been a sad trial to her, Papa. My step-mama tried very hard to establish me, but I do so hate being around strangers that I was excessively awkward with almost everyone."

She slipped her arm through his and they began to walk slowly towards the house. Lord Sheringham looked down at her, a worried look in his eyes. "I can't understand why you are so shy with strangers, Selena, when you always used to adopt your brother's friends as if they had been your own."

"Yes, but I have known most of them forever. I was not shy with Charles when he came to Town, of course, and through him, I became acquainted with Lord Allerdale and Miss Edgcott, who is now Lady Allerdale. And then I became friends with Lord Carteret."

"Only friends?" Lord Sheringham enquired gently.

"Yes, only friends."

He patted her hand. "Never mind. You will always have a home here, you know that. But I thought you were not happy here anymore and hoped that you might meet someone you could admire and who would make you comfortable. Are you quite sure this Lord Carteret could not do so? Your stepmother wrote to me of him, and Gregory tells me he's a fine fellow."

They paused in the lofty entrance hall. Selena looked up into her father's troubled brown eyes and said, "No, I am not *quite* sure that he could not."

"Selena! Have you been setting the Town by its ears and behaving like the regular hoyden you are?

What's this I hear about you sending poor Carteret off to find Charles?"

She smiled as her handsome brother came bounding down the stairs two at a time, his hazel eyes so like her own, laughing.

"Gregory! I do not behave like a hoyden!" A qualm of conscience made her add, "At least I do not do so anymore."

Gregory, Viscount Perdew, was unimpressed by this outburst. He threw an arm about her shoulders and dropped a kiss on her head. "Perhaps not when you are in strange company, but you have been leading my friends about by the nose for years. Carteret's not the only chap you've got in a regular fix, is he? I haven't forgotten the time you persuaded poor Adolphus Bassington to rescue that kitten from the river only he couldn't swim, and he nearly drowned, whilst the kitten made its way to the bank unaided."

"But, Gregory, I didn't know he couldn't swim!"

"Or the time you begged Ralph Mawsley to let you drive his curricle only because I had refused to teach you and dash it if you didn't drive into a tree and break his arm!"

Selena bit her lip, trying not to laugh. "That was very bad of me," she admitted. "But it was my very first lesson."

"And as for poor Edward, you scarred him for life when he tried to stop you taking my horse for a ride!"

"That is an exaggeration," she protested, "my stirrup caught him above the eye, but you can hardly see the scar anymore! Is Eddy at home?"

"No, brat!" Gregory said. "He has gone on a tour of the West Country with some of his university chums to celebrate his liberation from the hallowed portals of Oxford."

Selena turned back to her papa, who was smiling indulgently at this interchange. "Has Lord Carteret sent any news to Bassington Hall yet?"

"No, there has hardly been time. But don't you go fretting about Charles," he said cheerfully, "I have never known the luck favour a fellow more."

"Lord, yes," agreed Gregory. "If you are going to sit around moping, Selena, I shall have no patience with you. Scores of fellows go missing after a battle, you know. Mostly they have suffered some trifling injury and their names have not been recorded correctly, if at all, and sometimes they have not gone missing, but it is just a clerical error."

Selena was not proof against their combined arguments and began to feel more optimistic. "Yes, of course."

"And I tell you what, Selena," Gregory continued, "I've acquired a new phaeton, and if you promise not to show me a Friday face, I'll let you drive it! Now, you'd best go up and change for I'm famished, and I'll be devilish put out if cook has to put dinner back!"

Selena mounted the stairs in a happier frame of mind than she would have thought possible only an hour before. She found Albina hovering a little uncertainly at the top of the stairs and was surprised to see a hint of shyness in her stepsister's dark eyes.

"Albina, how nice to see you. How happy you must be that your mama has returned."

"Yes, I am of course. But I am also happy to see you, Selena."

The words sounded a little awkward, but there was

an earnest look in Albina's gaze that proved their truth. Selena smiled. "Has it been dreadfully flat?"

"It was at first," she said, looking a little conscious, "but Gregory and your papa have been very kind."

"I am pleased to hear it," Selena said. "But remember he is also your papa now, and Gregory is your brother, so I should hope that he has been kind." Despite her words, she was intrigued. Before she had gone away, her brother had not shown much interest in his new sister. She took Albina's arm. "I see you are already dressed for dinner. Will you come with me whilst I change? I would like to hear all your news."

"Of course," Albina said. "And I yours."

"So," she said as her maid helped her out of her dress, "tell me about this brotherly kindness that Gregory has shown you."

Albina's smile held a hint of guilt. "He has been giving me riding lessons and he escorted me to my very first grown-up party."

"Albina!" Selena said, surprised. "Do not tell me that Mrs Farley has allowed you to escape the schoolroom! Whatever will your mama say?"

"I'm not sure," Albina admitted, flushing a little. "But even if she is cross, it will be worth it! Lord Sheringham—"

Selena wagged an admonitory finger at her.

"Very well. Papa said that now I am seventeen, I should learn how to go on in society a little, and when he took me to visit Lady Bassington, I realised he was right."

"Oh? Is that where you met Charles?"

"Yes," Albina confirmed, "before he and Lady Bassington went to Town for Lady Brigham's ball. I am afraid I was very stiff because I felt a little nervous."

Selena was bent over her washstand but she glanced up at his and reached for a towel. "I would not have expected you to be nervous, Albina."

"I did not think I would be quite so tongue-tied. But I have spent most of my time in the schoolroom with Mrs Farley, and on the occasions I have been sitting with Mama when she received visitors, I was always told to remain firmly in the background and only speak if I was spoken to. What have I to say, after all? My head is full of schoolroom stuff."

"And yet you went to a party. How brave of you."

"I was determined to do better. I have always found that if only I apply myself to the things I find difficult, they become steadily easier. I think it helped that Gregory had started chatting away to me in a very easy manner during my riding lessons."

Selena felt a sudden pang of conscience. When she had joined her in her French lessons, Albina had always seemed so calm, confident and proficient, that Selena had felt quite inadequate. Still reeling herself from the changes at the court, she had not perhaps given as much thought as she should have to how her new sister had been feeling. She had certainly not made any great effort to get to know her well, and Albina's cool demeanour had not encouraged her. But now she realised that it had all been a front and that whilst she had been wandering about the grounds, her head in the clouds more often than not, or visiting her friends, Albina had probably been longing to join her. Not that her mama would have let her; Lady Sheringham seemed determined that Albina would sally forth into the world with a good education behind her and every accomplishment. Selena smiled. It seemed that in their absence, Albina had begun to blossom.

"Did you enjoy your party?"

"Very much," Albina said, her eyes brightening. "It was given by Mrs Mawsley. I met her daughter Sarah, who is not much older than me, and I sat next to Ralf Mawsley at dinner. He was very polite and amiable."

"Yes, you could not have done better than to go to the Mawsleys for your first party. Ralf is a particular friend of Gregory's, you know. I expect he regaled you with all the antics I used to get up to?"

Albina nodded, her expression a little grave.

"I see they have shocked you," Selena said, sitting in front of her mirror so her maid could brush out her hair.

"Yes." Albina met Selena's eyes in the glass. "But not in the way you think."

"Oh?"

"He made you sound so gay, Selena, so happy and carefree. But you have not seemed so since we came to live here. It saddened me to think we had made you so unhappy."

Selena nodded dismissal to her maid and turned to face Albina.

"You did not," she said firmly. "Losing my mama made me unhappy. When you came, well, it took a little while to get used to it, that is all. And then, I did not wish to go to Town. But I am very happy to have a sister. I am determined we shall get to know each other much better now that I am home."

A small smile curled Albina's lips. "I would like

that. It has only been Mama and me for many years, and I had not realised until I came here, quite how lonely I was."

Selena stood and pulled Albina's hand through her arm. "Come, let us go down to dinner. And if your mama is cross as crabs that you have been liberated from the schoolroom, I shall fight your corner."

Lady Sheringham would never have ripped up at her husband whatever her grievance, but when Lord Sheringham informed her of Albina's doings, she discovered that she had no desire to do so. If anything beneficial could be said to have come out of the wasted weeks in Town, it was the knowledge that nothing could be more harmful to a girl's chances of acquiring a husband than excessive shyness.

"I fully approve of Albina getting to know some of our neighbours," she said. "I would have suggested it myself if you had not already taken matters into your own hands. I do not mean to criticise Selena, but I would not wish Albina to appear as socially inept when she has her season, as I am afraid to say, Selena did."

Lord Sheringham smiled ruefully. "I should not have forced Selena to go, of course. But it was always her mama's intention for her to have a season. We thought she would grow out of her dislike of strangers."

"Well, she has not. And even if she had, I am not at all sure it would have made any difference. Selena thinks herself in love with Captain Bassington."

"That is nothing but a child's hero worship. If she had spent as much time in his company in the last few years as she did when she was a girl, she would have outgrown it. As it is, she will probably have to fall in love with someone else before she realises it. But it looks as if it will have to be one of the local young men whom she has been acquainted with for years."

Lady Sheringham raised a brow. "Is that likely? Would she not already have done so if she was going to? Might I suggest, my lord, that it might be more profitable if you encouraged her to consider a gentleman on his merits rather than his ability to make her heart beat a little faster?"

Lord Sheringham's lips twisted. "Have you ever known love, my lady?"

"No, and I am glad of it. If you could have seen the passion Selena flew into when I suggested that Captain Bassington might not come back—"

Lord Sheringham groaned, but then took her hand and raised it to his lips, a look of compassion in his eyes.

"Was that really necessary, Elizabeth?" he said gently.

Lady Sheringham flushed and glanced at her hand in surprise. "It was perhaps not very well done of me," she conceded, her voice strangely uncertain. "I spoke without thinking and I am sorry for it. I did not wish to cause her pain, only to make her face reality."

"I sincerely hope that Selena will never have to face that particular reality. We are all fond of Charles, you know. I hope very much that he will come back, and that Selena may have the opportunity to discover that she has mistaken her feelings, for he has never given me any reason to suppose that he is in love with her."

It seemed that Lord Sheringham's hopes were

unlikely to be fulfilled. The next afternoon Selena rushed into his study, her hair wild, the hem of her dress muddied, and her chest heaving as if she had been running. Her red eyes informed him that she had been crying. He stood immediately and enfolded her in his arms.

"Been to Bassington Hall, have you?"

"Yes, Papa. To see if they had any news."

"And?"

"Charles is seriously ill, Papa, of an inflammation of the lungs."

"That is unfortunate," he said calmly, "but not necessarily fatal, you know. Particularly not in a healthy young man like Charles."

Selena's chin wobbled, but she nodded.

"That is what Lady Bassington thinks. She said that it would not suit him at all to be carried off by such a paltry disease and so I might be sure that he wouldn't be."

Lord Sheringham looked down into her pale face and gave her a reassuring smile. "And she is quite right."

CHAPTER 4

Charles soon discovered the falsity of his confident assertion that it could not be much more fatiguing to sit all day in a carriage than lying in a bed. But if the rutted roads in France jolted him horribly, causing him considerable discomfort, he bore it all with a cheerful grin. However, he made no complaint when Lord Carteret insisted he take to his bed for the sea crossing.

"You can hardly stand, Charles," he said sternly. "The first time the ship pitches, you'll brace your legs only to discover they won't hold you up!"

"I know it!" he admitted sheepishly.

The weather remained benign, and although this lengthened the journey by several hours, the gentle rolling of the ship lulled Charles to sleep and he arrived on English shores much refreshed, claiming that he would do capitally now.

Lord Carteret was not so sanguine. He was not used to playing nursemaid, and Charles' rattling cough and weakened state concerned him. Knowing it would be useless to suggest that his friend rest a little more before they continued with their journey, he did not make the attempt. However, he wasted no time in hiring the most comfortable post-chaise and four that he could find. Even so, it took them a week to reach Bassington Hall. A week in which Charles' appetite improved very little but his cough began to be less frequent. Although his tanned face prevented him from appearing as pale and sickly as he would otherwise have done, he nevertheless looked drawn and haggard.

"Thank God!" Charles murmured as the long rambling house came into view. "If I never see the inside of a yellow bounder again, it will be too soon!"

"I hesitate to point out the illogical nature of your statement," Lord Carteret said, his relief quite as great as Charles'. "Regretting your impetuosity?"

"Not at all. I never could stand being stuck in a coach. I prefer to ride or drive myself." He suddenly laughed. "Sound dashed ungrateful, don't I? I'm not, you know." He held out his hand. "Thank you, Carteret."

Lord Carteret shook it but said, "You can thank me when we are certain that I have not killed you."

"You need not worry; there is nothing that our housekeeper Mrs Chivers cannot cure. She knows everything there is to know about herbs. If she had been born in another century, she would have been accused of being a witch!"

As they pulled up in front of the hall, the dark, oak door opened, and the butler came unhurriedly through it. Two strapping footmen followed him.

At an imperious nod from the butler, they came

forwards. One opened the carriage door and the other let down the step. He glanced upwards as he did so, his countenance impassive until he spied who was within. Then, his eyes widened, and an inappropriate but delighted grin crossed his face.

"Captain Bassington!" he said.

Charles had known the footman all his life as he was the son of one of their tenant farmers and near to him in age. He also acted in the role of valet for him whenever he was at home. He winked and said in a low voice, "Careful, Sam. If Pooley sees that silly grin, he'll have you polishing cutlery for a week!"

"I'm that glad to see you, sir," he said softly, "that I'd be happy to do it!"

He stepped away from the carriage to allow Charles to alight. As he did so, the butler caught sight of him. A muscle twitched in his jaw as years of training warred with his natural inclination to smile. Natural inclination won.

"Captain Bassington!" he said. "Welcome home, sir, welcome home."

"Thank you, Pooley," he said, his eyes twinkling. "It seems we have taken you by surprise. Did you not receive the letter Lord Carteret sent from Brussels informing you of our impending arrival?"

The butler bowed as Lord Carteret stepped down from the chaise.

"No, sir. The only letter we have received was the one informing us that you were dangerously ill." He frowned as something occurred to him. "Sam, take Captain Bassington's arm, he does not look at all well."

"Thank you, Sam," Charles said, surprising the

footman by accepting his proffered arm. He chuckled. "Thought I'd send you to the right about, didn't you? I would have, of course, in the normal course of events, but I'm afraid I am a little knocked up. Take me to my mother. I doubt very much she was thrown into a pucker by the news of my illness, but either way, I do not doubt she will be pleased to see me."

"Take Lord Carteret's baggage up to the red chamber, Jonathan," the butler said to the second footman, before turning to the unexpected guest. "Will you go with the captain, or shall I show you to your room, sir?"

"My room," Lord Carteret said. "I would rather change out of all my dirt before I present myself."

Charles threw a laughing glance over his shoulder. "Crying craven, Carteret? Afraid my mother will lay the blame for my condition at your door? You needn't worry, you know. She won't."

Lord Carteret raised an eyebrow. "I am merely allowing you some privacy for what will be, I am sure, a touching family reunion."

Charles grinned. "If you think my mother will weep all over me, you don't know her. She doesn't suffer from her nerves, thank heavens. As a matter of fact, I'm not sure she has any!"

"I should perhaps mention that Lady Bassington has a visitor," Sam said, as they made their way to a parlour in the east wing.

Charles glanced up at him, a look of dismay in his eyes. He had wished to enjoy the surprise his unheralded arrival would engender, but he did not feel up to talking polite nonsense with visitors.

"Who is it?"

"Lady Selena," Sam said. "She comes every day to see if there is any news of you."

"Oh, well that's all right. She's practically family."

The merest hint of a grin flitted across the footman's face. "She'll be out of reason pleased to see you," he murmured. "Be careful she doesn't bowl you over."

Charles laughed. "She's a young lady now, Sam. I hardly think she'll throw herself in my arms."

As the footman reached for the door handle, Charles shook his head. He was wheezing slightly and withdrew a handkerchief from his pocket and coughed into it. When he had recovered, he nodded and Sam opened the door. Charles sauntered through it, a jaunty grin on his face.

Lady Bassington was reclining on a chaise longue set before two doors that were thrown open, allowing the light summer breeze to fan her. Selena sat beside her, reading aloud from a book, which Charles had no doubt would be the latest romantic novel doing the rounds, and his sister-in-law, Caroline, appeared to be darning some sheets.

As Lady Bassington's eyes were closed, and Caroline was absorbed in her task, only Selena glanced up. He watched her eyes widen to their fullest extent, shock, relief, and then joy chasing through them. Her book thudded to the floor, she jerked to her feet uttering a little squeak, and flew across the room towards him. He laughed and put out his hands to ward her off.

"No, really, Little Squirrel."

Sam took a step forwards as if to protect him, but a mahogany occasional table came to his rescue.

Selena stumbled into it, causing the vase of flowers upon it to wobble precariously. She caught it before it fell and when she raised her eyes again, she seemed to have collected herself a little. She did not come any nearer but stood where she was, her smile a little dimmed.

"Charles," Caroline said in surprised tones, rising to her feet. "How like you not to have let us know you were better, or that you were about to descend on us. I will inform Mrs Chivers."

"Where have your wits gone begging, Caroline?" Lady Bassington said in a deep, lazy drawl. "Charles is clearly far from being well, and it would have served him right if Selena had knocked him flat. As for not letting us know he was on his way home, that would have robbed him of the element of surprise." A smile lurked in her grey eyes. "Well, Charles, you have not surprised *me*. I told Selena that you would not allow something as commonplace as an inflammation of the lung to carry you off. Come home to recuperate, have you?"

He crossed the room to his mother, ruffling Selena's hair on the way past. Bending, he kissed Lady Bassington's cheek, and it was he that was surprised when his mother briefly clasped him to her.

"Carteret did write, Mama, but I am not surprised his letter has not yet arrived. Everything is at sixes and sevens over the water. He brought me home."

"I don't suppose he had much choice," she said dryly. "But it is a pity he could not persuade you to wait until you were a little stronger. There's nothing to you, Charles, you're skin and bone. Never mind, between the doctor and Mrs Chivers, we'll soon have you on the mend."

A heavy hand suddenly clapped Charles on the back and his legs buckled. Sam seemed to have foreseen this possibility, for his arm was taken in a firm grip and he was hauled upright, before suffering the ignominy of being lifted into the footman's arms.

"Oh, I'm terribly sorry, old fellow."

Charles looked at the amiable but startled face of his older brother, a faint smile curling his lips. "Don't give it a thought, Adolphus. You can put me down, Sam. It was just that I was taken unawares."

"No, he can't," said a deep voice from the doorway.

All the Bassingtons were tall, but the head of the family was a huge bear of a man, with a florid but still handsome countenance.

"Pleased to see you, you young scapegrace, but it's plain as a pikestaff that the journey has knocked the stuffing out of you. Get him to bed, Sam, and then ask Mrs Chivers to have a look at him, will you?"

Sam bore Charles from the room as if he were carrying a rare prize.

"I had best be getting home," Selena said, "or I will be late for dinner. Would you thank Lord Carteret for me?"

Lady Bassington rose to her feet, revealing an ample figure. "Yes, of course. I will send him over to pay you a call tomorrow, Selena. Although I will miss your daily visits, my dear, I think it will be best if you let Charles rest for a few days before paying us another."

As disappointment flickered in her eyes, Adolphus

said, "I'll walk with you as far as the stile that takes you onto Sheringham land, Selena. Although I don't know why you insist on walking when you'd get here in half the time if you rode. You're a capital horse-woman, after all."

"I like the exercise," she said, accepting his arm and letting him lead her from the room.

Lady Bassington met her lord's eyes for a moment, and then he held open his arms and she walked into them. A small sob broke from her.

"Hush, my love," he said softly. "He is safe now, and it would never do if your children discovered that you had turned into a watering pot. Your unshakeable calm is legendary, and it would cause much disappointment if they discovered that you worry about them as much as any other mother."

She gave a watery chuckle, stepped away from him, and straightened her cap. "One sob does not a watering pot make, Bassington. And I do not worry about them as a rule, and well you know it."

"If you say so, m'dear," he said, with a meekness that did not deceive his wife.

"I do say so. Now, go and get ready for dinner. You stink of the stables."

A warm look came into Lord Bassington's eyes. "You never used to object. I can remember a very interesting evening with you in a hayloft above a stable, my dear. How could I ever forget it when it was there that I proposed to you?"

Lady Bassington's grey eyes became rather misty. "You were shameless, calculating, and altogether reckless. I don't know what possessed me to accept you."

If any of his children had been privileged to have

seen Lord Bassington's wicked grin, they would have been quite amazed. "And you, my love, were fearless, trusting, and gloriously abandoned!"

"Nonsense!" she said in a low voice. "Age has addled your brains, Bassington. I was naïve, curious, and clearly out of my senses!"

He suddenly pulled her against him and kissed her full on the mouth. When he raised his head, both of them were a little breathless.

"The first two I will allow," he said gruffly. "But I have never known a woman with more sense than you, Frances."

"It is just as well I had the sense to marry you," she said softly, "for otherwise you would have turned into a hopeless rake and been miserable as sin."

Lord Bassington took her hand and raised it to his lips. "I do not think I was ever a rake, but I will concede that I would have been miserable without you. The day I discovered you had persuaded your father to accept a mere baron into the family, was one of the happiest of my life."

"I would have married you with or without his permission," Lady Bassington said, smiling. "Something I am sure he was well aware of. Now, I shall go and see that Charles is comfortably settled." She chortled. "Trust Adolphus to welcome him so heartily."

Lord Bassington did not release her hand. "A moment, my dear. Are you aware that Caroline, having refurbished all the main rooms on this side of the house, has asked my permission to start on the west wing?"

She looked dismayed. After a moment's thought, she said decisively, "I have granted Caroline a great deal of leeway thus far, but I do not think that I can allow any more disruption to our lives at this present moment. I think we should send her and Adolphus to live at Horton for a while."

Her lord raised a brow. "But my aunt Cecelia has occupied it for the last thirty years. You know she was so eccentric that she would allow no maintenance to be done. And as she died only a few months ago, I have hardly had time to set it in order. It's barely habitable."

"Then it is time it became habitable, and I can think of no one better to set it in order. Caroline will be in her element. And I will say this for Adolphus, he understands the land, he takes after you in that respect. Together they will bring it about."

"That is true," he said thoughtfully. "The land is not in such a state as the house, but I should have retired old Farnaby years ago. Only Aunt Cecelia's dislike of change prevented me."

"That is decided then," Lady Bassington said. "As it is only some ten miles distant, they can go and view the house tomorrow."

CHAPTER 5

S elena thanked Adolphus for his escort, nimbly climbed the stile that separated their lands, and jumped down into the park of Sheringham Court. She walked with her head down and her brow creased in thought. The rapid beat of her heart was not only due to her quick strides. Her thoughts and feelings were rather jumbled and seemed to match pace with her steps.

Her uppermost feeling was happiness. Although Charles had looked rather drawn, his carefree grin and the twinkle in his eyes made it impossible not to believe that he would make a full recovery. But the burst of joy she had initially felt on seeing him had been tarnished a little when he had held out his hands as if to repulse her. Part of her was glad that he had, for he had made her recall the impropriety of her impetuous impulse to fling herself at him, but another part of her was saddened that he had not wished for her embrace.

She reminded herself sternly that she had vowed

that if only Charles was safe, she would be satisfied. She had already accepted that he would only ever be her friend, after all. She frowned as she remembered how he had carelessly ruffled her hair as if she had still been a child. It was how he saw her, she realised. That was why he had asked his cousin to watch over her; he had not thought her capable of looking after herself. She had to admit that her behaviour in Town had given him some reason to think so. Well, she was no longer in Town, and she determined there and then that she would finally overcome her reluctance to engage with gentlemen she did not know. She would follow Albina's example and take every opportunity to apply herself to the task. Instead of only attending parties where she knew everyone, which was her general habit at home, she would accept all invitations offered to her.

On reaching the house, she hurried to the drawing room, where the family would be sure to have gathered before dinner, to share her news. As all eyes swivelled in her direction as if to assess her mood, she smiled apologetically.

"I am sorry I am a little late. There was a little excitement at the hall, you see."

Gregory took one look at the glow in both her cheeks and her eyes and jumped to his feet.

"By all that's great, Charles is back, isn't he?"

"Yes, Lord Carteret has brought him home, although he is not quite well yet."

"Oh, you've no need to worry about that," Gregory said confidently. "Charles is never ill for long. Do you remember when we all had the measles?

Charles recovered far sooner than the rest of us. Are you satisfied now, sister?"

"I am, of course," she said. "Now that I know he is safe, I am content."

Lady Sheringham laid aside her embroidery. "I am very pleased to hear it. Perhaps now you will reconsider coming with Albina and me to the assembly in Alnwick the day after tomorrow."

"Oh, do say you will come," Albina said. "I will enjoy it so much more if you are there, Selena."

"Then I shall come."

"I say, that is very sporting of you, Selena," Gregory said. "Would you like me to join you?"

Selena felt touched at his offer; Gregory rarely attended such events. The thought of her brother's support to bolster her confidence was appealing.

"I would like that very much, Gregory. Thank you."

"We may as well make a family party of it then," Lord Sheringham said, smiling. "It has just occurred to me that I would not wish to miss Albina's first public outing and that although it is not Selena's first time at an assembly, I have never as yet enjoyed the pleasure of watching her dance."

Selena saw the shrewd look Lady Sheringham sent in her direction and suspected that she hoped that her husband would see for himself what a hopeless case she was. She did not begrudge her this hope but was determined not to gratify it.

When Selena awoke the next morning, she felt different, lighter somehow. It was a moment before she realised that it was the absence of anxiety that had wrought this change. A slow smile spread across her face. Charles was safe, and she was about to embark on a new chapter of her life. She did not feel happy precisely, but more content than she had been for some time.

She had barely dressed before Albina came to her room dressed in a buff riding habit that hugged her slim figure and suited her dark colouring admirably. Her eyes were big with news.

"Selena," she said softly. "Mrs Farley is leaving us today. She has received a letter from her sister. Unfortunately, she is ill, and Mrs Farley is going to nurse her. She will not be returning as she says that she has nothing left to teach me."

Selena took both of her hands. "So, you are completely free of the schoolroom. Congratulations."

"Yes, for Mama does not intend to replace her." Albina looked a little shamefaced. "Is it very wrong of me to feel so happy? Surely I should feel more upset to be saying goodbye to Mrs Farley?"

"Fudge!" Selena said. "I am sure she is a very worthy lady, but she is also dour and humourless."

"What was your governess like?" Albina asked.

"Exasperated! I was always slipping off to follow my brothers when they were at home and escaping into the park when they were not. Eventually, Mama dispensed with one and taught me herself." She suddenly laughed. "Mama was far too lenient with me, however, and I am afraid that I excel at nothing."

"That is not true. Gregory said that you are a clipping rider and a mean whip."

"Did he?" Selena said, surprised. "He doesn't say that to me although he taught me himself! But even if

I am, they are not essential accomplishments, you know."

"Even so, I would like to see you ride. Would you join us today?" A look of uncertainty crossed Albina's face. "No, that would be sadly flat for you when I have only just mastered a trot."

"Nonsense. I would like to see your progress. I can always gallop ahead now and again and then come back to you. I will change into my habit and see you at breakfast."

Lord Sheringham looked pleased when he saw Selena in her faded blue riding habit, an old favourite of hers.

"You have not ridden out since you came home, child," he said. "I think it was that which worried me above all."

Selena smiled at him ruefully as she took her seat at the breakfast table. "Oh, Papa, I am sorry. I did not mean to worry you."

Lady Sheringham looked at her a little doubtfully. "Whilst I am pleased you are taking up your interests, Selena, I hope you will not encourage Albina to push herself beyond what she is capable of."

"Don't worry, ma'am," Gregory said. "I shall not allow Albina to come to any harm. Besides, she is far too sensible to test her mettle against Selena. It's downright refreshing to teach someone who listens so attentively and does precisely what she is told."

"I am pleased to hear it," Lady Sheringham said. "Reason should always trump impulse."

"As a general rule, I would agree, my dear," Lord Sheringham said gently. "Although I believe that sometimes there is reason behind our impulses, it is just that one has not caught up with the other."

Lady Sheringham considered this. "Can you give me an example?"

He smiled warmly at her. "I can. I offered for you on impulse. I had not meant to do so until we had known each other a little longer. The reason is becoming ever clearer to me, however."

Lady Sheringham stiffened a little and glanced uneasily at the onlookers. "Oh?"

"You are a good woman, Elizabeth," he said. "You would not have encouraged Selena to go to the assembly in Alnwick with you after all she has put you through if you were not."

Selena hid a smile as colour rushed into her step-mother's face. She pushed back her chair and went to her, surprising Lady Sheringham by dropping a light kiss on her cheek.

"It is true. But I mean to do much better. Or at least, I will try."

"Well, good, good," she said rising to her feet, unusually flustered. "Now, if you will all excuse me, I must go and give Mrs Rudge my instructions for the day."

As the door closed behind her, Lord Sheringham smiled gently at his daughter. "Good girl, Selena. You have been raised with affection and love, and I am glad to see you are prepared to offer it to someone less fortunate than yourself."

"It is true," Albina said as they walked to the stables. "If you had ever met my grandparents, Lord and Lady Camberley, you would know it. They are stiff and cold, and they make me angry because they are always criticising Mama."

"And what was your papa like?" Selena asked.

"I don't remember him very well," Albina said. "He died when I was only eight, and I hardly ever saw him. Grandfather invited us to go and live with him after Papa died, but Mama said she would not subject me to the upbringing she had suffered. When I asked her what she meant, she clammed up and said she should not have said so much. She was left the use of a small townhouse in Harrogate for her lifetime, and we lived there very quietly until we came here."

"Well, I for one, felt dashed sorry for your mama, today," Gregory said suddenly. "She ain't one to wear her heart on her sleeve, but she never interferes with me, so I have no objection to her. I don't know why my father put her to the blush in that way."

Albina turned her dark, thoughtful eyes upon him. "I think that he was trying to reassure Mama that he is pleased with her and make sure that we all know it at the same time. Papa is very kind. He wanted someone to bring Selena out, but I also think he felt sorry for Mama. She is not as cold as she appears. Last evening, you talked of having the measles. Well, I too had them the year before last. I was very ill, and I awoke one evening to find her holding my hand and crying."

"Of course she would be crying," Gregory said. "All mamas worry about their children."

"What I am trying to say, is that she cannot easily show her feelings."

"Gregory," Selena said, suddenly struck by insight. "Our new mama is Papa's latest project!"

"Project?" Albina said.

"Yes. I am sorry if you do not like the term. I did

not mean to offend you. Papa *is* kind and he has a conscience. We have three other smaller estates dotted about the country. Papa has turned one into a refuge for the poor. Half of it is full of old people, and half full of orphans. Papa had a notion that they would be of benefit to each other. And they are. They all contribute to the work of the house and estate in some way. He has also invested in two mills, one in Manchester, and one in Newcastle. He has insisted on a fair wage for those employed and insisted that the children must have reasonable working hours and as safe working conditions as can be contrived." She glanced at her brother. "If I am not much mistaken, Gregory, Papa has started a campaign to thaw out our new mama. He wants us to show her love and affection and I think we should do it."

Gregory pulled a face. "If you think I am going to start kissing her and offering her compliments, you're fair and far off!"

Selena laughed. "Don't be so cork-brained! Just be your charming self with her. Do not stand upon ceremony or be overly polite. Laugh at her in a kind way when she says something you think foolish, like you used to with Mama. And pretend not to notice if she offers you a set-down."

"That's all right for you to say," her brother said. "And what are you going to do, may I ask?"

"I am going to ask her opinion on my dress. I am going to dance with anyone who asks me at the assembly this evening. If I need to, I might even confide in her."

"What about?" Gregory asked.

"Oh, I don't know. Perhaps I will ask what she

thought of this gentleman or that. We will see. I will know when the opportunity presents itself."

Albina spoke, her voice quiet and serious. "Thank you. We are fortunate indeed to have come here."

"Enough of this mawkish nonsense," Gregory protested. "We'll see if you still think that in an hour's time, Albina, for you are going to try a canter today."

Albina looked a little alarmed, but squared her shoulders and said, "If you think I am ready, then I shall certainly try it."

"Good girl," he said cheerfully. "I will explain it all and Selena can show you."

Albina did achieve her canter, and all three ended the exercise in very good humour with each other. Selena and Gregory saw Albina back to the stables, and then returned to the park for a good gallop.

"I tell you what, Selena," Gregory said when they pulled up not far from the Bassington lands. "I didn't think much of Albina, at first, but I was mistaken. I offered to teach her to ride at father's request, but it broke the ice. She stopped looking down her nose at me, and I realised that she just didn't know how to go on. She's game enough without being the reckless chit you used to be." He sobered for an instant. "As today seems to be the day for confidences, Selena, I'll tell you to your head that I'm dashed glad you seem to have come out of the mops. If it wasn't Mama – not that I blamed you for that; I was dashed cast down myself – it was accepting father had married again, then it was going to Town, and to top it all off, it was worrying about Charlie. I admit you have had reason enough to feel down in the dumps, but I'm glad you've found your way out of them. I never thought

I'd say it, but I miss the days when you were a reckless chit."

Selena forced words past the sudden lump that had lodged in her throat. "I don't think I will ever be a reckless chit again, Gregory, I am nigh on twenty, after all. But I am feeling more like myself."

"Well, I'm dashed glad of it," he said. "I wasn't that keen on father marrying again, but he's the better for it, anyone can see that. Some people ain't meant to be without a partner. He's one of them."

A mischievous glint brightened Selena's eyes. "And what about you, Gregory? Isn't it time you thought of finding a partner?"

Gregory looked horrified. "Now don't start getting ahead of yourself, Selena. You might need to think about it soon, but it's a different case for men. It might not be fair, but that's how it is. If you have any ideas of matchmaking in that head of yours, ditch them."

Selena threw him an arch look. "I haven't. I wouldn't foist you on any of my acquaintances!"

Gregory grinned. "That's the spirit."

As they were about to turn and make their way back to the house, they saw a man riding full pelt towards the hedge that marked the boundary of the Sheringham and Bassington lands.

"Now that's a fine horseman if ever I saw one," Gregory said, in admiring tones.

"It's Lord Carteret," Selena said. "I was expecting him to call today."

"So it is. I never knew he was such a goer! And if I'm not much mistaken, that's Spirit he's riding. Only Charles and Filbert, the head groom at Bassington Hall, have ever been able to handle him!"

Lord Carteret slowed his horse as he approached the hedge, and then cleared it with a foot to spare. He pulled up his mount, talking to him in soft tones when he shook his head and whinnied.

"Pleased to see you, Carteret," Gregory said. "I must admit though, that I didn't think you the man to be taken in by my sister's antics. Although I am very happy that you have brought Charlie home safe and almost sound, what possessed you to do it?"

Lord Carteret bowed and raised his hat to Selena, before offering Gregory a small smile. "Call it a whim, Perdew. I found I had nothing much else to do, and I had a fancy to see for myself how things stood. I have never completely trusted what I read in the newspaper. I find their accounts so often pander to those who desire the sensational."

"And did you find they had?" Gregory asked.

Lord Carteret's grey eyes suddenly darkened to the colour of wet slate. "Not in this case," he said softly. "I only saw the aftermath, of course, but I will not easily forget what I witnessed." He glanced quickly at Selena.

"Do not mind your words with me," she said. "I am aware that I lost my head a little, but I have now regained my senses. Thank you for bringing Charles back to us. How is he?"

"Weak in body but strong in spirit," he said with a wry smile. "He has been confined to his bed but is already chafing against this restraint. That he will recover does not seem to be in doubt, but it may take some time."

"If you think that, Carteret, you don't know Charlie. Mark my words, he will be right as a trivet before you know it. I shall ride over and see him tomorrow. Or do you think that is too soon?"

"Do, by all means," Lord Carteret said. "He needs distraction. I dare say he will be very happy to see you, but perhaps leave it until the day after tomorrow as he is a little knocked up by the journey."

They began to make their way back towards the house.

"That is a very nice mare, Lady Selena," Lord Carteret said.

"Yes. And she is still rather fresh. I am afraid I have been neglecting her sadly. She would like another run, I think. Shall we?"

"By all means," Lord Carteret said. "Spirit could do with the exercise."

When they dismounted in the stable yard, Lord Carteret looked at Selena with new respect.

"I never suspected that you were such a superb rider, ma'am."

"Neck or nothing!" Gregory said. "Always has been."

"Yet you never, to my knowledge, rode in the park whilst you were in Town."

"No," she agreed. "I would have found no pleasure in dawdling along amongst the throng."

"I quite understand," he said. "And neither did you wish to put yourself on display, I suspect."

"That too," she acknowledged.

As they entered the house through the door that led most directly from the stables, they encountered Lord Sheringham, clearly on his way there himself.

Once the introductions had been made, Lord Sheringham said, "I am pleased to make your acquaintance, Lord Carteret. I have heard good things about you."

"I am pleased to hear it, sir."

"Yes, that is all very well, but I always like to form my own opinions. Come to my study and take some refreshment, if you will."

"It would be my pleasure, sir."

Selena and Gregory exchanged a surprised look. It was not like their father to be quite so interrogatory of a new acquaintance.

CHAPTER 6

C harles looked up as the door to his chamber opened. He raised a brow when the second footman entered carrying a tray as Sam always waited on him when he was at home. He smiled at Jonathan in a friendly fashion, however. He had little appetite but discovered that he was looking forward to tasting a few mouthfuls of home-cooked food; their cook, Mrs Gough, was an excellent practitioner of her art. He glanced down with some interest at the tray that Jonathan placed carefully on his lap. After a moment, his gaze returned to the footman whose face was suitably wooden.

"What in the name of all that is holy, is this?" he said softly.

"I believe, sir, that it is vegetable soup and a glass of milk."

"That is patently obvious," Charles said, dipping his spoon into the broth, a look of distaste twisting his lips. He raised it halfway to his mouth before turning it so that a watery stream of peas and turnips fell back into the bowl with a small splash. "Perhaps, I should rather have said, what the deuce do you mean by bringing me such pap?"

Jonathan was a relatively new addition to the Bassington household, and his acquaintance with Captain Bassington was superficial at best. He gulped. "I'm only doing as I was told, sir. I overheard the doctor recommending Mrs Chivers to provide you with a diet of vegetables and milk until both your cough and your appetite improve."

"My appetite is hardly going to be tempted by such fare as this!"

"No, sir," the footman said, eyeing him warily.

Charles had always had a lively sense of humour and he suddenly grinned.

"There's no need to stand there looking so dashed worried. I'm not the sort of rum fellow who would hurl a bowl of hot broth at you merely because I did not like it. You may take yourself away and don't go blabbing that I was displeased. I would not like to upset Mrs Chivers or Mrs Gough."

A small sigh of relief escaped the footman. "I will not say a word about it, sir, you may be sure."

As the door closed behind him, Charles dutifully took a spoonful of the broth. It was not quite as bland as he had expected, but neither was it tasty enough to tempt him to take another. He was just contemplating rousing himself enough to get out of bed and pour the remainder of it into the chamber pot when his door opened again. Sam entered the room carrying another tray. The smell of bacon and eggs assailed Charles' twitching nostrils.

"That's more like it," he said. "Well done, Sam. I

should have known you would find a way to bring me something edible."

The footman laid the tray on a table and grinned. "Mrs Chivers asked me to bring it. But I am under strict orders not to give it to you unless you drink all of the milk and take at least some of the broth. She says she is sure that Doctor Shilbury knows what he is about and that she would not dream of going against his orders, but she can't for the life of her see how you are to get stronger on vegetables alone."

Charles chuckled. "I can hear her saying it. I have already taken some of the broth." He drank his milk and nodded. "Now, bring me that tray."

"I'm afraid it's only a small portion, sir."

Charles tucked into the single rasher of bacon and the small pile of scrambled egg. A rueful smile twitched his lips as he finished his repast. "I could not have managed more. Mrs Chivers knows what she's about. Now, help me into a dressing gown and bring me my slippers."

"I ought not to," Sam said in a resigned tone. "You know you're supposed to stay in bed for at least a week, but I know you well enough not to argue."

"You're an impudent dog to even consider the notion!" His smile took the sting from his words. "I'm only going to sit by the fire, Sam." He threw off his covers and slipped out of bed. "I'd as lief stay in my room today. I find Caroline dashed unrestful!"

"You won't for much longer, sir," the footman said as he shrugged him into a black, silk dressing gown. "She and Mr Bassington have gone to look over Horton Manor. The word is they are going to live there whilst they bring the place up to scratch."

"Are they, by Jove? Well, I'll give Caroline her due, if anyone can bring that place about, it's her. It's a shame it's been allowed to become so shabby. I rather like the house."

Sam picked up a footstool but put it back down when Charles raised a brow.

"If you are going to try and mollycoddle me, Sam Crake, I'll ask Jonathan to wait on me."

"Nah, you'd never do that," Sam said reproachfully. "You've not had him twisted around your finger since he was seven years old." He shook his head. "When I think of all the beatings I endured for slinking off to join you on some escapade or other when I should have been doing my chores."

"Poppycock! You never needed any persuading! Besides, your father isn't a violent man. I don't believe it."

The footman grinned. "No, he's a good 'un. It was Mother who always boxed my ears."

"I won't hear a word said about your mother, Sam. She makes the best apple tart I've ever tasted. I shall pay her a visit as soon as I'm able."

"She'd like that right enough," Sam said, collecting the trays. "Can I do anything else for you, sir?"

"You can ask Carteret to come to me. I fancy a game of cards."

"He's gone over to the court to visit Lady Selena. I saw him ride out astride Spirit. He handled him very well too."

"Yes, he's an excellent horseman. How I envy him."

"Oh, I'm sure Lady Selena will be over to see you before long."

"I envy him for being able to take Spirit for a gallop, you dolt," Charles said, a little testily. "I can hardly entertain Selena in my dressing gown! Besides, she's useless at cards."

Charles had never been a good patient. He hated to be inactive, but although a night spent in his own bed had restored him somewhat, he still felt deplorably fatigued. Lord Carteret found him dozing by the fire when he finally put in an appearance and would have left the room as quietly as he had entered it if some instinct had not warned Charles that he was not alone. His eyes opened and he smiled sleepily.

"Hello, old fellow. Did you enjoy your ride?"

"Very much. Spirit is a fine horse."

"I know it, damn you. Not only do you leave me here with nothing to do, but you take my horse into the bargain! A fine friend you are! It would have served you right if he had thrown you."

Lord Carteret's lip curled up at one corner. "Feeling sorry for yourself, Charles?"

"I should think I am! I never could bear to be invalidish."

"I suppose it would be useless for me to point out that if you followed the doctor's orders a little more closely and remained in bed, you might recover more quickly?"

"Quite useless," Charles agreed. "I'd fret myself to flinders and that would not do me any good at all."

"No, perhaps you are right," he said, seating himself on the other side of the fire.

"What news is there from the court? I expect Selena has been bombarding you with questions?"

"Not at all. She did ask me how you were, but that is all. The Sheringhams are going en famille to the assembly at Alnwick tomorrow evening. Lord Sheringham has invited me to join them."

"Good God!" Charles said. "Poor Selena. Is it not enough that she has been dragged to any number of assemblies these last few months? I expect it is Lady Sheringham's doing."

"Again, you are mistaken," Lord Carteret said gently. "Lord Sheringham informed me that it is for Albina's benefit and that he had been most surprised that Selena had volunteered to go. She told me herself that she was looking forward to it."

"Did she, by God? Then all I can say, is that she must have changed considerably since I left Town."

"Oh, I would not go that far, Charles. But I will admit that she became a little more comfortable in company as the weeks went on."

"I'm glad to hear it," Charles said, frowning a little. "I expect that was because you took her under your wing. I'm dashed grateful, Carteret. Thank you."

"You have no need to thank me," Lord Carteret said. "It was Allerdale who asked me to do it, and I would not have done so if I had not wished to."

Charles looked at him intently. "Have you fallen for her, Carteret? I've nothing to say against the match, dash it, I told you I encouraged Selena to think of you as a suitable husband." He pushed his hand through his hair and shifted a little in his chair. "She had spoken of you in her letter, said that you were easy company or some such thing. I knew this encounter with Bony would be brutal, and I thought I'd give her a little nudge in case I didn't come through it. I was afraid her stepmother would push her into marriage with someone she didn't like."

"Yes, I was there when you said as much to Allerdale. But I think you underestimate Lady Selena, Charles. Although she was rather aloof and shy when in Town, I would say her timidity was a shield to keep unwanted suitors at bay rather than a natural character trait."

"You may be right," he admitted. "But she was far from her family and friends, and Lady Sheringham is rather formidable."

Lord Carteret pushed himself to his feet. "No more so than a dozen other mamas who were determined to find husbands for their offspring. Now, I must go and change out of my riding gear." He laughed at the look of disappointment on Charles' face. "Do not worry. I had barely entered the house before Sam informed me you wished to play cards. I shall return presently."

It was not until he had left the room that Charles realised Carteret had not answered his question. He did not look like a man in love, but then Carteret was such a reserved fellow that it was nigh on impossible for anyone, except perhaps Allerdale, to gauge his feelings.

Charles was not able to support more than two days in his room, and so when Gregory visited him the day after the assembly, he found him downstairs in his mother's sunny parlour.

"Charlie!" he said, striding across the room to shake his hand. "I knew you'd be up and about in a pig's whisper. I've never known anything to lay you about the heels for long. How are you feeling?"

"A little stronger every day," Charles said, taking the hand offered to him.

"Charles may be up, Gregory," Lady Bassington said, not looking up from the letter she was writing at a desk set in one corner of the room, "but I would thank you not to encourage him to do more. He has, as usual, defied Doctor Shilbury's advice, but he is not yet fit to go riding or join any sort of expedition."

Gregory turned and bowed. "No, of course not, ma'am. I didn't see you there. How do you do?"

"Very well, I thank you," she said, laying down her pen and offering him a smile. "I need not ask the same of you. You appear to be in fine fettle."

"Oh, Lord yes, ma'am. Never better."

"Yes, well, you've always have had more energy than is good for you. Sit down, if you please, and tell us how you enjoyed the assembly at Alnwick. Lord Carteret went out with Adolphus early this morning and so I have not had an opportunity to ask him."

Charles laughed. "What possessed you to go? You've always said that dancing with a pack of girls you've known all your life is a dead bore!"

"It is, of course," he admitted. "But I thought I'd support my sisters. Albina's a good girl when you get to know her, and you know what Selena is like."

"None better. How did she do?"

"Very well," Gregory said. "They both did. I was proud of the pair of them."

"Your feelings do you credit," Lady Bassington said approvingly. "Was it very well attended?"

"Bursting at the seams!" Gregory said. "There is a

house party at the castle. At least a dozen of the guests came, although Hugh Percy was not there. I didn't know any of them."

"That is hardly surprising when you rarely go to Town these days," Charles said. "Can you remember any names or is that hoping for too much?"

Gregory grinned. "Far too much. Even when I did go to Town, I did not attempt to move in the first circles; it would have been a dead bore. Besides, they were all too high in the instep for me. I kept clear of them. There's only one thing more tedious than dancing with a girl you've known all your life, and that's dancing with one you don't know at all! But ask Selena when next you see her, she proved very popular and danced with three of them. She seemed to thoroughly enjoy herself too. In fact, dashed if she didn't sparkle! I know she didn't wish for her season, but it's done her a world of good."

"I'm very happy to hear it," Lady Bassington said. "I must say, I am surprised Selena didn't accompany you today, Gregory."

"Oh, now that she knows Charles is not at death's door, I think she'll give you some peace. She has begun a charm offensive on my stepmother and has taken her and Albina to see Dunstanburgh Castle."

"I wish her luck with that!" Charles said dryly.

"Charles!" Lady Bassington said, her soft chuckle robbing her words of any semblance of severity. "Remember to whom you are speaking."

"Do not worry, ma'am," Gregory said cheerfully. "Charlie knows he can say what he likes to me. Thought she was a little starched up myself at first, thought Albina was too, but I was mistaken. They just weren't used to our ways."

"And they are now?" Charles said sceptically.

"Well, Albina is, and her mama is a work in progress."

"I really must pay Lady Sheringham a call," Lady Bassington said.

"I'm sure she'd be very glad of it. Now, I must be off."

"Already?" Charles protested. "You have only just arrived!"

"I'm sorry, but I promised my father I'd meet him at the home farm, before sitting in on his meeting with his secretary."

Charles sighed. "If you must, you must, but come again tomorrow, will you?"

"I'll come the day after. Ralf Mawsley has arranged an expedition to Kimmer Lough. Both the girls are going so I can't cry off."

"Don't want to cry off, more like," Charles said wryly. "You want to go fishing."

"Don't I just! I'm still determined to catch the monster pike that is rumoured to be in there!"

"I know you wish you could go, Charles," Lady Bassington said when he had gone. "But you know it would be the height of foolishness. You may try and win back all that you lost to Carteret from me, instead. You might even go for a short walk in the garden. Doctor Shilbury said that when you feel up to it, you might take a small amount of exercise."

"I can hardly wait," Charles murmured.

"Ungrateful boy. It is not as if I want you under my feet, but do you see me complaining?"

Lord Carteret and Adolphus just then came in.

"At last," Lady Bassington said. "Charles is heartily bored. Do what you can between the pair of you to entertain him."

"Chomping at the bit to be out and about, I expect," Adolphus said.

"How right you are," Charles agreed. "I have the giddy pleasure of being allowed to take a turn about the garden tomorrow to look forward to. Care to join me, Carteret?"

"I would, of course, but we came across Lady Selena out for her ride, and she invited me to join the party going to Kimmer Lough. I am not sure when we shall be back."

"Then don't spare me a thought," Charles said, a little pettishly. "I would not like to interfere with your pleasure."

"Thank you," Lord Carteret said softly. "I thought that is what you would say."

Charles suddenly laughed. "Does anyone ever get the better of you, Carteret?"

"Rarely."

"I shall take you for a walk in the garden," Adolphus said. "I'll even take you for a drive if you think it won't tire you out too much. Just about the grounds, you know."

Charles' eyes lit up. "You're a good fellow, brother," he said. "Just make sure you don't mention it to anyone, or they'll all get in a pucker!"

"Can't see why they would," Adolphus said. "But mum's the word if that's what you want."

"I tell you what, brother, I shall be dashed sorry to see you go off to Horton."

Adolphus looked gratified. "It's kind of you to say so. You must come and stay."

"Oh, there's no need for me to do that, but I shall certainly ride over to see how you go on. When do you go?"

"Oh, not for several days yet. I shall be able to take you on a few more outings before I do, never fear."

"I very much hope that I will be able to take myself before many days are out."

CHAPTER 7

The group that left Sheringham Court was made up of seven people. The Sheringham party, Lord Carteret, Ralf Mawsley, his sister Sarah, and Miss Jane Rowland, an old friend of Selena's. It was only a few miles to Kimmer Lough, and a pleasant ride across open farmland brought them to the edge of the glimmering stretch of water. Rough moorland rose on the far side of the lake, its barren appearance softened by the occasional flash of yellow gorse or purple heather. A stretch of stunted trees lined the far side of the water, but the ground there was always too marshy to take advantage of their shade whatever the season. As all the ladies had been warned to bring a parasol, this was not felt to be any great inconvenience.

They left the horses to graze on the rough stubble that covered the field, and whilst the ladies spread out two large blankets and went for a gentle stroll, the gentlemen prepared their rods and chose a spot along the bank of the lough from which to fish. As all of the ladies had gone to the assembly at Alnwick, it was only natural that this should form a large part of their conversation.

Neither Sarah nor Jane had enjoyed a season in Town, and so had been most impressed by both the modish raiment of the visitors who had graced it, and their haughty bearing.

"I felt positively dowdy," Sarah said.

"I thought your dress very pretty," Albina protested.

"Yes, so did I," Sarah said, smiling wryly, "until I was introduced to Lady Filbert. Her eyes swept over me in a way that made me want to sink!"

"I know just what you mean," Jane said, laughing. "The master of ceremonies presented me to Lord Whitchurch as a desirable partner, and although he bowed politely and led me onto the floor, he hardly said a word to me."

It was typical of both girls for them to shrug off the experience with a laugh. They both came from good families who were comfortable rather than rich and had been brought up to be happy with what they had. They were pretty enough without being anything out of the ordinary, although Sarah's glossy black hair and Jane's fine green eyes were generally admired.

"It is my belief," Jane said thoughtfully, "that they only came to puff off their own consequence and laugh at us. What do you think, Selena? You had perhaps met some of them when you were in Town."

Selena had only been listening with half an ear, but she smiled and said, "I had only met Lord Ormsley, but I had hardly spoken to him. He seemed very pleasant. I think I surprised him by how gay I was."

"You were not so gay when you were in London?" Sarah asked.

"Not as a rule," Selena admitted. "You know I do not like meeting strangers. But I discovered a trick that worked very well. I simply imagined that I was talking to Lord Carteret."

"What a good idea," Albina said. "But why did you not imagine you were talking to Gregory?"

Selena laughed. "That would not have done at all! I would not have liked to appear too familiar, after all."

"No, perhaps you are right," Albina said, considering the lively exchanges which frequently passed between them.

"Lord Carteret certainly has very nice manners," Jane said, approvingly. "Does he make a long stay with the Bassingtons?"

"I do not know," Selena said. "But I think he intends to bear Charles company for a little longer yet."

"Or perhaps it is you whom he wishes to bear company," Sarah said, a glint of mischief in her eyes.

"I hope he may," Selena said lightly. "We became friends when we were in Town."

Jane looked at her rather searchingly but said nothing.

They turned as a shout of triumph came from behind them. Gregory held a large fish in his hands. The sun glinted off its green scales as if they had been jewels, and as they drew closer, they saw that it boasted deep orange fins.

"That's a guinea you owe me, Ralf!"

"Ugh! I don't know how he can bear to hold it," Albina said, shuddering.

"If you had grown up with brothers, you would not be so squeamish," Selena said, smiling.

As the girls retrieved the parcels of food they had brought with them from their saddlebags, they became aware of a cloud of dust in the distance. A gig emerged from it, and soon the sound of hooves beating against the compacted soil could be heard.

"It is Adolphus and Charles," Selena said.

The sharp tone of her voice carried to the anglers, and they put down their rods and came over to them.

Gregory began to laugh. "I knew Charlie would escape his leash before long."

"He was a fool to do so," Lord Carteret said, frowning. "Adolphus should have known better than to have brought him."

"Charles has always been able to persuade him to do his bidding," Selena said.

"He's always been able to persuade us all to do his bidding," Gregory said. "Especially you, Selena."

"When we were children, perhaps," she said with quiet dignity. "But no longer."

Her eyes met Lord Carteret's, and she thought she saw approval in them.

"I hope I haven't missed all the sport!" Charles said, descending from the gig.

"We've only just begun," Gregory assured him. "Although I've already bagged a fine perch."

"I'll wager you two guineas I'll catch a bigger one. Perhaps I'll even catch the elusive pike!"

"Done!" Gregory said, holding out his hand.

Charles shook it, nodded at Lord Carteret, and

exchanged greetings with Ralf, before bowing to the ladies.

"Sarah, Jane, what beauties you have turned in to."

Sarah giggled but Jane, who was nearer to Selena in age and so rather more assured, spoke to him in reproving tones, her clear, green eyes narrowing.

"I see you are still full of nonsense, Charles."

Lord Carteret gave a dry laugh. "Well said, Miss Rowland."

Charles paid him no heed but assumed a wounded look. "How can you say so?"

"Easily," she said. "Compliments trip off your tongue as smoothly as a knife slides through butter. I remember when I had just turned sixteen and you told me how wonderful I looked in my new dress."

"Then I am sure that you did."

"No, I did not. It was canary yellow and made me look horribly sallow, not to mention clashing with my red hair. But I was foolish enough to believe you and worked my fingers to the bone making myself two more in that particular shade. It was only when I heard Ophelia Frampton and her friends laughing at me that I realised quite how hideous I appeared."

"I am amazed you listened to her," Selena said. "She has always been spiteful."

"I didn't," Jane said, laughing. "I asked you, Selena, and you admitted that although it was not hideous, it did not become me."

"So I did! I had forgotten." She glanced at Charles. "It was really too bad of you. You should be more careful with your compliments."

His eyes widened in surprise and he held up his

hands as if to ward off a blow. "I shall be from now on. In fact, I shall compliment none of you from this day forth!"

"You have never been in the habit of complimenting me, Charles, and I now see that I should be extremely grateful for that circumstance," Selena said, a little archly.

"No, he always teased you instead," Gregory said, grinning. "He was far more likely to say that you had acquired another freckle, or that your hair looked like you had been dragged through a hedge. And I'll say this for you, sister, you didn't care a jot!"

Charles smiled fondly at Selena and she could not prevent her lips curling up, just a little.

"Of course you did not," he said, "or I would not have done it! Besides, it was true." His eyes dwelled on her face for a few moments, and his smile turned wry. "I could not say either of those things to you now, Selena."

Albina had been talking to Adolphus, but she turned her head at this and said, "You certainly could not, Captain Bassington. I think Selena is the prettiest girl of my acquaintance." She suddenly looked aghast and cast a fleeting glance at Jane and Sarah. "I mean, *one* of the prettiest girls of my acquaintance."

Charles laughed. "How can I answer that when I have vowed to offer no compliments? I will say only that you are clearly a girl of discernment, Albina. May I call you that?"

She inclined her head.

"And you may call me Charles when we are not in formal company. There is no need for punctilio here in the country when you are amongst a group of people who have known each other forever. Lord Carteret excepted," he said, sending his friend an amused glance. "He is a very correct gentleman, you see, very dignified."

"Something which you are not," Lord Carteret said. "What possessed you to come?"

Charles threw up a hand as if to swat him away. "Boredom. Now for heaven's sake, don't fuss. I am feeling much better. I've hardly coughed at all today, and you saw what a good breakfast I made." He eyed the packets that the ladies still held in their hands. "In fact, I do believe I am already feeling peckish again. I hope there is enough for me."

He sat down on one of the blankets and the rest of the party followed suit. Selena chose to sit on the other blanket with Lord Carteret, Albina, and Ralf.

Ralf shared his sister's dark hair, and his eyes were of a deep blue, but his nose was undistinguished, and his cheeks a little round, rendering his countenance pleasing rather than handsome. His disposition was generally easy going and his manners very gentle-manly. He picked up a bowl of cherries and offered it to Albina.

"Considering you have only been in the saddle a matter of weeks, I thought you rode very well, Miss Tate."

"Albina," she said, taking a few of the cherries. "I will feel very much the outsider if I am the only lady present you do not address by her first name." Her eyes suddenly widened, and a blush stole into her cheeks. "Oh, that is, unless like Lord Carteret, you are also more dignified than Charles?"

Ralf smiled kindly at her. "I should hope I am.

Anyone must be I should think. He has never liked to stand on ceremony with anyone. When we were very young, he chose his friends by their willingness to join in with his games alone, whatever their background and whoever's estate they came from. And he would think nothing of paying a visit to whatever small holding or farm was nearest to him at any given moment to beg for sustenance. I shouldn't think there's any farmer's family within a ten-mile radius who doesn't know him personally."

"Did you find that a little awkward?" Albina asked. "If he expected you also to play with them, I mean."

"No. Just as I shall not find it awkward if you would like to call me Ralf. Are you missing your old friends, Albina? Tell me about them."

Seeing that they were happily ensconced in conversation, Selena turned to Lord Carteret, a smile in her eyes.

"Tell me, Lord Carteret, did you also play with all the waifs and strays who lived about your estate?"

"No," he said dryly. "You have heard twice in a matter of minutes how very dignified I am, so I am surprised you need ask."

"Do you not like to be called so?"

"Certainly, if it the epithet suggests I have a composed or serious manner that is deserving of respect, but the merest inflexion of tone can suggest that the person referred to is staid, haughty, stiff, or proud."

"As Charles meant it. It was very naughty of him. I think the first definition much more nearly defines you."

"Thank you, Lady Selena." He suddenly smiled. "But it was not so very bad of him, you know. A gentleman often teases or is downright rude to his friends, it is only those he does not like so much to whom he is meticulously polite."

"Of course," she said, her eyes momentarily straying in Charles' direction. His countenance was animated, and he had reduced Sarah to fits of giggles again. She smiled rather wistfully and returned her attention to her companion. "He seems much better."

"So it would appear." Lord Carteret's eyes were now upon Charles. "Forgive me if I am impertinent, but it occurs to me that it is a little strange that you did not choose to sit with him when you were almost mad with worry for him when you were in Town."

Selena felt her cheeks grow warm as his eyes suddenly swivelled to meet her own. She dropped her gaze. "How very missish I must have seemed. Almost hysterical. I am amazed that I did not give you a disgust for me."

"You may be certain that you did not," he said softly.

Her eyes remained fixed on the last remaining cherry in the bowl set before her as she said awkwardly, "You have been so good to me, so kind, that I will admit that I had feelings for Charles that were not... were not precisely sisterly."

"Had?"

She forced herself to meet his gaze. "I am trying very hard to overcome them. I know he does not feel the same way, you see."

"I think you very wise, Lady Selena." He smiled ruefully. "You may even find in time, that you were mistaken in your feelings. I thought I was madly in love with someone when I was younger, but I discovered that I was mistaken and now find myself very grateful that she refused me."

Selena felt honoured that he had shared something she felt sure was very private to him. "I wonder if she feels the same?"

"I believe she is now very happy in her situation. And I am glad."

"You *are* dignified," she said impulsively, "and honourable, and obliging, and everything any sensible woman would want in a husband."

She inwardly groaned. She should not have spoken so to him. She did not wish him to think that she was throwing out lures. She covered her confusion by again rushing into speech. "Now that Charles is so much better, will you be leaving us soon?"

"Not quite yet. I will do what I can to prevent him from trying his strength too far for the next week or so."

"You are a good friend. As I have cause to know."

"I hope that I will prove to be very much your friend," he said, an enigmatic look in his eyes.

He rose and she watched him join the other gentlemen who had started to return to their sport, a puzzled expression on her face. She suddenly wished he were not quite so dignified for it made it very difficult to discern the meaning, if there was any, behind his words. Albina broke into her reverie.

"We had better tidy what remains of the food away or we will be beset by flies. You may call me squeamish if you wish, Selena, but I will admit that I cannot bear them."

They decided to throw the remnants of the picnic to the fish, before rinsing the bowls and returning them to their saddlebags. Sarah and Albina returned to the blankets, but Jane hovered by the grazing horses and took Selena's arm.

"No doubt it is very selfish of me, but I am very glad to have you home again, Selena."

"And I am glad to be back," she said. "It is so very comfortable to be amongst old friends."

Jane glanced across to where Lord Carteret sat on an upturned bucket. "And new ones?"

Before she could answer, Charles called to her.

"Selena! Will you hold my net for me?" He was leaning backwards, and his rod had bent under the strain as he tried to pull in his catch.

Compliance warred with a reluctance to show herself as much at his beck and call as she had ever been. Even as she wavered, the other fishermen put down their rods and came over to him.

"If it isn't just like you, Charlie, to have the devil's own luck!" Gregory said in exasperated tones. "You were not even supposed to be here. It is the outside of enough!"

Charles grinned unrepentantly, staggering a little. "Old Mister Pike must be huge; I can hardly hold him!"

"Give me the rod," Lord Carteret said imperatively. "You should not be exerting yourself in this foolish way."

"Not a chance," Charles replied cheerfully. "We've been after this old fellow for years."

Gregory stepped up to him and placed his hands on the rod just above Charles'.

"We will do it together. It would never do if we let him get away."

As they strained to bring in the fish, Lord Carteret picked up the net.

"I think I see something," Ralf suddenly said.

The water several feet in front of them rippled and all eyes focused on the spot, their anticipation palpable.

"It is nothing but a dashed branch!" Ralf said, his voice heavy with disappointment, as a bunch of twigs poked through the glassy surface. "It must have been lodged in the mud at the bottom of the lake which is why you nearly broke your rod in an effort to land it!"

Charles gave a ragged laugh and sat down.

"See if you can pull it in, will you, Gregory? It should be easier now. My line appears to be well and truly caught."

"It seems to be floating this way of its own accord," Gregory said, adding his might to the current's efforts.

It was not a mere branch but the best part of a tree trunk with several branches still attached. Gregory knelt and grabbed one of them. Lord Carteret lent him his aid and between them, they managed to pull it ashore.

"So this is your great catch," Selena said dryly, bending down to unravel the line that was twisted around a slender branch. Her nimble fingers worked at it for a few moments before she straightened, saying, "It is no good; it is hopelessly tangled. I will have to cut it."

"I have some scissors in my reticule," Albina said, hurrying over to the blankets.

She returned swiftly and handed a small pair of scissors to Selena. As she bent over the branch again, they slipped from her slick fingers and disappeared into a gaping hole in the trunk. She looked at it doubtfully. There was something very daunting about putting your hand inside a dark cavity.

Charles laughed. "Are you afraid that a fish will be inside waiting to nibble your fingers, Selena? You did not used to be so faint of heart!"

"Let me, Lady Selena," Lord Carteret said.

"No, no," she said quickly, sending Charles a glinting glance. "I am not such a poor creature."

She thrust her hand into the aperture, jumping a little when her fingers encountered something slimy. She would have snatched it back if she had not just then encountered Charles' mocking look. Instead, her fingers curled around the object and she drew it forth.

"Oh," she said surprised. "It is a necklace made of flat glass beads. They are the sort you find on the beach, I think, but it is so dirty it is difficult to tell."

"Treasure!" Charles said, pushing himself to his feet. "Let us see if there is more!"

Lord Carteret dipped a bucket into the water and presented it to Selena. "Perhaps you would like to wash it."

"Yes, thank you."

As she did so, Charles took off his coat and rolled up his shirt sleeve. He plunged his hand into the hole and brought out the scissors.

"It extends for some way," he said, laying them aside and again putting his hand inside the cavity. When his arm had disappeared almost to his elbow, he gave a crow of delight. "There is something else in here, but it appears to be wedged in and is slippery into the bargain. If only I could get some purchase."

He closed his eyes as if he were concentrating and when they snapped open again, they were alight with triumph.

"I've got it!"

All eyes were fixed on his arm as it emerged slowly from the hole.

"Do not keep us in suspense," Gregory said. "Pull it out, man!"

"Your wish is my command," he grinned, raising his hand with a flourish.

A stunned silence descended on the group. Charles dropped his prize, his eyes suddenly bleak. Albina gave a small shriek and Jane put her arm about her. Everyone stared at the bleached, white skull that lay staring blindly up at them, its gaping mouth seeming to offer them a grizzly grin.

Lord Carteret dropped a large handkerchief over it and said calmly, "There is no need for alarm. It may well have been there for hundreds of years."

"The poor, poor, creature," Selena murmured, her gaze dropping to the simple necklace in her hands.

Charles removed it from her nerveless fingers, his eyes never leaving hers. His gentle gaze steadied her, and she offered him a small smile of thanks.

Now the gruesome object had been covered, Albina regained her composure. "Even if it has been there for a thousand years, I think we should all say a prayer for the lost soul."

"That is a very good notion," Ralf said approvingly. "Very thoughtful of you too."

Everyone closed their eyes and offered up a silent prayer.

"What now?" Ralf said. "Should we put it back in its watery grave?"

"I think not," Gregory said. "Although anyone is free to fish the lough, technically we are on Sheringham lands and as my father is a justice of the peace, I think I should show it to him."

CHAPTER 8

By general consensus, the party broke up. Once the horses had moved off, Charles climbed into the gig, a grim set to his mouth. He had been pleased to come home, glad to leave the blood-drenched soil of the battlefield and the stench of death far behind. But it seemed it had followed him. His hand slipped into his pocket and his fingertips ran over the smooth glass beads. He should have given them to Gregory to take to his father, but by the time he had helped Selena into the saddle, it had slipped his mind.

He took out the necklace and absentmindedly began to play with the beads as if they had been a rosary. She had smiled and offered him her thanks, but he had sensed that she was troubled, and he did not think it was due to the discovery of the old skull alone. Whatever it was that was bothering her, she did not seem to wish to confide in him, but in Carteret. Although he had been entertaining Sarah Mawsley, he had kept a covert eye on them. He had not missed the flushed look on her face or the earnest way in which she had spoken to him. He would have to have another word with Carteret about his intentions; it would not do for him to raise her expectations if he did not intend to offer for her.

His fingers had finished their exploration of the beads and as he came to the hard, small, leather knot which bound them, his eyes dropped to the necklace. When he had taken it from Selena, he had not so much as glanced at it, but closed his fist about it, wishing to dispel the look of sadness which had filled her eyes. But as his eyes roamed over the different coloured pieces of glass bound together by a thin strip of leather, his breath caught in his throat and he felt the thud of his heartbeat in his ears.

"It's a pretty thing, ain't it?" Adolphus said.

Charles returned it to his pocket and agreed that it was, his voice bland.

"Are you all right, Charles?" Adolphus asked gently. "Feeling a little knocked up? Was I wrong to bring you?"

Charles turned his head and met the concerned gaze of his brother. It was like looking at an older, gentler version of himself. Adolphus' hair and eyes were the same hues as his own, only Adolphus' blue orbs were kinder and his red-gold hair much shorter. He forced a smile to his lips.

"No, you did not do wrong. It was a very good thing I did come, and I am not feeling any worse for the outing."

"I'm pleased to hear it," Adolphus said, his worried frown lifting. "I knew Caroline and Mama would not approve, but I couldn't see how allowing you to become so bored you were blue as megrim would help your recovery."

Charles gave a surprised laugh and his brother grinned.

"I'm not as slow-witted as you all think."

"I do not think you slow-witted," Charles protested. "Just not awake on every suit. And very obedient; you married Caroline, after all, just as Papa wished you to."

"I wanted to marry her," he said, surprising Charles again.

"I am glad you are content, but I could not be happy with someone who would try and order my life," Charles said.

"She don't," Adolphus said. "When have you seen her try to?"

Charles realised that he had not, in fact, witnessed Caroline do so. It was just her habit of reorganising everything at the hall that had made him think it. When he explained this to Adolphus, he nodded.

"Caroline was on the shelf gathering dust when I met her," he said. "When her mama died, she took over the reins of her father's house. Papa took me to stay with Sir Walter for a few weeks' hunting. He lives in Leicestershire, you know. I liked her. Simple as that. She's a straightforward sort of girl. You know where you are with her. She has a brusque demeanour, like Sir Walter, but she doesn't want to order anyone about, just make them comfortable."

"I don't think she's made Mama comfortable," Charles said dryly.

"No," Adolphus said, grinning. "But she's only done what Mama would never have got round to. I didn't want to discourage her so soon after we were wed, but before we return from Horton, I will drop a word in her ear. I'll find a new project for her, one that will not turn the house upside down."

Charles looked at his brother with new respect.

"It was a pity we found that old skull when the ladies were present," Adolphus said, turning the subject.

"Yes," Charles agreed.

"I was surprised to see it gave you a bit of a fright. You would have thought it a great joke when you were a boy and would probably have used it to play pranks on our sisters."

"I've seen a lot of skulls cracked open with their brains spilling out since then," he said grimly.

"I suppose you must have. Do you know what I think, Charles?"

Charles smiled wryly. "I would not dare hazard a guess. It seems I don't know you as well as I thought I did."

"Stands to reason you wouldn't when you've been away so much, only popping home now and again. I expect you still think of people in the same way you did when you first left, but we all change, you know."

"So it would seem. What is it you think, Adolphus?"

"I think *you* have changed, and not for the better. I saw the way you dropped that skull as if it had been a hot poker, and how white you went about the gills. I say again, it's not like you, and if that is what years of being in the army has done to you, it's time you sold out and found something else to do. Besides, your luck won't last forever, you know."

They had by now arrived at the stables.

"You may be right," Charles said softly. "But I'm not sure what else I could do."

"Well, think about it. I'm sure you'll come up with something."

When they entered the house, Sam informed them that Lady Bassington wished to see them immediately.

"Now we're in the basket," Adolphus said, winking at his brother.

But when they entered the parlour, they found Lady Bassington completely unperturbed. Caroline was seated at the writing desk, and Lady Bassington reclined in a chair close by it.

"Ah, there you both are. We are writing invitations. We thought we would hold a dinner to celebrate Charles returning to us more or less in one piece. It can double as a farewell to you and Caroline, Adolphus, before you go to Horton at the end of next week. We wished to know if either of you had anyone, in particular, you wished to invite."

Adolphus smiled at his wife. "You must invite anyone you wish, my dear."

She returned his smile. "As you please. I fancy I know who your intimates are. And what about you, Charles?"

"Oh, just the usual crowd. Mama will know."

He turned to her and raised a brow.

"Are you not going to give me a dressing down, Mama, and tell me what a tiresome boy I am?"

"Is it my habit to give you a dressing down, Charles?"

He crossed the room and dropped a kiss upon her

cheek. "No. You have always been the best of Mama's."

She looked up at him intently. "You do not look much the worse for your truancy, just a trifle hipped, perhaps."

"We discovered something rather unexpected," he said abruptly. "Adolphus will tell you of it. There is something I must do."

Charles went into the hall and nodded at Sam. "Come up to my room."

The housekeeper came through the door that led down to the kitchens before he had reached the stairs. Mrs Chivers was a neat, plain-spoken woman, with a particular fondness for Charles. The martial glint in her eye did not betray this, however.

"If you wish to go gadding about the first day you've managed to swallow a decent breakfast, I'm sure it's no business of mine, Captain Bassington, but you might have at least sent to the kitchen for some supplies first."

A twinkle of appreciation lightened Charles' eyes. "And would you have given them to me?"

"You may be sure I would. No one's ever been able to talk any sense into you when your mind is made up, however mad the scheme."

Charles attempted to look penitent. "How right you are, Mrs Chivers. But content yourself with the knowledge that I have not been gone so long without sustenance."

"I'm glad to hear of it," she said, thrusting a glass filled with a greenish liquid at him. "I would be obliged if you would drink this. I have been informed that your cough is much improved, and it may be conceited of me, but I am certain it is my herb tea that has done the trick."

Charles took the glass from her. "I quite agree," he said, gulping it down. "Thank you. If I go on any more excursions, I shall request a hamper."

"Make sure that you do," she said severely. "Now that you've got your appetite back you will be right as rain before you know it, but you are not there yet."

As they mounted the stairs, Sam sent him a sympathetic glance.

"I've never heard Mrs Chivers give anyone such a dressing down as that. And it is not like her to be so disrespectful to a member of the family."

"It is a sign that she is greatly moved," Charles said. "She was worried about me."

"Then I hope she is never worried about me. Did you enjoy your fishing, sir?"

They had reached Charles' room. Sam followed him in and closed the door behind them.

"No, Sam. I did not. We caught more than we bargained for." He took the necklace from his pocket. "We found this, and I thought I recognised it. Do you, Sam?"

The footman stared at it for a moment. All semblance of colour drained from his face. He reached out a hand that was not quite steady and took it.

"O'course I do." He gulped and licked his lips as if they had suddenly gone dry. "It was our Ellie's. You made it for her when she fell over and chipped her tooth on the front step. Such a rumpus she made, saying as how no one would ever like her now. She hardly ever took it off from the day you gave it to her."

Charles sighed and slumped into a chair. He dropped his head into his hands.

"I thought it was the one I made for her, but I hoped I might have been mistaken."

"Where did you find it?" Sam asked, his voice not quite steady.

"Sit down, Sam," Charles said gently.

"It wouldn't be fitting—"

"Sit down, Sam!"

The harsh note in Charles' voice persuaded the footman to take the chair opposite him.

"It was found in a cavity in a tree trunk we fished from the lough."

Sam looked perplexed. "I can't believe she would throw it in there," he said. "She hated the place. Said it always gave her the shivers."

"That is not all we found, Sam," Charles said heavily. "We also found a skull."

Sam sat as if turned to stone, his eyes fixed on the necklace.

"So she didn't run off," he finally murmured. "She drowned."

Charles looked into the face of his childhood playmate and felt pity flood through him.

"We do not know that for sure. It could be a coincidence. Perhaps she did throw the necklace into the lough, and perhaps the skull has been there for hundreds of years."

When Sam finally raised his eyes, they were glistening with unshed tears.

"It's no coincidence," he said. "She left us the briefest note, telling us not to worry because she was going to a better place. We thought she had found a position somewhere, that she would write and tell us about it once she was settled. But she never did. She hadn't been right for a while. She'd turned sullen, snappy, and secretive. It weren't like her." His face suddenly twisted into a grimace. "It seems she didn't go so far, after all."

"Sam. We cannot know that for certain," Charles said gently.

"No?" Sam said. "Well, you tell me this. Did that skull have a chipped front tooth?"

"I don't know," Charles admitted. "Once I realised what I was holding, I dropped it. I couldn't bear to look at it."

Sam nodded and got to his feet.

"Where is it now, sir?"

"At Sheringham Court. Gregory thought his father would wish to see it."

"As do I," Sam said. "I don't want to say anything to Ma until I am sure. May I go?"

Charles stood and clasped Sam on the shoulder. "We shall both go. I'll have the gig brought round."

They were just crossing the hall when Lady Bassington and Caroline came into it.

"Charles!" Caroline said. "You cannot mean to go out again!"

"I must go to Sheringham Court," he said curtly.

"But—"

Lady Bassington glanced from the white-faced footman to her son and put a hand on Caroline's arm to silence her. Charles had thrown off the mantle of scapegrace and bristled with the purpose and determination of the soldier.

"You will find your father there," she said calmly.

"I am glad," Charles said. "For he will wish to hear what we have to say."

They found Lord Bassington, Lord Carteret, and Gregory in Lord Sheringham's study.

"Ah, Charles," Lord Sheringham said, rising to his feet. "I believe you are in possession of a necklace. Could I see it? It might help us determine just how old this skull you found is."

"I know exactly how old the necklace is," he said, dropping it on the desk. "I made it some six years ago."

"But you said nothing about it," Gregory said, surprised.

"I did not look at it closely until I was almost home, and I could not be sure until I had consulted Sam. I made it for his sister, Ellie Crake."

Lord Sheringham shot a look at the footman. "You are sure it was hers?"

"Yes, milord. She always wore it."

"Might I ask, Charles, why you would make such a thing for one of our tenant's daughters?" Lord Bassington said quietly.

Charles' eyes widened. "Sir! You cannot think that I would… for God's sake, she was hardly more than a child!"

"I don't wish to talk out of turn, milord," Sam said. "But I can tell you why he made it."

Lord Bassington nodded. "Go on."

"Charles had dropped in at the farm to see Ma, in the hope she had been baking I expect. He'd always been a prime favourite with all of us, and Ellie rushed across the yard to greet him, tripped, and broke her front tooth. She was that mortified. She was fifteen and beginning to think of her appearance more than she used to. Charles came back the next day with the necklace to cheer her up. There was nothing havey-cavey about it. It was just kindness on his part."

"I hope that Ellie was fully aware of that," Lord Bassington said gently. "She wouldn't be the first girl to be thrown into flat despair by unrequited love."

"Can you be suggesting, sir, that Ellie threw herself in the lake because she was in love with me? It is impossible! I never so much as flirted with her," Charles exclaimed.

"I am not suggesting you did, Charles. But you are not perhaps always aware of the feelings you inspire in others."

Charles opened his mouth as if to protest but shut it again as he recalled what Jane had said to him earlier. One careless compliment from him had influenced her far more than he could have imagined.

"It weren't that, milord," Sam said. "He wasn't home above once or twice a year by then, and Ellie was perfectly happy when he went back to fight the Frenchies. It were the following year, when she had just turned sixteen that she became unhappy, and she disappeared before Captain Bassington came home again. I was working up at the hall by then, so although I don't know what caused the change in her; Ma never told me or my brothers, I know it wasn't him."

"I'm much obliged to you, Sam," Charles said, eyeing his father resentfully.

"It seems my theory will not fly," Lord Bassington said. "I am glad of it."

"We still cannot be sure that the remains we found were Ellie's," Lord Carteret said.

Lord Sheringham steepled his fingers. "No, not without some further proof. But the lake is very deep, and I fear it would be a useless task to try and find more remains. And what could we discern from a pile of bones, in any event?"

"Sam wished to see the skull," Charles said. "To see if the front tooth is chipped in the same way Ellie's was."

"Of course! Where have my wits gone begging?" Lord Sheringham said, opening a deep drawer in his desk. He picked up the skull and examined it for a moment, before turning it so everyone could see for themselves the chipped tooth.

"Well, Sam?"

The footman grasped the back of a chair and drew in a deep breath.

"It's her," he said flatly, closing his eyes.

Lord Sheringham put the skull back in the drawer.

"Sit down in that chair, Sam," he said gently. "Pour him a glass of wine, Gregory."

"I'll do it," Charles said, turning to a sideboard, and pouring himself one whilst he was at it.

"It seems I have something to investigate, after all," Lord Sheringham said.

"Investigate?" Sam said blankly.

"Don't you want to know what happened?" Lord Sheringham said gently. "As she has been found on my land, I most certainly do."

"Yes, of course. But how would you find out after

all this time? She disappeared five years ago leaving the briefest letter behind."

"Does your mother still have it?" Lord Sheringham enquired.

"Yes, milord. She keeps it in a wooden box Pa made for her."

"Then I have somewhere to start. I think, however, that we should keep this as quiet as possible until I have completed my enquiries. If this gets out, speculation will be rife, and we want to cause as little upset to Mr and Mrs Crake as we can." His frowning gaze fell upon Gregory. "Not a word to anyone, especially not your sisters. I would not have them upset. We will allow the assumption that it is an ancient specimen to prevail."

Lord Bassington rose to his feet. "You may take a few days off, Sam."

The footman looked appalled at the prospect. "Oh no, sir. I must go and tell Ma, but you may be sure she will not wish me under her feet. We mourned Ellie's loss to our family years ago. It was just the shock of her discovery that had me reeling. No doubt Ma will be too when I tell her, but at least the news will stop her wondering if she'll walk back through the door one day." He shook his head. "I'll leave her to tell Pa. He was the one that suffered the worst. She couldn't do no wrong in his eyes."

"I shall come with you," Lord Bassington said. "To offer my condolences. Your parents are my tenants, after all. I shall warn them to expect a visit from Lord Sheringham."

CHAPTER 9

Selena had been pleased when Gregory had invited Lord Carteret to accompany them into the house for some refreshment. She had quite recovered from her initial shock at seeing the skull. The necklace had been a poignant reminder that it had once belonged to a living, breathing, human being, and it was that reflection that had unsettled and saddened her. She realised now that the trinket had been rather primitive in both design and execution, however, and could easily imagine that both it and the skull had been hundreds, if not thousands of years old. Thus, the remains were transformed from a rather gruesome discovery to objects of interest, and she would have enjoyed listening to any theories Lord Carteret might have had as to their origin.

But they had found her stepmother, father, and Lord Bassington in the drawing room, and no sooner had Gregory explained what he had in his bag than the gentlemen had disappeared into her father's study. Selena felt a little resentful. If they were talking of its archaeological probabilities, she could not see why they needed to be private. Her thoughts were given another direction when Trinklow entered bearing Lord Ormsley's card.

"Show him in," Lady Sheringham said, checking her cap was straight.

A few moments later, a tall, handsome man, with powerful shoulders entered the room. The fine lines about his clear, light brown eyes, his assured air, and serious demeanour suggested that he was somewhere in his late thirties. He wore the traditional country wear of buckskin breeches, top boots, and an olive riding coat, but there was no doubting the quality of every item, and his informal attire did not encourage him to relax his very correct manners. As the ladies stood, he offered them an elegant bow and bestowed upon Lady Sheringham a polite smile.

"I hope I do not presume upon your good nature too far by paying you a visit, Lady Sheringham. I am fully aware that our acquaintance is slight, at best."

"Do not talk such nonsense," Lady Sheringham said, returning his smile. "We had met before the assembly, after all. But perhaps you do not remember meeting us in Town?"

"I assure you that my recollection of meeting both you and Lady Selena is quite clear in my mind, ma'am."

"I do not think, however, that you had the opportunity to meet my daughter, Miss Albina Tate, at the assembly. She was not in Town as she has only just begun to go into society a little."

As his cool gaze alighted on Albina, she dropped into a polite curtsy.

"I am honoured to make your acquaintance, Miss Tate."

"And I yours," she murmured.

"Please, won't you be seated?" Lady Sheringham said. "Trinklow, a glass of wine for our guest, if you please."

"Thank you, no," Lord Ormsley said. "I am aware the hour is growing late, and I must return to the castle in the next few minutes." He softened his words with a smile. "Country hours, you know. I am afraid I am a most lamentable guest and have absented myself rather than be roped into the archery contest the younger members of the party are so set on. I outgrew enjoyment of such sport many years ago."

"Such a greybeard as you are," Selena said, her thoughts out of her mouth before she had considered her words.

She was relieved to see a spark of amusement in his eyes.

"Precisely," he said. "I was very happy to renew my acquaintance with you, Lady Selena, and wondered if I might perhaps persuade you to ride with me tomorrow?"

"What is it that you wish to avoid tomorrow?" she said, smiling.

"Charades," he said. "I really cannot be expected to join in such a childish game."

Selena laughed and sent Lady Sheringham an enquiring look.

"I can see nothing to object to in the scheme, as long as you take your groom."

There was something about Lord Ormsley that reminded Selena of Lord Carteret. He was older, of course, but had the same dignified demeanour, the faultless manners, and perhaps most importantly of all, a gentlemanly quality that suggested he would never step outside the bounds of propriety.

"Certainly, Lord Ormsley. Had you anywhere particular in mind?"

His rueful grin momentarily robbed his face of its usual austerity. "I am afraid the choice must be yours. It is your country, after all."

"Then we shall ride towards Eglingham. The countryside is quite lovely in that direction and you might be interested in the church. It is of ancient origins, although it has been modified somewhat in recent times."

He stood and bowed, showing a strongly muscled leg.

"I shall look forward to it. Now, I must take my leave. Lady Sheringham, Miss Tate, Lady Selena."

The ladies stood, Lady Sheringham nodding, and the girls dipping into a curtsy.

Lady Sheringham sank back into her chair and looked at Selena, a slight uneasiness in her eyes.

"Selena, it can only add to your consequence that Lord Ormsley, who has been one of the most desired prizes on the marriage mart for some years past from all I gathered when we were in Town, has sought out your company. We must show him every observance. He is not only an earl but also a man of good princi-ples and great integrity."

Lady Sheringham's brow furrowed as she sought for her next words. Selena watched her with some interest. Rather than the calculating look Lady Sher-ingham had worn whenever a potential suitor has approached her in London, her eyes were pensive, even uncertain.

"The thing is, Selena, although Lord Ormsley is clearly still in his prime, unless I am much mistaken, he is some years your senior."

"But, Mama," Albina said. "If Selena likes him, what is that to the purpose? Was not Papa some years older than you?"

Lady Sheringham's cheeks paled.

"That is beside the point, Albina," she said sharply. "I am not suggesting that Selena should dismiss him out of hand, but merely that she should think carefully before considering him a… a possible prospect."

Selena understood by these words and the ashen look that accompanied them, that not only had her stepmother married a man some years older than herself but that the marriage had not prospered. She was aware of a spurt of sympathy towards her and felt touched that Lady Sheringham's desire to please her second husband by securing for Selena a great match, seemed to have been supplanted by a stronger desire not to see her so unhappily circumstanced as she had been.

She smiled warmly. "Thank you for your advice. I am more interested in widening my experience with the opposite sex, however, than in viewing every new gentleman who crosses my path as a prospective husband."

"I am pleased that your confidence is growing, Selena," Lady Sheringham said, her voice unusually gentle. "But as Lord Ormsley proposed to Miss Edgcott, Lady Allerdale as she is now, when we were in Town, it would appear that he is looking for a wife."

"Did he?" Selena said surprised. "I had not realised. Eleanor said nothing of it to me."

"That is to her credit. The news got about somehow, however, and it was not long afterwards that he left Town. Of course, that led to speculation that he was heartbroken, but he does not appear so to me. I think it far more likely that he discreetly withdrew to avoid any further embarrassment to either himself or Miss Edgcott."

"I am sure you are right, ma'am. It cannot have been pleasant for him. I will not encourage him to think his suit would prosper if he does appear to favour me. It would be horrid for him if he were rejected twice in swift succession."

"But you might discover you like him," Albina pointed out.

"In which case, I might not discourage him," Selena said cheerfully. "But for now, I shall merely enjoy being able to be in the company of someone I do not know at all well, without turning into an insipid miss."

Selena knew that she must have appeared so to him when they had met in Town, if not at the assembly.

The following afternoon, she donned a fetching jade riding habit that brought out the green tints in her eyes. Her mama had persuaded her it would suit her to admiration not many months before she died, but when it had been delivered, Selena had decided it fitted her form too closely and would not wear it. However, when she ran her eye over her other two riding habits with an objective eye, she realised they were rather shabby. It could not add to Lord Ormsley's consequence to be seen riding about the countryside with a dowd. She picked up the miniature she kept on her dressing table and smiled down at the beloved face of her mama.

"You were right," she murmured. "I have always liked it, you know, but I felt it was too dashing. I have several other dresses my stepmother ordered for me when we were in Town that I have not yet worn for the same reason. I think I shall begin to wear them too. I am turning over a new leaf, Mama. I am only sorry that you are not here to see it." She gulped and blinked away the sudden tears that sprang to her eyes.

She put the portrait down gently and picked up the hat that matched her habit. It was decorated with a single golden plume which curled up over the brim. She glanced quickly in the mirror, gave a satisfied nod, and headed for the stables. She felt certain that Lord Ormsley would be punctual and decided she would ride out to meet him.

Lady Sheringham was overseeing Albina arranging some flowers in the hall, and as Selena ran lightly down the stairs, her stepsister glanced up.

"Selena! You look magnificent!"

"Oh, this old thing," she said lightly. "It has been hanging in my wardrobe for a long time and I thought it was time I gave it an airing."

Lady Sheringham raised an eyebrow, but there was a note of approval in her voice as she said, "It has given you quite a new touch, my dear."

Selena felt a moment's doubt. "You do not think it too much?"

"Not at all," Lady Sheringham said. "You will certainly match Lord Ormsley's elegance."

"That is what I thought."

She met him halfway down the drive and saw at once that he rode very well.

He took off his hat to her. "I hope I am not late, Lady Selena. I thought I had set out in good time."

"It is I who am early."

"If I were a conceited fellow, I might take that as a compliment."

Selena quashed the slight feeling of unease these lightly uttered words engendered, and said with some spirit, "Then I hope you are not conceited, for it was the fine day that drew me out early as much as any desire to be in your company sooner, sir."

He laughed and ran an assessing glance over her frisky mare. "That is a fine horse, Lady Selena. It appears she is itching for a run."

"She is, as am I."

On these words, she turned the mare into the park and gave her her head, leaving Lord Ormsley and her groom to follow in her wake. It was not many moments before he came alongside her.

"Trying to give me the slip already?" he said, amused.

She raised her chin. "Not at all. Just leading the way."

"And testing my horsemanship, perhaps?"

"Hardly. You ride very well."

"As do you, ma'am."

They were approaching a hedge.

"I would ask if you wish me to open the gate, but I think I already know the answer."

Even as he spoke, Selena slowed before taking the hedge in a graceful leap. She pulled up on the other side, wishing to give her groom a chance to catch up. Quite used to her ways, he was not far behind.

Having galloped her horse's fidgets out, Selena led them down towards a collection of houses that could be seen in a dip in the valley, at a more dignified pace. The church stood on the edge of the village. They dismounted and left the horses to graze on a nearby patch of grass, supervised by her groom.

"It may not be very grand," Selena said as they walked towards the modest church, "but the tower and chancel are thirteenth century. The tower has an upper chamber where people could take refuge when the village suffered border raids."

"I see you are something of a historian, Lady Selena," Lord Ormsley said.

"Not at all," Selena admitted with engaging frankness. "My brothers and their friends would enact such raids when they were boys."

Her companion raised a questioning brow. "Do not tell me that you also took part in these games?"

"I would have done so, for I was always following them about. But as the only role they would give me was that of the fleeing maiden, I declined."

He laughed. "I am finding it increasingly difficult to match the shy young lady I met in Town with the young lady who is standing beside me now."

"I am much more comfortable on my own patch."

"I am pleased then, that chance led me onto your patch, ma'am."

Selena did not know quite how to answer this, and so walked quickly towards the church. It would, she realised, be very easy to fall into the habit of light flirtation with Lord Ormsley, and there was no doubt that she could do with the practice, but she must not encourage him, at least not until she knew her own mind better.

They paused for a moment in the porch, allowing their eyes to adjust to the dim light. As they began to walk down the aisle, Selena took refuge in what she felt sure must be a safe topic of conversation.

"There is a rather splendid octagonal font which dates from 1663—"

"So there is, so there is," came a deep, booming voice from the shadowed chancel ahead. "Although I am amazed and impressed that you know the precise date, Lady Selena."

"Oh, Mr Harbottle, I did not see you there. I hope I am not interrupting you. I thought I would show Lord Ormsley your fine church."

The kindly-faced vicar strode out of the gloom, his white locks gleaming as a ray of sunshine found its way through an arched window.

"You are not disturbing me. I have finished my business here and am at leisure to show Lord Ormsley around the church and discuss some of the finer points of its architecture with him." He bowed. "Pleased to meet you, sir."

Lord Ormsley returned his bow. "That is very kind of you, Mr Harbottle, but I am sure Lady Selena—"

"Allow Mr Harbottle to be your guide," Selena said. "I meant it when I said I was no historian."

The vicar began to lead his visitor to a squat doorway. "Perhaps you would like to see the tower, Lord Ormsley?"

Lord Ormsley looked over his shoulder. "Are you not coming, Lady Selena?"

Selena smiled. "No, I have seen it many times. I shall await you here."

As they disappeared through the door, a faint cough alerted her to the fact that she was not alone.

"Who is there?" she said.

Another figure strode out of the gloom. The locks that were now burnished by the beam of sunlight slanting through the window were that odd mix of blond, red, and gold that belonged to only one family in these parts. Selena felt her unruly heart flutter.

"Charles! Why did you not make yourself known?"

As he came closer, she realised that his eyes were unusually sombre.

"I had been baring my blackened soul to the vicar and did not feel like making polite pleasantries with a stranger."

"I am sure your soul is not black, Charles." She suddenly thought of all the men he must have killed in battle, and added gently, "Perhaps just a bit charred?"

He smiled wryly. "Just so. Is Gregory waiting for you outside?"

"No, just Dixon, my groom."

His smile faded.

"Just how well do you know this Lord Ormsley?"

Selena was a little taken aback by the interrogative note in his voice.

"Not well. I saw him in Town a few times, and at the assembly in Alnwick."

"And yet here you are, careering all over the countryside with him."

"Charles! He is a very respectable person, and there is nothing at all out of the way in a young lady accompanied by her groom going for a ride with a gentleman."

"You were not accompanied when you came into the church though, were you?"

Selena had never seen this side of Charles. He had teased her often but had never spoken to her so sternly. She felt a flash of annoyance at his proprietorial attitude. However he saw himself, he was not her brother, and for him to rip up at her when she was trying very hard to make new friendships was too bad of him.

"Stop being so absurdly prudish, Charles," she said. "It is none of your business what I choose to do. I am not a child, and I would ask you to remember it."

Charles' eyes suddenly swept over her attire.

"I could hardly forget it when you are wearing that habit as if it were a second skin."

Selena gasped and her eyes blazed. "You are not only prudish but positively gothic and extremely rude into the bargain!"

Charles' eyes held hers for a long moment, the challenge in them turning to a look of bemusement. "So I am. I do apologise. Forgive me, Selena. I do not know quite what came over me. You look extremely fetching in your habit, I assure you."

She unbent a little. "Very well. I accept your apology. People do often have unexplainable crotchets when they have been very ill."

He gave a soft laugh. "Selena, I do believe we have just had our first row."

"You should be pleased," she said acidly, her anger

and hurt not quite spent. "I have no desire for another brother, two are quite enough, but if you must insist on taking on the role, you now have the satisfaction of knowing that I can quarrel with you just as easily as I do with both Gregory and Eddie."

Mr Harbottle's voice penetrated the door to the tower. Selena did not know if she was sorry or glad.

Charles bowed to her. "I shall leave you to your respectable gentleman, Selena."

CHAPTER 10

C harles nodded briefly to Selena's groom and strode towards the village inn. He always prayed for all those lost in battle and begged forgiveness for his part in it after an engagement, usually seeking out a quiet corner of a church or chapel soon afterwards. He liked to be alone during these private moments of painful reflection and had felt a twinge of annoyance when Mr Harbottle had discovered him today. He had, however, derived much comfort from his soothing words and prayers. But the unexpected insight he had shown had unsettled him.

"Yes, yes, I know you are wishing me at Jericho, Captain. Heaven forbid anyone should know that behind your light-hearted raillery lies a wealth of remorse, sorrow, or regret, eh?"

"It is not quite so bad as that, Mr Harbottle," he had said quietly. "I usually make my peace before I come home and like to leave that side of my life far behind me."

"I have a feeling that that is not so easy as you

suggest. You are the sum of all your experiences, Captain Bassington. If you only allow people to see a part of you, then you allow no one to truly know you."

He had grimaced. "I would not wish my family and friends to be tainted by horrors they neither can nor should, know anything of."

"Of course you would not," Mr Harbottle had said gently. "But you must not underestimate those who love you either. They will not think any less of you for sometimes glimpsing the shade beneath your light. If you try to separate different aspects of life into neat compartments indefinitely, your true self will become fractured beyond repair. If you are already feeling such a dislocation, then perhaps it is time you left the soldiering side of your life behind for good. It seems our fight against Napoleon is finally over, after all."

"I sincerely hope so," Charles said. "But being a soldier is a huge part of my life."

"Indeed it is. I am not suggesting that you deny that aspect of yourself but learn how to best use it in a more peaceable way. You must have learned many skills and developed several aspects of your character that could be put to good use. I suggest you make a list of your strengths and consider how they could best serve you."

First Adolphus, and now Mr Harbottle had suggested he sell out. Was he ready to do so?

"Here you are, sir."

Charles smiled at the gap-toothed ostler who had clearly seen him coming and brought his horse down the road to meet him.

"Very efficient," he said, handing him a few coins.

"Thank you, sir. I'd have looked after such a fine beast for nothin'."

Charles quirked a brow. "He caused you no trouble?"

The ostler grinned. "He aimed a kick at old Filey, but he's such a sour boots I can't say as he can be blamed for that. I soon settled him down."

"As I see. You have a way with horses. What is your name?"

"Ned Wilkins, sir, and if you ever need to take on another hand, I'm your man."

"Thank you, Ned, I shall bear that in mind."

He mounted his horse and trotted out of the village before turning onto a rough track that would lead him to a path through the woods that bordered his father's lands. It was fortunate that Spirit knew the way, for Charles again lapsed into reverie.

It was not unusual for one of the greener recruits to reconsider his career after a particularly brutal battle. Unless they were clearly unsuited to a military career, Charles always advised them against making a hasty decision, but to wait until enough time had passed that they were sure they were thinking clearly. He was not a green recruit, of course, but a battle-hardened veteran, and it was not fear or even horror he felt after a battle – one eventually became numb to that – but weariness. A rueful smile touched his lips. Mr Harbottle had been right; remorse, regret, and sorrow he felt in full measure. Each time worse than the last. He had felt quite drained by the time they had finished their prayers, and he had groaned softly as they had heard the scrape of the church door opening.

The vicar had said gently, "I doubt you wish to be sociable just at this moment, so I will distract our visitors whilst you make good your escape."

He had intended to do so through a side door, but then he had heard Selena's voice. Shielded by the darkness and a pillar, he had watched her smile and introduce the tall, elegant figure beside her to the vicar. His name sounded familiar, but Charles could not remember where he had heard it. Selena had appeared poised and quite as elegant as her companion, who had seemed disappointed that she was to be denied the role of guide by the vicar. And well he might; Charles had not known Selena could look quite so alluring.

When he had seen her in Town, her gowns had been of undoubted quality, but conservative. Her riding dress was far from it and revealed a womanly figure that he had not realised she possessed. What had wrought this change in her appearance? He might have thought it was to attract Carteret if she had not appeared with this Ormsley fellow.

These thoughts had swiftly chased themselves through his head and, not quite ready to don his usual gay aspect, he was still undecided as to whether to approach her or not when he had been betrayed by his cough. There had been a faint quiver of alarm in Selena's voice as she had asked who was there, which had suggested she was not quite as confident as she appeared, and before he realised what he was about he was on his feet and moving towards her, instinctively wishing to allay her fears.

He had not been at all surprised when she had refuted the idea that his soul was blackened; she had never been able to bear hearing a word said against him. But he had not expected her addendum, that it might be a little charred. The words and the sympathy he had seen in her eyes had suggested that she had some inkling as to what might have brought him to the church, some understanding that when he was not at home kicking up a lark with his friends, he was doing something far, far less pleasant. They also suggested a maturity he had not credited her with.

He had first gleaned that she might not idolise him quite as much as she once had at Kimmer Lough, when she had sided with Jane and gently remonstrated with him for being too careless with his compliments, and then had ignored him and bestowed her confidences on Carteret. This had felt a little strange after the open friendliness of her letter and the fuss and rumpus she had made that someone must go and find him, but it had occurred to him that she might feel some embarrassment at her overreaction.

He winced. What about his overreaction? It felt natural for him to protect her if her brother or father were not there. But she had been right; his words had been both prudish and rude. If it had been Carteret or Ralf Mawsley with her, he wouldn't have kicked up a fuss. He should be glad that she was beginning to spread her wings. He was glad. It was just as she said, he had the crotchets from being so long ill, and on top of that she had caught him at a difficult moment.

A slow smile spread across his face as he remembered her eyes flashing with fire after he had told her that her habit fitted her like a second skin. He had seen that look many times when she was a girl, but it had usually been aimed at Gregory or Eddie when they had teased her too far. It had never before been aimed at him.

What was it she had said? *I have no desire for another brother, two are quite enough, but if you must insist on taking on the role, you now have the satisfaction of knowing that I can quarrel with you just as easily as I do with both Gregory and Eddie.*

He chuckled. He rather liked Selena in spitfire mode, and if she no longer saw him as perfect, all the better, for he wasn't, far from it. As he approached the ride that would lead him through the woods, he met his father coming in the other direction.

"Hello, Charles," he said, coming alongside him. "Glad to see you astride Spirit. Now I know you are feeling much better, but I hope you won't rush off back to your regiment too soon. Once Adolphus goes off to Horton, I would be grateful if you would take on some of his duties. I'm not as fit as I once was, you know."

"You're as strong as an ox," Charles said, grinning. "Besides, I know as much about estate management as you know about how to stalk an enemy without being seen."

Lord Bassington gave a hearty laugh. "What do you know about it? I've practised stealth in my time, although not for such serious stakes. As for not knowing anything about estate management, it's time you learned. If anything happened to Adolphus, you would inherit, and I'd like to think you'd be capable of filling his shoes."

"His shoes have always been far too large for me," Charles quipped.

His father smiled but said, "They would indeed be

difficult to wear, for he loves and understands our land almost as much as I do."

"I know it," Charles said. "And it would be the most outrageous twist of fate if he should not step into your boots, sir. I have never begrudged him his inheritance."

"You have no need to tell me that, Charles. But you of all people must know that fate picks its victims with no regard for merit or justice."

"I do indeed know it," Charles said, his expression turning serious. "But let us hope that Adolphus will sire many healthy sons and live to a ripe old age."

"It is my dearest wish," Lord Bassington said. "But even if he does, if he were to have some unfortunate accident before they were out of short coats, they would need someone to ensure the estate was still profitable by the time they were ready to take the reins. As their uncle, you would be the obvious choice."

"Very well," Charles said. "I never could win an argument against you. I accept the role of uncle to Adolphus' unborn children and will endeavour to learn anything you wish."

Lord Bassington put his hand on his youngest son's shoulder. "You've always been something of a free spirit, Charles, and more often than not, I've let you have your head. But I have seen you far too seldom over the last several years, and I would enjoy taking you about and teaching you a thing or two."

"I would also enjoy that, sir." His lips twitched. "I know all of our tenants, of course. Mrs Blacky bakes fresh biscuits on a Thursday, Mrs Stranmore generally makes a plum cake on a Friday, Mrs Crake bakes an apple tart on a Saturday——"

Lord Bassington smiled but said sternly, "It is time you learned what you can do for them rather than what they can do for you, my boy."

"I'd be happy to do anything for them," Charles said. "Especially Mrs Crake. How did she take the news? I didn't like to ask Sam."

"She shed a few tears but soon pulled herself together."

"Perhaps there *is* something I can do for her," Charles said slowly. "If Lord Sheringham wishes to keep his investigation discreet, he can hardly go about questioning everyone about Ellie. But no one would think it anything out of the way at all if I dropped in on them, even if I wasn't carrying out your business. If we could discover who Ellie was friendly with, I am sure I could bring her up in a quite natural manner."

Lord Bassington considered this for a few moments and then nodded. "I think we should put your scheme to Sheringham. There's no time like the present, unless you've tired yourself out?"

"Hardly, sir. Walking any distance tires me, but riding comes as naturally to me as breathing."

He turned his horse on the words and cantered back down the track, waving his hat in the air as he shouted, "En avant!"

When they were shown into Lord Sheringham's study, he was sitting back in his chair, a rather pensive look on his face. But he smiled warmly at his visitors and came forwards to shake their hands.

"I've just returned from visiting the Crakes," he said. "Mrs Crake has confirmed that the necklace was the one Ellie always wore. Apparently, the girl thought of it as a good luck charm."

Charles' lips twisted. "It didn't bring her much luck, did it?"

"Apparently not," he said, indicating that they should sit. "Mrs Crake is adamant that her daughter would never have taken her own life."

"She said as much to me," Lord Bassington said.

"I agree with her," Charles said. "Her nature was sunny, and her character robust. When I took her the necklace she was already laughing about her accident."

"But Sam did mention that she had changed, Charles. That she had not been happy. Is it possible that she was not in her right mind? That she was suffering from melancholy?"

Lord Sheringham sighed. "I would say that it is entirely possible. When I asked Mrs Crake about the source of Ellie's unhappiness, she said that she had developed a tendre for one of the seasonal labourers Mr Crake had taken on, a Mister James Rowe. Ellie always worked in the fields when she was needed, but begrudgingly. When Mr Rowe arrived, she went very willingly and followed him about."

"And did he return her feelings?" Lord Bassington asked.

"Mr Crake says not. His view both then and now is that Mr Rowe was an honest man and a hard worker who knew what he was about. Ellie was his employer's daughter and barely more than a child and so he was kind to her. Mr Crake claims it never occurred to Mr Rowe, who was in his late twenties, that her friendliness towards him was romantic in nature. And when he did suspect it, he discussed the matter with Mr Crake, which seems to support the idea that he was honest. There were only a few weeks' work remaining by then, and Ellie was told to stay at the house and help her mother. They were of the opinion that as long as they were kept apart, Ellie would soon recover from her infatuation."

"And did she?" Charles asked.

"It seems not. Mr Rowe left a week early, saying that his mother was ill, but Ellie remained sullen for another month." Lord Sheringham held up a sheet of paper. "And then she left leaving this behind."

Charles stood and took it from him.

Dear Ma and Pa,

I have gone far away. Do not look for me and do not worry. I have gone to a better place where I hope I will no longer feel so miserable.

Ellie

Charles passed the note to his father. "This tells us nothing. It *could* be construed as a suicide letter, I suppose."

"But neither Mr nor Mrs Crake read it as such at the time," Lord Sheringham said. "They were sure that she had found a position somewhere. Ellie had begun to grumble that she wished they lived near a bigger town, that she found her life dull."

Lord Bassington frowned. "I can understand why they would not like to think Ellie had taken her own life; they are good Christian people, after all. But that only leaves murder, which seems even more improbable."

"Or it could have been an accident," Charles pointed out. He frowned. "Except that she didn't like Kimmer Lough. She said it always gave her the shivers."

"If she were contemplating something as serious as putting a period to her existence, perhaps that would not weigh with her," Lord Sheringham said. "But everything is conjecture. I was considering how best to proceed when you arrived."

"Charles has an idea about that," Lord Bassington said.

"Go on."

When he had explained, Lord Sheringham said, "I think it a good plan. I had been wondering how to make my enquiries without raising any suspicions."

He picked up a notebook and tore a sheet from it. "I asked Mrs Crake for a list of Ellie's particular friends. It has only a few names, so your task should not be too arduous. I think I should see what I can discover of this Mr Rowe. It seems unlikely that he could have had anything to do with it as he had left the area some five weeks before Ellie's disappearance, but he is a loose end I would like to tie up. Unfortunately, the only information Mr Crake had, is that his family live somewhere in the vicinity of Newcastle."

"Not quite the only information," Charles said. "We know that he knew what he was about, which suggests a farming background. I would enquire for Mr Rowe at the farmers' market and also at the inns that the farmers frequent on such days."

"An excellent idea," Lord Sheringham said.

A knock fell upon the door and the butler entered.

"I am sorry to interrupt you, sir, but Lady Sheringham requests your presence in the drawing room. She is entertaining Lord Ormsley, Lady Bassington, and Lord Carteret."

"We will come directly, Trinklow," he said, glancing at his guests. "You will join us, I hope?"

"Certainly," Lord Bassington said. "I knew his father. He was a high stickler and thought a great deal of himself. I'll be interested to see what sort of a chap his son is."

"As will I," Lord Sheringham said. "He seems to have taken a shine to Selena."

Charles would have liked the opportunity to speak to Ormsley himself, but once bows had been exchanged, the older gentlemen monopolised him, manoeuvring him a little way apart from the main party.

"I am pleased to see you looking so well, Captain Bassington," Lady Sheringham said. "It must be a great relief for your family and friends."

Her eyes flickered towards Selena as she spoke, but she was engrossed in something Lord Carteret was saying. Lady Sheringham smiled and indicated a chair near Albina. "Please, won't you sit? Tempting though it must be, you really must not overtax yourself."

Charles felt a spurt of irritation at this reference to his weakened state.

"A short ride is hardly likely to have done so, ma'am."

He did, however, take the chair indicated.

"I hope I find you well, Miss Tate?"

Albina smiled at him. "Indeed, you do. I am very much looking forward to the dinner that is to be held at the hall in your honour."

"It is not only in my honour—"

"You should be honoured."

Charles glanced over at Lord Ormsley who had spoken the words.

"From all I hear, all the cavalry regiments performed most gallantly in our latest and hopefully our last engagement with Napoleon. You might be interested to know that he has given himself up to the English. News reached us at the castle last night. He has been taken aboard the Bellerophon. The word is, he hopes to seek asylum on English shores."

Charles looked suddenly grim. "Then I hope he will be disappointed. It is outrageous for him to make such a request."

"Oh, there can be no question of it," Lord Ormsley agreed.

"But why would he think such a thing possible?" Selena asked.

"Because we treated his younger brother Lucien so very well," Lord Carteret said. "He too was brought to English shores as a prisoner of war, and then allowed to live in some luxury with his family on a nice little estate near Worcester. He was treated with great civility and became something of a celebrity."

"Oh, I'm sure the local gentry came flocking," Lord Ormsley said. "The fact that he was at odds with his more dangerous brother and had refused to accept the princely title offered him, giving them an excuse to extend their hospitality to him." He gave a dry laugh. "Conveniently forgetting that the young Lucien Bonaparte was a staunch supporter of Robespierre and that he helped his brother Napoleon to power in the first place, however much he fell out with him afterwards."

Charles found himself reluctantly warming to

Lord Ormsley. The man seemed very well informed and spoke a great deal of sense.

"What do you think his fate will be?" he asked.

"I expect there will be a great deal of argument about that," Lord Ormsley said. "He will most likely be exiled again but let us hope that this time the spot chosen will be so remote that escape will be impossible."

"Yes, well, this is all very interesting, but perhaps not a suitable topic for the drawing room," Lady Sheringham said coolly.

"Come to our dinner next Thursday," Lady Bassington said. "Then you may enjoy discussing Napoleon's fate to your heart's content over the port."

Lord Ormsley bowed. "I would be honoured, ma'am. The party at the castle will come to an end on Wednesday, but I am sure I can find a suitable inn in Alnwick to put up in."

"Oh, there is no need for that," Lord Bassington said with his usual good humour. "Come and stay at the hall."

Lady Bassington's deep chuckle rang out, although no one could quite see what had caused her amusement.

"Bassington," she said, "you are a constant delight."

CHAPTER 11

Selena released a slow breath, feeling the tension ease from her shoulders. She had half expected her father to invite Lord Ormsley to stay at the court and was glad that Lord Bassington had beaten him to it, for although she had enjoyed the earl's company, she did not wish it to be forced upon her. It was one thing to be in the company of a man with whom she did not share the ease and familiarity of long-standing acquaintance for an hour or two, but quite another to have to entertain him for perhaps several days.

"Thank you, sir," Lord Ormsley said, looking from Lord Bassington to his wife with a slightly bemused expression. "I would be delighted to accept your invitation."

"Capital!" Lady Bassington said, chuckling again. "I think Caroline and I should perhaps tweak our arrangements a trifle. Do you like dancing, Lord Ormsley?"

His brows rose. "Yes, of course. But I would not

wish you to make any changes to your evening on my behalf."

"Nonsense," she said, waving a languid hand. "I really should have thought of it before."

"In that case, I shall look forward to it, ma'am. Now, I must take my leave, or I will be in disgrace with my hosts. Thank you, Lady Sheringham for your kind hospitality, and Lady Selena, for a very pleasant afternoon."

All eyes turned to Selena, who responded as her stepmother had, with a smile and a gracious nod.

After he had left the room, Lady Bassington said, "Selena, you have been neglecting me sadly."

Selena raised surprised brows. "That is hardly fair, ma'am, when you asked me not to call for a few days."

"Yes, but now Charles is so much improved, you may resume your visits. You have not finished reading Emily and the Wicked Marquess."

"A novel?" Lady Sheringham said, a hint of disapproval in her voice.

"Yes, they are my weakness. Selena takes on all the parts so very well. Why don't you and Albina come and listen? I am sure you must enjoy it."

Lady Sheringham looked uncomfortable. "I thank you for your kind invitation, Lady Bassington, but I am not sure that Albina would benefit from listening to highly improbable events that most likely lead to an equally fantastical, not to mention, unsuitable, conclusion."

"Have you ever read a novel, Mama?" Albina asked.

"I have not."

"Oh, now I insist upon you coming," Lady Bassington said, a twinkle lightening her grey eyes. "You do not know what a treat you are missing. Do not disappoint me, I beg of you. We may enjoy a stimulating discussion of the parts read that may prove very instructive."

Lady Sheringham looked sceptical. "Could you not enjoy a stimulating discussion of them with your daughter-in-law?"

"Alas, no. She will be far too busy planning and making all the necessary arrangements for our dinner and the several guests we are expecting."

"You are fortunate indeed, Lady Bassington, to have a daughter-in-law who is willing to take on such a responsibility, but surely you will wish to supervise her? The success or failure of your party will be laid at your door, after all."

Lady Bassington chuckled softly. "Caroline will do much better without my interference. I trust her implicitly. She enjoys giving her attention to all those little details that I would not even consider. Please, say you will come. Shall we say tomorrow, at two o'clock?"

Lady Sheringham's eyes turned to her husband as if seeking support.

"Go," he said, smiling. "You really should not denigrate a whole body of writing without having any knowledge of it, and Albina has been brought up with such good principles that I do not fear her being corrupted."

Having run out of excuses, Lady Sheringham offered a rather tight smile. "If you see no objection, then I shall certainly go."

"And are gentlemen permitted to attend Lady Selena's reading of this novel?" Lord Carteret said.

Lady Sheringham, Lady Bassington, and Selena spoke as one.

"No!"

"Is it so very shocking?" he asked, amused.

"It is not at all shocking, you horrid boy!" Lady Bassington said. "But we will be able to enjoy a franker discussion without your presence."

Selena's eyes flew to Lord Carteret's at this disrespectful form of address. She saw a smile lurking in them and laughed.

"So much for your dignity, sir."

"My pride has taken a severe blow, I assure you, Lady Selena."

"Then perhaps you might condescend to accompany me on a visit to a few of our tenants," Charles said.

The words were polite enough, but Selena thought they had an edge to them. She glanced across at him but could read nothing in his expression. Lord Carteret's, on the other hand, was one of sardonic amusement. She could not fathom what might have caused it.

"It seems I am quite at your disposal, Charles."

"Very good," Lord Bassington approved. "I will be interested to hear your opinions of our farms, Carteret."

"You shall have them, sir, for what they are worth. I am afraid my steward is always complaining that I do not take enough interest. I must admit that now my sisters are wed, and my mother is no longer with us, I find the prospect of any length of time alone at Westerby, a lowering one."

"Then you should consider taking a wife," Lady

Sheringham said, her eyes going from him to Selena and back again.

Selena felt her cheeks heat with embarrassment at such an obvious ploy. Lord Carteret's lips curled in a faint smile.

"Perhaps."

"Trust in serendipity," Lady Bassington said. "When the time is right, the lady will appear."

"But how will I know the time is right, or which lady to choose?" Lord Carteret said flippantly.

Selena felt grateful that he had not taken the bait her stepmother had offered him.

"When you no longer need to ask those questions, you arrogant pup! Now, take me home. We must return to the court if I am to have time for my customary nap before dinner."

As the Bassington party took their leave, Charles approached Selena. He took her hand and dropped a light kiss upon it. His hair was even longer than Lord Carteret's, and it fell forwards and tickled her arm as he did so. She shivered and glanced down at the natural curls that many a female would envy and was aware of a desire to reach out and curl one around her finger. Fortunately, he straightened before she could give in to the impulse.

"Am I forgiven for being such a bore earlier?"

Selena tried to retrieve her hand, but although his grasp remained light, Charles did not release it and, unwilling to enact a tug of war in front of everyone, she merely raised her brows and said with stiff politeness, "Of course. I accepted your apology at the time, did I not?"

"Yes, but admit it, Selena, you were still as cross as crabs," he said, grinning.

She was quite unable to prevent her lips curving up in response. "Perhaps."

They stood for a moment smiling at each other, Selena feeling as if a ray of sunshine had broken through a cloud.

"Come along, Charles," Lady Bassington said. "You should also have a rest before dinner."

As Charles rolled his eyes and moved away, Selena discovered two things; that she could breathe again and that her papa was watching her closely, a surprised look in his eyes.

"Papa? Is something wrong?"

"No," he said softly. "Far from it. It has just occurred to me how lovely you look today. So grown up, so like your mama."

Selena's eyes went quickly to her stepmother, dismayed at her father's unusual lack of tact.

"Do not look so concerned, Selena. Your father has only spoken the truth," Lady Sheringham said quietly. "You are very like her. I have always thought so. It must be a great comfort to your papa."

Lady Bassington still hovered by the doorway. She smiled warmly at Lady Sheringham. "I shall see you tomorrow. It is time we became much better acquainted."

When they climbed into the barouche the following afternoon, Lady Sheringham seemed tense. Selena felt her discomfort and smiled encouragingly at her.

"Anyone would think you were going to have a

tooth drawn, please do not look so forbidding. I am going to try my best to entertain you."

Albina followed her lead and took her mama's hand. "I am sure it will not be so bad as you suppose, Mama. You might even find that you enjoy Selena's performance."

"It is not Selena's performance that I question," Lady Sheringham said. "But the material she will be reading."

"It is all nonsense," Selena said, "but very enjoyable nonsense. The plot is as improbable as you supposed, but that is part of the fun. Lady Bassington and I like to predict what unlikely events will happen next before I begin. We do not take it at all seriously, you know."

Lady Sheringham looked bemused. "Then why do you read such stuff?"

"Because we enjoy it, and it gives us something new to talk about."

"It will be like arriving at the play halfway through the first act. We will not understand a thing that is happening."

Selena laughed. "Then I shall summarise the story so far."

Lady Sheringham frowned, and Albina listened intently.

"Let me make sure I understand you," Lady Sheringham said. "Emily was swapped at birth for her nursemaid's child and ended up in the poorhouse. On her deathbed, the nurse admitted the deception and Emily was restored to her rightful family at the age of twelve. The poor child who had been brought up as their own was relegated to the position of maid, and Emily found herself in a more privileged position than she could ever have imagined. Yet when five years later, a marriage was arranged for her, to a marquess no less, she fled this life of luxury, opposing her parents in a quite reprehensible way, even though the marquess had been meticulously polite and offered her no sign that he would be a bad husband."

"But do not forget," Selena said, "that Emily had felt a darkness within him from the moment they met."

Lady Sheringham gave a dry laugh. "I find that as unlikely as all the rest. I am not disputing the possibility that the marquess may not be as charming as he first appears but think it highly unlikely that Emily would have been able to discern anything beneath his polished manners at the tender age of seventeen."

An unwelcome memory made Selena frown. "I will admit that there is some truth in what you say."

"But I do not think it impossible," Albina interpolated. "Remember that she had endured many years of privation and been exposed to a great deal of unhappiness. She had not been shielded from all the unpleasantness in the world."

"You may have a point, Albina, but I think her experience of hardship makes it even more unlikely that she would choose an uncertain future over an extremely advantageous marriage."

"But, Mama, if she is right, and he is not a good man, even if she married him, her future would still be uncertain, or at least her future happiness would be."

Lady Sheringham's lips tightened but she offered no answer.

"This is precisely what Lady Bassington meant

about the text generating a stimulating discussion," Selena said. "It is a way to consider concepts, that however exaggerated, can have some application to real life. The heroes in such stories are perhaps too heroic, and the villains are perhaps painted too black, but she says the truth generally lies somewhere in between."

"That is all very well," Lady Sheringham said, "but unless the reader has the wit to realise it, such stories could set a dangerous precedent."

"Perhaps," Selena admitted. "But not if the reading is shared and the events discussed openly."

"Who is the hero of this tale?" Albina asked.

"We have not reached that part yet. Emily is at present on her way to Bath to take up the position of companion to Lady Parsonby."

"But who wrote her reference?" Lady Sheringham said.

"I see you are not one to overlook any detail," Selena said. "I must say that I think your enjoyment of the story might be severely hampered if you do not endeavour to do so."

When Lady Sheringham merely raised a brow, she said, "Her governess. Emily is not only beautiful but extremely gifted as well."

Lady Sheringham raised her eyes to the heavens. "Of course she is."

"I think it must be quite a burden to be very beautiful," Albina said thoughtfully.

Lady Sheringham looked at her in astonishment. "Why?"

"Because you would never know if somebody liked you or the image you presented. And although everybody ages, it must be particularly difficult for those who have been used to attracting a great deal of attention. Think of Lady Callow."

"Who was Lady Callow?" Selena asked, intrigued.

"She was an acquaintance of Mama's in Harrogate," Albina explained. "She had clearly been a beauty in her time, but she was sadly faded. She tried to make herself interesting by acquiring illnesses that made it necessary for her to visit various spa towns. She said neither Bath nor Cheltenham had agreed with her, but she had high hopes for the waters of Harrogate." A smile both wise and mischievous curled her lips. "But I must admit that the thought crossed my mind that she was more hopeful of finding a susceptible bachelor there than in any of the more fashionable watering places."

"Albina!" Lady Sheringham exclaimed. "I only took you to the pump rooms on a few occasions when you were recovering from the measles. How can you have so accurately summed up her character?"

Albina shrugged. "I so seldom met people that I was naturally interested in them."

"But you saw her so clearly."

"Perhaps because she did not see me at all, and so I had every opportunity to observe her."

Lady Sheringham looked stricken. "I should have encouraged you to make more friends of your own age."

Albina captured her mother's hand for the second time and squeezed it gently. "You would have had to send me to Mrs Laycott's seminary, Mama, and I am glad you did not. When you arranged for me to join their dancing classes during our last year at Harrogate,

I felt most awkward. I was either too plain or too intelligent to be popular with any of the girls there."

Burning resentment briefly flared in Lady Sheringham's eyes.

"I begin to think that this visit was not such a bad idea, after all. I have discovered more about you in the last five minutes than I have in the last five years, Albina. Why did you not tell me they were unkind to you?"

"I did not wish to worry you, and I had to learn to dance, after all," Albina said, her tone matter of fact.

"Why should you not wish to worry me?" Lady Sheringham demanded. "It is my prerogative to worry about and protect you."

"As it is mine to do the same for you," Albina said gently.

Selena saw pain and guilt distort her stepmother's features and looked away, feeling as awkward as if she had seen her naked.

They found Lady Bassington reclining in her usual place in front of the window. She smiled at her visitors but did not stand.

"I'm so glad that you came," she said, waving her hand at another chaise longue she had had brought into the room. "Let us not stand on ceremony. Please, make yourself comfortable, Lady Sheringham. You will find that if you lie back and close your eyes, you'll be able to envisage all the characters so much better."

Lady Sheringham perched on the edge of the chaise longue, her back ramrod straight, whilst Selena took her usual chair beside Lady Bassington and picked up the book. Albina chose a seat midway between them.

Selena opened the leather-bound novel and turned to the correct chapter. "I have explained the story so far."

"Excellent," Lady Bassington said. "Then we may all predict what happens next. I believe we must allow Lady Sheringham to begin."

That lady looked pained but said, "If Lady Parsonby proves to be a woman of firm moral fibre, then I very much hope she will write to Emily's parents and let them know where she is."

Selena sent her an apologetic glance. "Oh, I forgot to mention that she did not use her real family name or address."

Lady Sheringham gave a sniff of disapproval. "So, not only is this young lady ungrateful and disobedient, but she is also dishonest. How charming."

"You are severe," Lady Bassington said, chuckling. "You must take account of her exquisite sensibility and the dire peril she thinks she is in."

"Must I?" Lady Sheringham said coolly.

"Yes, I insist upon it," Lady Bassington said, smiling kindly at her guest. "I beg you will enter into the spirit of our little game."

Lady Sheringham unbent a little. "Very well. I think that one look at her youth, extreme beauty, and the quality of her clothes will be enough to alert Lady Parsonby to both her unsuitability for the role of companion and to the possibility that she is practising some subterfuge. If she's a warm-hearted person she may take her in whilst she tries to discover her true circumstances, if she is not, I suspect she will send her packing."

"I think Lady Parsonby will take her in," Albina

said. "But she will have a son and they will form an attachment to each other."

"Very good," Lady Bassington said approvingly. "I see you are a quick learner. I agree. And although Lady Parsonby is sympathetic, she does not wish to see her son throw himself away on a penniless companion and so sends her away."

"I think she will fall into a scrape on the way to Bath," Selena said.

Lady Bassington groaned. "You are too clever for your own good, Selena! I should have thought of that."

All but Lady Sheringham's predictions proved to be correct. After several minor mishaps, which included the stagecoach overturning and Emily having to deter the advances of a determined gentleman, she eventually arrived in Bath, only to be sent packing again when Lord Parsonby fell in love with her.

"I cannot help but think," Albina said, "that if Lord Parsonby had revealed his feelings to Emily as well as his mama, she might have then revealed her true identity and Lady Parsonby would realise that the match was not so unequal after all."

"It is to his credit that he did not show any undue warmth to a female residing in his house," Lady Sheringham said. "And that he should consult his parent before revealing his feelings to her."

"It might be proper," Lady Bassington said, "but when he returns home and discovers her gone, he will only have himself to blame. And if he is prepared to consider his mama's feelings over the dictates of his own heart, I shall think Emily better off without him. Some thought that as the daughter of a marquess, I had married beneath me, but I did not regard it for an instant."

"And did you marry against your parents' wishes?" Lady Sheringham flushed as she realised the intrusive nature of her question. "I am sorry, I should not have——"

Lady Bassington's rich chuckle rang out. "Do not be embarrassed. I am determined we are to be friends. Our families have always had such close ties that it could not be otherwise. That being the case, we are bound to find out much about each other."

Lady Sheringham's flush faded as she paled.

"The answer to your question is no," Lady Bassington said. "The situation did not arise as they put my happiness ahead of ambition, and my husband's birth was respectable after all."

"You were fortunate," Lady Sheringham murmured.

"Yes, I am fully aware of it. We have followed the same policy with our own children, although we may have given Adolphus a little nudge. You will meet my daughters at our dinner. They are a few years older than Adolphus and found their own husbands without any effort on my part at the assembly in Alnwick. I am glad of it, for they both live within a day's drive so I see them and my grandchildren often. Their husbands are great friends who live some fifteen miles the other side of the town. They decided to come together to the assembly one evening and the girls snapped them up." She smiled softly. "They had a joint wedding. I should have expected it, I suppose, for there is only a year between them and they have always done everything together."

"It sounds very romantic. Were they love matches?" Selena asked.

Lady Bassington sighed. "It is not as romantic as it sounds. I would rather say their unions were based on friendship and mutual respect. My girls seemed to have firm ideas of what they wished for in a husband."

"They sound like sensible young women," Lady Sheringham said approvingly.

Selena laughed. "You make it sound as if their chosen partners had nothing to say in the matter, Lady Bassington."

"I am not at all sure they did. Once the girls had made up their minds, they reeled them in in very short time."

"How?" Selena asked.

Lady Bassington shrugged. "I am not entirely sure. It was certainly not by using any of the usual feminine wiles. They did not preen and pout or pretend to be helpless. They were always just themselves, which probably means they were very direct."

"You cannot mean that they were the ones who proposed, surely?" Selena asked.

"I do not know for certain," Lady Bassington said regretfully. "They just laughed when I asked for the details and said it was better that I did not know, so I suspect they either did take matters into their own hands or pushed their partners into it."

"And what rank are their husbands?" Lady Sheringham asked.

"One is a baronet and the other a plain country squire, although he is most certainly a gentleman."

"Do you think rank so important in a husband,

Mama?" Albina asked. "Would you place it above happiness?"

Lady Sheringham opened her mouth and then shut it again, her brow furrowing as she considered her answer.

"I would certainly not encourage anyone to marry someone I felt sure would make them unhappy," she said, "but I do not see why it needs to be a choice. It is possible to be happy with someone who is of rank, after all." She smiled at her daughter. "A marriage is an alliance of two families, designed to benefit both so that wealth and land may be secured and old blood lines preserved."

Lady Bassington snorted. "If you ask me, more than one old blood line would benefit from having new blood in it, judging by some of the idiots such alliances produce!"

Albina stifled a giggle as her mama gave her a stern look.

"When you have your season, you will meet many gentlemen of rank. I am sure you will find a few to choose from that will have qualities that you must admire."

"But Selena did not."

"No, but her crippling shyness made it difficult for her to get to know any of them at all well. She would do much better if she were to have her season again."

"But you said I was not to have another season," Selena said without rancour.

A faint flush stole along Lady Sheringham's high cheekbones.

"I was vexed when I said that," she admitted. "If you do not receive an offer that you feel you can accept before it is time for Albina to make her come out, you may, of course, come to Town with us."

"Thank you," Selena said softly. "I do not think I will come, but I am happy that you would be prepared to take me."

Lady Bassington had been listening to this interplay with interest, a small smile playing about her lips.

"I have found this afternoon very enlivening," she said. "But now it is time for my nap. I do hope you will all come again."

CHAPTER 12

The first two names on Charles' list bore no fruit. The third was Rachel Blacky. As they rode into the farmyard, Mrs Blacky came out of the house and stood on her freshly scrubbed front step, a pristine apron tied around her plump waist and a rolling pin lightly dusted with flour clutched in one hand. The array of fine wrinkles on her face deepened as she smiled.

"Captain Bassington! We heard that you were mortal ill!"

"As is the nature of rumours, it was something of an exaggeration, as you see."

"That's as maybe, but you're a great deal thinner than when last I saw you." She gave Lord Carteret an assessing glance. "Mr Blacky will be in for his break in a moment, if you'd like to come in and wait for him. I'm about to put some biscuits in the oven and they'll be ready in no time. You're both welcome to some if your friend don't mind simple fare."

"Thank you, Mrs Blacky," Lord Carteret said,

dismounting. "The captain speaks very highly of your biscuits."

"Captain Bassington!"

They turned and saw a ruddy-faced gentleman hurrying across the yard.

"I'm happy to see you up and about. I expect you've come to eat me out of house and home."

Charles grinned. "I will admit that I was hoping your good wife had been baking, but I also wished to show Lord Carteret some of the farms and to enquire if there is anything that you require of my father."

Mr Blacky's thick eyebrows shot up. "He's putting you to work, is he? I'd have thought you were due a rest."

"I've had quite enough of resting," Charles said.

"Aye, you never could sit still. You and Lord Carteret are most welcome to have a look around. Bring your horses into the barn while Mrs Blacky gets the biscuits ready. Your visit is most timely, for now Rachel's had her first child, she and Jonas have moved into the cottage down by the river, but it needs a few repairs."

"She finally agreed to marry Jonas Fielding then?"

"Aye, she put him out of his misery just over a year ago. It's a weight off my mind as the good Lord hasn't seen fit to give me a son of my own and my family has run this farm for three generations. I think she always meant to have him, but it was common knowledge that he had been mooning over Ellie Crake only she would have none of him. Not long after she went off, he started making sheep's eyes at Rachel, but she was that upset that Ellie had disappeared without a word to her that she wasn't interested, besides, no girl likes to think of herself as second best. He's proved his constancy, however. Never looked at another girl for the four years it took him to wear her down."

Charles felt a stab of disappointment. It seemed that Rachel was unlikely to prove a likely line of enquiry.

"Will we find Rachel at the cottage?" he said.

"No, she'll be in the dairy at the back of the house, but we all take a break at this time nowadays, so you'll see her soon enough." He wagged a playful finger. "She'll be pleased to see you, sir, but don't you go making Jonas jealous."

Charles gave a surprised laugh. "Could I?"

Jonas was one of the blacksmith's sons, but all Charles knew of him was that he had a taciturn manner which even Charles' easy-going manners had never managed to pierce.

Mr Blacky laughed. "Aye, you could at that. Not that you'd mean to, of course, but a smile and kind word from you has always put her in a twitter."

Charles met Lord Carteret's eyes and saw a satirical gleam in them.

They found a dark-haired, wiry man, tethering cows to brass rings spread along the wall of the barn ready for milking.

"Good day to you, Jonas," Charles said.

The man nodded but did not smile.

"Good day, sir. I'm glad to see your luck hasn't run out after all."

"Thank you. Unfortunately, it has not held for all of my regiment."

"You want to quit whilst you're ahead," Mr Blacky

said. "Follow Jonas' example and settle down and raise a family."

Charles smiled ruefully. "I am hardly in a position to support a wife."

"I expect his lordship can find you something to do. Why else would he be training you up?"

"Against the very long odds that I might one day inherit or need to guide my future nephews."

Mr Blacky laughed. "Them there's very long odds to be sure. But it's a good idea, think on. There's plenty of gentlemen who are far too idle to look after their own affairs."

Charles returned Carteret's satirical glance. "So there are."

Spirit seemed to take objection to sharing the barn with the cows. He snorted and skittered.

"You go on into the house, Captain," Jonas said. "I'll put them in the meadow."

"Thank you, Jonas."

Mrs Blacky was taking the biscuits out of the oven as they entered the kitchen.

"Rachel's just wrapping up a cheese I promised her ladyship," she said. "She won't be above a minute."

Charles seized on this opportunity. "Do you mind if I take a look in the dairy? I'm attempting to broaden my knowledge of how things work on a farm."

"I've no objection," she said, putting the biscuits on a wire rack to cool. "But don't be long; Jonas will be back in a minute." She smiled kindly at him. "It took him that long to get her, that he don't want to give anyone the chance to take her away from him. It's all nonsense of course, but it happened to his own mother, after all. She ran off with another man, leaving poor Mr Fielding to raise three boys and run the Smithy."

Charles went back into the yard and strode to the small dairy that was housed in a lean-to building attached to the end of the house. It occurred to him that if Jonas was the jealous type and he had been fixated on Ellie, he would not have liked her mooning over Mr Rowe. When that gentleman left the Crake farm, did he renew his efforts with her? Could he perhaps have killed her in a jealous rage when she again spurned his advances?

He found Rachel securing the paper she had wrapped around the cheese with a bit of string. She was plumper and prettier than he remembered. She finished tying the string before glancing up. A smile crossed her face as she dipped into a curtsy.

"You look well, Rachel," he said, returning her smile. "Motherhood suits you."

Her smile widened and a faint touch of colour warmed her cheeks.

"It's kind of you to say so, sir."

He was about to refute that it was kindness that made him say so when he recalled her father's words.

"Can you tell me something of how you run the dairy?" he said instead.

"Why would you want to know that?" she said, laughing. "Don't tell me you've gone and fallen in love with a farmer's daughter, after all?"

"After all?"

She blushed rosily. "A group of us used to meet up after church on a Sunday. We were all soft in the head about you. We used to daydream that one day you'd pick one of us to marry." She gave a self-conscious laugh. "We had some heated arguments about who you would choose."

Charles looked a little shocked. "Do not tell me that I gave any of you reason to think so?"

"Don't be daft. It was just a game. You always had a laugh, a wink, and a smile for all of us, but we knew you didn't mean anything by it."

"I'm glad to hear it. You were all just children to me."

"Girls grow up faster than you think, sir," she said knowingly. "And just as well, for although we knew we had nothing to fear from you, some so-called gentlemen would ruin us without a thought."

"I hope you would report any such attempt to my father."

"We would have if we needed to. It was only when Mr Rowland, as he was then, had his friends staying that we had to be on the watch, but thankfully there's been no sign of them since he came into his title. But enough of this nonsense. It won't do for Jonas to find me talking in such a way to you."

Charles frowned. "So I hear. I hope he does not mistreat you?"

"You've no right to say so," she said, stiffening. "He worships the ground I walk on. It took me a while to realise it because I thought he was sweet on Ellie Crake." A hint of sadness passed over her face. "But that was all long ago." She gave a rueful smile. "You always did have a way of making us forget that you were well above our station and talk to you as if you were a friend."

"Sam still misses Ellie," he said.

"So do I," she said softly.

"Do you ever hear from her?"

She shook her head. "No, never a word. One day she was here and the next she was gone and that's all I know. I did wonder…"

When she trailed off as if in thought, Charles prompted her. "What did you wonder?"

"Well, in the weeks before she left all she could think about was one of the farmhands who worked for her pa. I did wonder if she'd gone looking for him."

She picked up her cheese and moved towards the door. "If she did, I hope she found him and she's as happy with him as I am with Jonas. Sally Stranmore was her closest friend, she's Sally Grant now and lives up in the woods behind the court. If anyone might have heard from her, it would be Sally. I'm afraid there's no time to explain what I do here just at the moment; I need to give little Joe his feed."

Sure enough, when they entered the kitchen, tiny high-pitched cries could be heard coming from a wooden box tucked in one corner of the room. Rachel smiled at her husband, scooped the baby up, and went out of the room.

"Did you find out all you wanted to about the dairy?" Jonas asked, his voice sullen.

Charles smiled broadly at him. "I didn't learn a thing, Jonas. Rachel was too busy telling me how happy she is with you. Now, I do hope there are some biscuits left for me."

"That's exactly what I used to say after you'd been visiting," Mr Blacky said dryly. He passed him a heavily laden plate. "It looks like you need them more than me today, so get stuck in, Captain."

After he had eaten his fill, they accompanied Mr Blacky and Jonas along a cart track that ran between fields lined with rows of cut grass, crops or stubble. Mr Blacky explained his rotation system to them as they strolled down towards the river. He nodded at a freshly ploughed field. "We'll be sowing the turnips soon. Very popular my turnips and good feed for the cows."

Lord Carteret seemed not to be quite as ignorant as he had professed for he asked several pertinent questions.

"What are these repairs that the cottage needs?" Charles said to Jonas.

"It's nothing too serious," he said, "and I'm quite capable of doing the work myself, but Mr Blacky thought we should get your father's permission first."

"If you wish to do the work yourself, you may, of course. I can understand it might be more convenient for you to do so, but you must give me a list of materials that you need. We shall provide them, at least."

When some half an hour later they collected their horses and began to ride back towards the hall, Lord Carteret said, "Did your charm still put Mrs Fielding in a twitter?"

Charles met his mocking gaze and his lips twisted in a wry smile. "I reined it in. I had no desire to put her in a twitter. Believe it or not, I never did."

Lord Carteret raised a sceptical brow. "You cannot meet a female without wishing to make her like you."

"Carteret!" Charles protested, laughing. "It is not true! You make me sound like a veritable coxcomb!"

"I do not think you that; you do not do it out of

vanity or conceit but because you are an inveterate flirt."

"No… well yes… but not because I wish to make every girl I meet fall in love with me."

Lord Carteret's laugh was as dry as sandpaper, and it seemed to graze Charles' temper. His eyes flashed. "Damn you, Carteret! I have never tried to make anyone fall in love with me. I am not so ramshackle!" His spurt of temper quickly died, and when he continued his voice held a hint of solemnity. "Besides, what would have been the point when I was away so much, could hardly support a wife, and would likely make them a widow before the year was out?" He sighed. "When I am home, I like to surround myself with fun and laughter. I like to make the people around me smile, I like to make them happy, and not because I wish them to love me, but because it makes me feel happier."

"As an antidote to your other life," Lord Carteret said quietly, his tone gentling.

"Yes, I suppose so. But I never distinguish one lady or girl above another, and I have never given any lady reason to suppose that I love her."

"No, I do not accuse you of that, and I admit you were the perfect choice for this mission. You have a knack for getting through people's defences. They like and trust you and not many can resist your smile. I have seen the frostiest matron succumb to it and be confiding in you within five minutes. I sometimes envy you that skill."

"Selena appears to confide in you," Charles said, looking searchingly at him. "I noticed her speaking to you very earnestly when we were at the lough."

Lord Carteret gave him an enigmatic glance. "I do believe, Charles, that some of Jonas Fielding's jealousy has rubbed off on you."

"Don't be ridiculous."

Even as he said the words, Charles remembered the smile he had coaxed from Selena when he had begged her forgiveness the day before. It had been warm and intimate, hinting at the special bond that had always existed between them. He had felt a moment's fierce pleasure that the one she had offered Ormsley had been almost perfunctory in comparison. It was not jealousy that had provoked this reaction; the thought was ludicrous. It was merely that he had been relieved that the harmony between himself and Selena had been restored and pleased that she had not had her head turned by a man who must be at least sixteen years her senior. He would admit he was a little piqued that she had seen fit to confide in Carteret instead of him, but only because it rendered him unable to help her.

"It is just that if something is worrying her, I would like to know of it."

"Then I suggest you ask her. A gentleman does not give up a lady's secrets."

"Then she does have some?"

"Everyone has secrets, Charles."

"What are your intentions towards her?" Charles asked abruptly.

A sardonic smile hovered about Lord Carteret's lips. "How very inquisitive you are this afternoon."

Charles looked belligerent. "You are not going to tell me, are you?"

"No, I do not believe I am, Charles. I will only say

this, I enjoy Lady Selena's company in no small measure."

Charles' irritation grew, partly because although it seemed nonsensical, he could not rid himself of the notion that Carteret was intentionally trying to get under his skin. "That much I already know. If you are not interested, I beg you will not raise her expectations, but if you are, I would take care that you do not lose out to a rival. What do you know of Ormsley?"

"I have never heard anything to his detriment. He is a good man and well respected. I have heard him make many a stirring speech in the House of Lords when he is passionate about some bill or other."

This reinforced Charles' good impression of the man, but it still did not make him a suitable candidate for Selena's hand.

"Do you think his intentions are serious? He is too old for Selena."

"I think his interest is piqued, and he is certainly considering matrimony as he proposed to Allerdale's bride quite early in the season."

Charles suddenly remembered a conversation that he had not really been paying attention to. It had been before his aunt's ball. Lady Brigham had been bombarding her son, Miles, with a run-down of all the ladies he might be interested in. She had mentioned Ormsley's wealth and good looks, but there had been something else. What was it? His eyes narrowed as his aunt's voice sounded in his head. *I was surprised to hear he had offered for Miss Edgcott as he is very starched up and she is, after all, only the daughter of a baronet and a lively girl. I would not have thought she would have suited him at all.*

If he had discovered that he liked lively girls, he

would discover soon enough that Selena fit that description, and she was the daughter of an earl and so of equal standing with him. Charles was suddenly glad he was coming to stay at the hall and not the court; it would be much easier to keep an eye on him. Selena may have seemed to suddenly grow up, but she was as innocent as a lamb and certainly not up to countering the moves of a man of Ormsley's experience.

Lord Carteret turned the subject. "Did you discover anything from Mrs Fielding?"

"Only that she thought Ellie might have gone to find Mr Rowe. You don't think Jonas could have murdered Ellie in a fit of jealous rage because she would not have him?"

"It is not outside the realms of possibility, but I don't think it. He waited for years before Rachel accepted him, after all. It seems he does not lack patience."

"Then it appears that all our hopes must be on the last name on my list, but I will leave it until tomorrow; I'm loath to admit it, but all that walking has tired me."

The admission brought some comfort to Charles. It was surely his fatigue that was causing him to be so irritable.

CHAPTER 13

When Lady Sheringham had commented that Lady Bassington was fortunate to have a daughter-in-law who would take on so many responsibilities, Selena had felt a stab of guilt. Her shock and resentment that her mother's place had been filled so soon by another, had kept her from offering her stepmother much support. She knew the comment had not been directed at her, but nevertheless thought she should make an effort to be more helpful. Lady Sheringham may not appear to need any help, but that did not mean that she would not be grateful for the offer. She resolutely stifled any feeling of disappointment and asked her maid to replace her riding habit in her wardrobe and instead bring her a morning dress.

Gregory looked up in surprise as she entered the breakfast parlour. "Are you not joining us for our ride this morning? Albina insists that we must practise her canter as we are to go with the Mawsleys and

Rowlands to Chillingham tomorrow, and she does not wish to slow the party down."

"Oh? Is Cedric coming too?"

Selena's tone was disapproving, and Gregory shook his head. "Selena, you cannot hold a man's youthful follies against him forever. Cedric may have run with a wild crowd for a time, but he settled down once he assumed his baronetcy."

Lady Sheringham spoke sharply. "I am not sure I wish Albina to go on an expedition with anyone whose character is questionable."

"It was not so much Cedric's character that was questionable, my dear," Lord Sheringham said, "but his friends. I used to feel very sorry for him. His nature is sensitive, like his mother's, and his father bullied him into becoming something he wasn't. Only Jane Rowland ever had the backbone to stand up to Sir Graham on his behalf. When Cedric assumed his title, the combined influence of his mother and sister allowed him to be the man he was meant to be, instead of the caricature his father created." He turned his glance upon Selena. "Cedric deserves compassion for the many unhappy years he suffered rather than censure for obeying his father's wishes. If you were not quite so prejudiced against him, you might have realised it. You stayed often enough with Jane when you were a girl, after all, and must have had opportunities enough to realise Cedric's true nature."

Selena gasped, unused to such a raking down from her papa, but found she could not defend herself. She was surprised to see sympathy in her stepmother's keen glance.

"I am surprised you allowed Selena to stay in such a household."

"Sir Graham may have been hard on his son, but as a gentleman, he would not have offered Selena or the other females in his household any incivility. And she did not visit when Cedric had friends staying as a rule."

Sensing Selena's discomfort, Albina asked quietly, "Why do you not ride today? I hope you are not ill?"

She forced a smile to her lips. "I am perfectly well, thank you. I thought I would make myself available to Mama, in case there was anything I might do for her."

It was the first time she had addressed her stepmother in such a way, and it had slipped from her mouth without thought or intent, but it somehow felt right. She could not be sorry for it, for the eyes Lady Sheringham turned towards her held surprise but also something akin to gratitude.

"I would be glad of your company, Selena," she said. "I am to visit Mrs Grant today, to take some salve for her son who has grazed his legs. Her sister-in-law is a maid here, and she told me of it."

Selena's smile became more natural. "What has little Oliver been up to now?"

"I believe he attempted to jump up behind a moving cart but was instead dragged behind it."

"That sounds like Oliver," she said. "He is full of pluck but cannot be brought to understand that his ability does not match his nerve."

"You will still come tomorrow, won't you?" Albina asked.

"Yes," Selena said, taking a deep breath. "Papa is

right. Cedric should be given the benefit of the doubt."

Lord Sheringham got up to leave the table, placing a comforting hand on Selena's shoulder as he passed her. "That is better, Selena. I am also pleased you are to accompany Elizabeth. You know our people well and will be able to fill her in on many small details."

Gregory winked at her from across the table and she saw devilry in his eyes. "I tell you what, Selena, you may take our step… our mother in my phaeton."

A look of amusement passed between them, but she said in a tone of sincere gratitude, "Thank you, Gregory. I find it so exhilarating to be perched so high above the ground, and your horses have such a wonderful turn of speed."

"That will not be necessary." Lady Sheringham said quickly, her eyes widening in alarm. "I will be quite happy in the gig."

Albina had been watching them closely and now became the recipient of Gregory's wink. Taking her cue, she said, "But, Mama, think how fashionable and dashing you would appear. I am quite envious."

Lady Sheringham raised her brows. "Albina, if allowing you the freedom to go into society a little has filled your head with such frivolous—"

Lord Sheringham chuckled. "It would be the height of foolishness to take the phaeton on such an expedition as they all know. I am afraid our reprehensible offspring are roasting you, my dear."

Lady Sheringham's mouth dropped open, but when she found four pairs of laughing eyes alight with expectation trained on her, she relaxed and smiled.

"Horrid children."

Lord Sheringham smiled indulgently at them. "It is good to hear you funning in quite your old way, but I must go to Newcastle on business and will be away overnight. Do not tease my good lady too much whilst I am away."

The Grants' cottage lay beside a road that ran through the woods to the north of the court. A wide track ran beside the house, leading to a yard and a long, low barn, before disappearing into the trees. Mr Grant was the estate carpenter and as Selena brought the gig to a halt, the sound of sawing could be heard, its grating notes somewhat offset by the cheerful whistling that rose above it. As they climbed down, the whistling stopped, and a thickset man in his mid-twenties, with a thatch of thick brown hair, liberally coated in sawdust emerged from the barn. When he saw his visitors, he quickly ran his hands through it and specks of dust danced through the dappled sunlight that filtered through the trees behind the barn.

"Lady Sheringham, Lady Selena," he said, bowing his head.

"We have brought something for Oliver's leg," Lady Sheringham said a little stiffly. "Your sister Molly informed us of his accident."

"That's mighty kind of you, milady, but it's only a few scratches."

"A few scratches can become a more serious affair if they are not treated properly."

Selena broke the awkward formality that hung between them. She offered him a friendly smile and nodded at the dray across the yard, still loaded with several lengths of wood.

"Is it that he fell from?"

Mr Grant grinned. "Aye. He was set on coming to work with me. Sally only turned her back for a moment and he was off like a terrier after a rabbit. The daft thing held onto the back of the cart for a mite too long. You go along in and I'll look after the gig. Captain Bassington has taken Oliver for a ride on his horse, but I doubt he'll be long."

As they walked towards the back of the house, Lady Sheringham said, "What business has Captain Bassington visiting our tenants?"

"Sally is the daughter of Mrs Stranmore, who is one of Lord Bassington's tenants, so it is not as surprising as it seems."

"Oh, I see."

Selena glanced at her. Her tone was not disapproving but guarded.

"Charles knows everyone," Selena said, "and he has always had the freedom to roam Sheringham lands, as we have had the freedom to roam Bassington lands."

They entered through the back door which gave directly onto the kitchen and discovered Mrs Grant wiping at her eyes with a handkerchief. Lady Sheringham took a half-step back, clearly uncomfortable to have intruded, but Selena rushed forwards.

"Mrs Grant! What has occurred to distress you so?"

Mrs Grant's youthful face flushed with embarrassment as she blew her nose and curtsied at the same time.

"I do beg your pardon, Lady Sheringham, Lady Selena. It is nothing. Please, won't you sit? I still have some of the tea from the Christmas box you very kindly gave me, my lady, if you would like some."

"Certainly not," Lady Sheringham said, "it is for your personal use and we have no need of refreshment. But I would like you to share with us what has distressed you. I hope Captain Bassington is not responsible for it?"

Selena stiffened at the suggestion but saw that a look of dismay had already replaced the one of suspicion her stepmother had worn when she had asked the question.

"He is in a way, although he would be mortified, I'm sure, if he knew. It is just that we got talking of old times and he asked me if I had heard from Ellie Crake, who used to be a close friend of mine."

"Sam's sister?" Selena said.

Mrs Grant nodded. "That's right, my lady. Did you know her?"

"No, but I know Sam well enough. He used to be Charles' shadow when I was a girl."

"Yes, they were always thick as thieves. I don't know if you remember, but Ellie just up and left five years ago, without a word to any of us."

"Ah, I see," Lady Sheringham said. "Well, now we know that the cause of your distress is nothing we can help you with—"

Selena's interest had been caught, and she interrupted. "Do you know what became of her?"

"That's what Captain Bassington asked me." She suddenly smiled reminiscently. "She thought the world of him. I remember he made her a necklace out of glass beads and she never took it off from the day he gave it to her." She sighed. "As far as I know, no one has ever heard from her again. Her ma thought she had found a position somewhere, but if she had, I'm sure she would have written to tell us of it, which made me think something might have happened to her." She shook her head. "It was that thought that upset me. But I'm probably being foolish; people change, after all, don't they?"

"Indeed they do," Lady Sheringham agreed.

Mrs Grant gave a dry chuckle. "No matter how much she's changed, I'd lay odds she still wears that necklace. It was only a simple little thing, with green, red, and white glass beads, but you'd have thought it was made of the finest jewels the way she loved it."

"Yes, well, we mustn't take up too much of your time, Mrs Grant," Lady Sheringham said. "I have brought you a salve to put on Oliver's leg. It would not do to let it become infected."

Selena let the words flow over her head as Lady Sheringham began to explain its properties and how often to use it. She felt cold prickles run along her forearms. Mrs Grant had exactly described the necklace she had found at the lough.

A firm stride was heard on the gravel path outside and Charles came through the open door, ducking so that the small boy set upon his shoulders would not bang his head upon the lintel. He had a mop of hair much like his father's and an engaging grin. Charles clasped his skinny legs above the knees, avoiding the rash of grazes that extended down both shins.

"Here you are, Sally. I've brought him back safe and sound."

He reached up and clasped the boy about the

waist before setting him carefully on the floor as he spoke.

"The captain says I'm a very brave soldier!" the little boy cried, running to his mother.

Charles wiped at a smudge of dust on his boot. "Yes, but do not forget what I have told you, young Oliver. A good soldier does not rush headlong into action without considering the consequences, and he certainly does not disobey orders!"

He straightened as he spoke, and for the first time saw the company. His eyes widened slightly, but he smiled and said cheerfully, "Follow my lead, Oliver."

Selena bit back a smile as he bowed and the four-year-old followed suit.

"Good day, Lady Sheringham, Lady Selena."

As Oliver parroted the words as best he could, Lady Sheringham's face softened.

"I have brought something to make your leg better, young man."

Oliver looked at her uncertainly. "Will it hurt?"

"It might sting, just for a moment, but your leg will heal much faster."

"Brave soldiers do not fear having their wounds tended, Oliver," Charles said gently.

Oliver stood a little straighter. "Thank you, Lady Sherry."

"Lady Sheringham," Mrs Grant said quickly.

The boy sighed. "But, Ma, it is such a long word."

Selena watched in some surprise as her stepmother leaned forwards and brought her face very close to his, saying in a loud whisper, "You may call me Lady Sherry, but it must be our little secret. It would not do if everyone did so."

"I shall take my leave of you," Charles said, bowing again. "Mrs Grant, Lady Selena." He unleashed his smile on Lady Sheringham before adding, "Lady Sherry."

Although Lady Sheringham raised a haughty brow, Selena thought she saw her lips quiver. She rose to her feet. "I shall come and say hello to Spirit as I am sure Oliver does not wish for an audience."

She closed the door behind them and walked beside Charles along the path that led through the small garden. When they reached the gate that led to the yard, she paused with her hand on it and turned to face him. As usual, his grin drew a smile from her.

"I do not think your step-mama approves of me, Selena."

"Then you have received a salutary lesson, Charles."

He quirked a brow. "How so?"

"It will do you a great deal of good to realise you cannot charm every woman who walks this earth."

He shook his head and heaved a dramatic sigh. "It is a blow, I must admit, but never fear, I will come about! I do believe that I may have made a very small dent in Lady Sherry's icy reserve just now."

"She was not at all icy with Oliver," Selena pointed out.

"No, she wasn't, was she? I wouldn't have believed she could look so... so kindly."

"Just because she does not wear her heart on her sleeve, it does not follow that she does not have one."

"I shall take your word for it. I am pleased that you seem much more comfortable in her presence, at any rate."

"When you saw us in Town, we were at odds a little," she said quietly. "But we understand each other better now."

He suddenly reached for her hand and squeezed it gently. "I am glad, Selena."

Even through her glove, the back of her hand tingled at his touch and she withdrew it a little more quickly than was polite. "As am I."

She opened the gate and hastily stepped through it, needing to put a little distance between them. He followed her, a small frown between his eyes.

"You are surely not still angry with me?"

She did feel a sudden, unexpected flash of anger. She was determined to accept their status as friends, to enjoy it even, as she had always done, but how was she to do so when he smiled at her, touched her, and spoke to her so tenderly? It made her feel that she was special to him, but she knew full well that she was not. She had seen his charm in action at Lady Brigham's ball, after all. She had watched him dance with a succession of creatures far more beautiful than she and saw how they smiled coquettishly, their eyes sparkling, also feeling that they were special no doubt. But then he had asked her to write to him, a request that should not have been made to any other than a family member, and she had been led to hope.

These thoughts only served to intensify her anger and she whirled around, about to fling them in his face, only to discover he was barely a step behind her. They inevitably collided and as she stumbled, he wrapped his hands around her arms to steady her. Heat chased over her shoulders, up her neck, and into her cheeks, and all the breath seemed driven from her lungs. As she opened her lips to take a deep gulp of air, his head descended towards her, and for a moment she vacillated between fear and hope that he would kiss her. But he stopped a few scant inches from her face, his glowing eyes narrowing a little.

"Selena," he said softly.

"Charles," she breathed.

"I do believe your freckles have come back."

The absurdity of the comment defused both her anger and the strange sensations coursing through her. She took a step backwards and gave a ragged laugh.

"Charles, you beast."

He released her and put up his hands. "No, no, Selena, I have always liked your freckles. In fact, I was disappointed that they had disappeared."

"Oh, stop it, you… you idiot!" she gasped through another laugh. "They were always there, only my step-mother gave me some lotion to disguise them."

She felt a surge of relief that she had not voiced her feelings to him. Their friendship would have been ruined and she would not have liked that. It was not his fault, but her own unruly feelings that were to blame. She gathered herself and her laughter dried up as she remembered why she had wished to speak with him.

"Charles, did the necklace I found belong to Ellie Crake?"

He sobered in an instant. "How did you find out?"

Her hand flew to her mouth and sudden tears started in her eyes.

"This is precisely why we did not mention it. We did not wish you or Albina to be alarmed."

She shook her head and sighed heavily. "I am not

alarmed, only sad for Sam and his family. That poor girl. I wonder what happened to her?"

"That is what your father and I are trying to discover."

Her brow wrinkled. "But why were you asking Mrs Grant if she had heard from Ellie when you already knew that she was dead?" She gasped and her voice dropped to a whisper as her brain caught up with the ramifications of her discovery. "You do not mean to tell me she was murdered?"

"No, I do not mean to tell you that," Charles said. "She had thought herself in love with one of the farm labourers, who did not return her feelings. It was some weeks after he left that she disappeared."

"So you think she killed herself?"

Selena was not sure which scenario she found more shocking.

"All possibilities are being considered, including accident. Your papa has gone to try and find the man Ellie was infatuated with. Perhaps we will know more when he returns." He sighed. "It was unfortunate you visited Sally today and discovered the truth. Your father does not wish his investigation to become general knowledge, Selena."

"I am so glad you informed me of it," she said, her sweet tone at variance with the exasperation in her eyes, "or else I might have mentioned it in passing to everyone I met."

His lips twitched. "It would only be natural that you might wish to discuss it with your particular friends."

"You may be sure, Charles, that I will not. I am quite adept at keeping secrets, I assure you."

Her voice had turned flat and hard, and his eyes suddenly bored into hers as if trying to reach inside her and draw every last one of them out. She dropped her gaze and shook her head.

"Selena," he said in an urgent under voice, but Mr Grant brought his horse to him and the moment passed.

"I shall go and prepare the gig. Goodbye, Charles."

Selena became aware of her stepmother's eyes on her on more than one occasion as they drove back to the court. She remembered how she had looked dismayed after she had asked Mrs Grant to explain her distress, and how she had tried to turn the subject away from her conversation with Charles.

"You already knew about Ellie, didn't you?"

"Yes," she admitted. "Your father likes to keep me informed of his affairs, to discuss them with me."

Selena heard the note of bemusement in her voice, and despite the seriousness of the topic at hand, she smiled.

"You are not used to that, I think."

"No. I am not used to my opinion being sought on topics that are generally thought to be the purview of men."

"You do not like it?"

"It is not that I do not like it, it is more that I am not used to being treated as an equal."

Selena remembered the words she had spoken to her in Town. *There is no such thing as friendship between men and women. Such a notion is preposterous! What have they in common?* She could not resist saying, "Or being treated as a friend?"

"Or as a friend," Lady Sheringham acknowledged, becoming busy retying the ribbons on her bonnet. "It appears that it is not such a preposterous notion, after all." She suddenly reached out a hand and placed it on Selena's arm. "Thank you. That was the easiest visit I have yet paid."

Selena looked at her in some surprise. "But surely you are used to the role? Did your husband not have tenants to visit?"

"He did, and I have been brought up to do my duty to any dependents. But I was taught to do it with condescension and no real feeling. I find it hard to change old habits, but it was easier with you present today. You have a natural way about you." She smiled, but it was the tight smile she gave when uncomfortable. "I think it also helped for the Grants to see you with me. I have felt a little resentment from some of our tenants. It seems your mother was well loved."

Selena felt a wave of shame wash over her. "I am sorry. I should have thought of that and come with you sooner."

Lady Sheringham released her arm and drew her shawl more firmly around her shoulders.

"That is what your father said. But I would not have him force you into it. I was fully aware that it was not an easy time for you."

"For any of us," Selena said gently, feeling simultaneously touched and remorseful that her stepmother had shown her such consideration at a time when she had shown her none.

"That is true." Lady Sheringham's smile was tinged with sadness and regret. "I wish to also thank you for befriending Albina. I have never seen her smile or laugh so much as she does now. She has always been a quiet, serious little thing, seemingly content with her own company, but it is quite clear that she is enjoying being part of a larger family."

"And I am enjoying getting to know my little sister." They had wandered some way from the original topic of their conversation but mention of Albina put Selena in mind of it. "I think we should tell Albina of Papa's investigation. In some ways, she is older than her years, and I do not think she will be overset by it, on the contrary, I think she would feel more upset to have been left out of something everyone else in the house knows about."

"Whilst I appreciate your concern for Albina's feelings, I am not convinced that is sufficient reason to inform her of such unsettling events, but I shall consult your father when he returns tomorrow."

CHAPTER 14

Charles took a path through the woods, feeling frustration and relief in equal measure. He was now certain that Selena was keeping something from him, and he had been so close to discovering what it was he could almost taste it. He groaned softly. That was not the only thing he had so nearly tasted. When he had felt Selena's warm skin beneath his palms, her slender body pressed to his as he briefly held her, he had felt a sudden jolt of desire. For a moment, the wide eyes looking up at him had not seemed like hers, but those of a vibrant, passionate creature begging to be kissed. He had very nearly granted that imagined plea, but as he had bent his head, he had seen something very like fear in those large hazel eyes, and it had been Selena before him again.

He felt a brute for frightening her, but at least it had prevented him from making an irrevocable mistake. He gave a heartfelt sigh. It had been some time since he had bedded a woman, and a man could not ignore his basic needs indefinitely. To think he could have ruined years of friendship by a single moment of madness. Worse, if he had kissed Selena, it was entirely possible that not only Tom Grant, but also Sally and Lady Sheringham might have seen them, and then they might have been forced into a union that neither of them desired and no one could possibly have approved of. The disparity in their fortunes was so great it was not to be thought of. He had no wish to make such an unequal marriage, to be beholden to his wife for every penny he spent; no man's pride could bear it. After his mother's dinner, he might take a trip to Newcastle and sate his needs with a very friendly widow whom he occasionally visited when he was at home.

The dim light that surrounded him gradually brightened as the trees thinned and he came to the park of Sheringham Court. He leant forwards, kicked his heels, and flew across the grass towards his father's lands, putting the rather unsettling episode from his mind.

When he walked into the hall, he discovered Doctor Shilbury about to take leave of his father.

"So, there you are, Captain," he said. "I had given up hope of examining you… again!"

Charles handed his hat to the butler, before saying in clipped tones, "I am perfectly well. I need neither a posset, a mustard bath, nor anything else."

Lord Bassington regarded his son coolly. "You will let the doctor be the judge of that. And it seems, Charles, that you have forgotten your manners."

Charles offered the doctor a small bow, a flush of colour staining his cheeks.

"Good morning, sir. I meant no disrespect. I am very grateful for your diligence, but I really am much better."

The doctor smiled knowingly at him. "There is no need to apologise, Captain. You have never had any patience with being quacked, as you have often told me! I can see for myself that as usual, you have defied my expectations and are looking in fine fettle, but I would feel easier in my mind if I could listen to your heart and lungs and ask you a few questions."

Lord Bassington bent a stern eye upon his son. "And make sure you answer them honestly, Charles. You may come to my study afterwards."

When Charles dutifully arrived there some twenty minutes later, he found his father signing a series of letters on his desk. Lord Bassington waved a hand at a chair, scribbled his signature on the last one with a flourish, bundled the papers together and slid them into a drawer, before looking closely at his son.

"Well? Have you been given a clean bill of health?"

A faint smile touched Charles' lips. He detected the note of concern behind his father's bluff manner.

"Not quite, sir. The good doctor has confirmed I am doing very well and has now prescribed that I begin to exercise my lungs a little more vigorously by taking longer walks."

Lord Bassington gave a short bark of laughter. "That is medicine that should not prove unpalatable to you, at least. And what of your visit this morning?"

"There was nothing more to be learned from Sally,

but I am afraid that Selena arrived whilst I took young Oliver for a short ride and she discovered the purpose of my visit."

His father raised a brow. "That was unfortunate. Not too alarmed, was she?"

"No, sir," he said, firmly banishing the thought that the only alarm she had suffered was thanks to him.

"I'm pleased to hear it. I'm very fond of her. She has a few odd quirks in her character, but she's a good girl for all that."

Charles thought that his father's gaze was rather probing and wondered if the guilt he felt at nearly kissing Selena had shown on his face, but he relaxed as Lord Bassington turned the subject.

"If you think you are up to it, I would like you to accompany Adolphus to Horton tomorrow morning. The estate lands are not in as good order as those here, and he will be able to show you why not and explain the improvements that need to be done."

Charles leant forwards, an eager look in his eyes. "I would like that. I have always had a fondness for the place."

"I know it." Lord Bassington smiled wryly. "You were the only one of us your great aunt Cecelia liked to visit her."

Charles laughed. "She was queer in her attic, so I can hardly take that as a compliment."

"I would not go that far, Charles." He sighed reminiscently. "She was a great beauty when she was young, you know, had scores of admirers, but chose to live a quiet, bookish life with her sister instead of marrying. But it was only after Margaret died that she moved to Horton and became a complete recluse."

Charles smiled fondly. "She told me that she could not bear to live in the house they had shared, that it had too many memories, yet she surrounded herself with pictures of Great Aunt Margaret, and often looked at the portrait of her set over the fireplace in the green parlour, almost as if she were including her in the conversation."

"Yes, she was much more comfortable living in the past. Your mother tried every now and then to make her more outward looking. After Lady Sheringham died, she often took Selena with her when she visited Cecelia. Selena had become so withdrawn she thought it might do her some good."

Charles looked surprised. "I didn't know. I hope she didn't terrify her."

"On the contrary, Cecelia took a shine to Selena. Said she reminded her of Margaret."

Charles' eyes lost focus as he brought the image of his great aunt's portrait into his mind. "There is a resemblance," he finally said. "In the colour of her hair and eyes."

"And her freckles, apparently," Lord Bassington said. "Cecelia said she could almost believe Selena had been Margaret's daughter."

"Really?" Charles said. "I must admit I never looked that closely at the portrait. I shall ask Selena what she made of Great Aunt Cecelia when next I see her."

Horton Hall lay a few miles east of the small market town of Wooler. It was a solid square edifice, its only claim to distinction being the elegant Doric porch and the delicate pink tinge of its stones. The estate encompassed the two small hamlets of East and West Horton, and its acres were divided by Horton Burn and bounded by the river Till to the south, so it was not perhaps surprising that they were lush and fertile. The Cheviot Hills rose to the west, adding a touch of drama to the undulating rural landscape.

"We shall not bother old Farnaby," Adolphus said, as he led him across the fields towards the modest park that surrounded the house. "I do not wish to embarrass him by airing his shortcomings in front of him."

"No," agreed Charles. "It is not his fault that his years have caught up with him."

Adolphus led him up a steep bank and reined in at its top. From this vantage point, they could see many acres of land spread out before them, and the glint of the river as it bent around in a loop in the far distance.

"Tell me what you see," Adolphus said.

Charles let his eyes flow over the patchwork of greens, browns, and golds before him.

"Too many fields are lying fallow," he murmured.

"Very good," Adolphus said. "And it is unnecessary. Turnips or clover can be grown to keep down weeds, replenish the soil, and provide fodder for livestock. What else?"

Charles' gaze was caught by a field of wheat, its golden stalks rippling in the breeze. He suddenly put his hand to his eyes to shield them from the glare of the sun and discovered it was not wheat, but grass that had been allowed to grow, presumably for haymaking.

"That grass should have been scythed when it was still green," he said, "and laid out to dry."

Adolphus leaned over and put a hand on his shoulder. "That is a good start. We farm many of these acres ourselves and in addition to having a word with our farm manager, we have two tenant farmers I intend to visit today. Keep your eyes and ears open. They have a duty to keep our land in good order, on top of that; if they are not productive enough, they will not be able to pay their rent. The tenancies come up this September and will be renewed for anyone who is doing a good job, but the farms we shall visit are in arrears. If they have a reasonable explanation or are willing to listen to sound advice then we may keep them on, but if not, they will have to go."

By the time they rode up to the house to partake of the luncheon Mrs Lantern, the housekeeper at Horton, had prepared for them, Charles had a growing respect and admiration for his brother. He had handled the tenants with a gentle but firm hand. His questions had been incisive, his knowledge better than theirs, and he had left them with a list of things that they must do, divided into two columns, one marked urgent, the other important. He had left them in no doubt that if things had not improved by September, they would need to move on.

"I never knew you could be so ruthless," Charles said, as they left their horses with the single groom who was in charge of the stables. "What about loyalty?"

Adolphus smiled, but his eyes were serious. "Loyalty cuts both ways. How did you deal with soldiers who did not pull their weight?"

Charles spoke without hesitation. "I'd give them a dressing down, tell them in no uncertain terms what was expected of them and give them a chance to shape up. If they did not do so, I would report them to a higher authority. We were a team, and if even one member did not perform his duty to the required standard, lives could have been put in danger."

Adolphus nodded his approval. "It seems to me then, that running an estate is not much different. Lives might not be lost, of course, but livelihoods might be. Our dependents each have their own role, their own place in the ranks if you will, but we must work together if we are all to prosper."

"You are right," Charles said slowly, as Mr Harbottle's words whispered in his head. *You must have learned many skills and developed several aspects of your character that could be put to good use. I suggest you make a list of your strengths and consider how they could best serve you.* He was used to being a leader of men, used to acting on his own initiative, used to making decisions based on reason, and even taking calculated risks. Carteret had commented on how people liked him, confided in him. All of these facets of his character could surely be put to good use here. He had lived a nomadic life for years and he was tired of it. It would be good to put down roots.

"I would like to run somewhere like this," he said softly, unaware of the yearning in his voice or even that he had spoken the words aloud until Adolphus answered him.

"I don't know exactly what is in Father's mind, but if you show yourself capable enough, perhaps you will. He will retire Farnaby when he finds a suitable replacement, I'm sure."

Charles felt something light up deep inside at this possibility. To be near enough to his family and friends that he could see them regularly, but far enough away that he could make his own life, was an extremely attractive prospect. He had always lived a life of service, but he had served his country long enough. He would enjoy devoting himself to his father's interests, to repaying him for purchasing his colours, for insisting on providing him with a small allowance on top of his wages.

He loved the countryside and knew every acre of both the Sheringham and Bassington lands, but here he could explore vistas new, breathe life into the land rather than soak it with the blood of his country's enemies. In that moment, a steely determination was forged within him, to not only apply himself assiduously to his new duties but to excel at them. He would not approach his father for this post until he knew he could fulfil its requirements. He wished to be granted the role of steward here, not as a favour or because he was a younger son in need of employment, but because he deserved it, in other words, on merit.

They found Mrs Lantern laying out their luncheon in the dining room with the help of a maid. She had been quite a young woman when she had first come here with his great aunt, but now her hair was peppered with grey, and her face was lined, but her eyes lit up as they entered the room.

"It is all ready for you, Mr Bassington, Captain Bassington."

Charles looked at the heavily laden table and chuckled. "But this is a feast fit for a king, Mrs Lantern. You should not have gone to so much trouble."

"Oh, it was no trouble, sir. It is very pleasant to

have someone to wait on. I am so looking forward to Mr and Mrs Bassington's visit." She cast an eye at the paint peeling above one of the windows. "This is a fine house, and it has wrung my heart to see it going to rack and ruin."

The brothers did justice to the spread set out before them, and after they had eaten their fill, Charles strolled around the house whilst Adolphus imparted the various messages Caroline had sent to the housekeeper. The rooms had spacious proportions without being so large that a fire lit in the grates would not easily warm them. Judging by the damp that had caused the paint or wallpaper to peel in several rooms, not many of them had been lit very often. The house was shabby and neglected, but there was no structural damage as far as he could see. The windows needed some attention and most of the rooms needed airing and redecorating, but beyond that only the presence of people was needed to dispel the rather melancholy air that hung over it.

In the nursery, he found a rocking horse, its colour undistinguishable beneath the thick coat of dust it wore. He gave it a gentle nudge and listened to the wooden rockers' rhythmic thud. A happy lively family would be best, he thought. He felt a sudden pang of sadness that it would not be his and pushed it firmly away. He was getting carried away and it would not do. It would make no sense for him to live in the house when once it had been put in order, a decent income could be made from renting it out. He would be quite happy in the lodge, the traditional residence of the steward here.

When he returned downstairs, he made for the

green parlour. He went straight to where the portrait of Great Aunt Margaret still hung and gazed intently at it for some moments. There *was* a marked resemblance between her and the young woman Selena had become. The rich, chestnut hair was dressed differently of course, but it framed the same oval-shaped face, and if the eyes that stared out at him were rather more piercing than Selena's, they were certainly of the same hue. Feeling a bit of an idiot, but somehow unable to resist the impulse, he pulled over a chair and stood upon it, the better to observe her freckles. A short laugh escaped him. They were lightly scattered across her nose and cheeks in the exact same pattern as Selena's. He jumped down hastily as he heard the steady tread of his brother.

"Are you ready to go, Charles? Have you seen all you wished to?"

"Yes," he said brightly. "Let us be on our way."

They had just come to a hill that led down to the village of Old Bewick when they saw a riding party some way ahead of them. Charles recognised the jade green riding habit immediately.

The trip to Chillingham Castle proved very successful. The housekeeper showed them around as the Tankervilles preferred their London abode and were rarely in residence. There were many fine rooms to be seen, and an interesting history attached to many of them. King Henry III had stayed in this room, James I in that one, yet there were chills and gloom enough in many of the medieval fortress's nooks and crannies to excite the most sluggish of imaginations.

Although none of the ladies present generally suffered from an excess of sensibility, the dungeon and torture chamber, replete with thumb screws, cages, and branding irons could not fail to send a shiver down anyone's spine. And when the housekeeper told them tales of ghosts that flitted across the courtyard when the moon was full, or of strange lights that many guests had witnessed in one of the parlours, usually accompanied by ghastly groans, in the most casual of tones, they found themselves torn between amusement and a rather delicious and tantalising fear that the stories might be true.

Gregory had not been able to resist playing a joke on them and had stood by a window and reflected the sun's rays from the glass face of his pocket watch so that a circular glowing light had danced across one of the dark tapestries that lined the walls of a bed chamber. But although the girls had gasped and clutched each other's hands, it was Cedric Rowland who had shrieked and backed out of the room.

Gregory had laughed and called him back.

"It was only me, you clodpole!"

Cedric was reed thin and had red hair like his sister, Jane, and as he came sheepishly back into the room, his scarlet face clashed horribly with it. His prominent Adam's apple bobbed up and down in his slender neck as he gulped, and Selena found herself feeling excessively sorry for him. He was the skittish, awkward boy she remembered, not the rather swaggering idiot he had later become, and she found herself going to him and placing a hand on his arm, a smile on her lips.

"Do not feel embarrassed, Cedric," she said gently. "I am sure I might have done the same thing if my feet had not been rooted to the floor as if they had been shackled by those leg irons we saw in the dungeon."

"And I thought my heart would burst through my chest," Sarah Mawsley said, eyeing Gregory resentfully. "You are the greatest beast in nature."

Cedric's eyes spoke his gratitude, but he said ruefully, "As females, it is quite understandable that you might have been terrified, but I should have stayed to protect you." He grimaced. "My father would have had me horse whipped for such cowardice."

"I am sure you would have returned of your own accord in a moment," Jane said calmly. "I am sure it is not to be wondered at that you were momentarily startled." She sent the perpetrator of the jest a withering glance. "It is Gregory that deserves to be horse whipped."

"Sorry," he said, with an unrepentant grin, "couldn't resist it. You must see that."

"I'm with Jane," Ralf Mawsley said sternly, "to scare poor Albina like that was uncalled for and downright mean."

Albina smiled up at him. "Do not be concerned on my behalf, Ralf. I was thrilled rather than afraid. What could a little light do to me, after all?"

Selena saw the warmth in her eyes and heard the admiration in Ralf's voice as he said, "You're a remarkable young lady, Albina."

She felt a little uneasy. She had grown fond of her

stepsister and would not wish her to be made unhappy. She had nothing at all to say against Ralf, she had always liked him, but her mama had her heart set on a good, if not a great match for Albina, she was sure.

Albina was the daughter of a viscount, and now the stepdaughter of an earl, and although Ralf Mawsley could ensure she was comfortable, his estate was small, and he had no title at all. But perhaps she was making too much of it. Albina did not hang upon his every word or attempt to attract his attention in any way, but divided her attention equally amongst the friends, as was proper. Even now she had moved on to take Sarah's arm to study a dark portrait of a rather morose looking woman, and they were happily inventing a story that might explain her sullenness.

As they made their way home, Cedric brought his horse alongside her own. He sent her an anxious sideways glance.

"Do you know, Selena, that today is the first time we have exchanged more than a passing greeting for years."

She felt a prickle of remorse but reminded herself that there had been reason enough for it. Not wishing to spoil the enjoyment of the day, she said lightly, "But then there was a time when you were rarely at home and then I was in mourning, so perhaps it is not so surprising."

She focused on his chin, careful not to meet his eyes in case her own revealed more than she wished him to see. She tensed as she saw his Adam's apple bob as he swallowed, as if he were preparing to say something difficult to her.

"I know my behaviour was not all it should have

been for a while, Selena, and I bitterly regret it now."
He gulped again. "It was unfortunate my friends
arrived a day early the last time you stayed with us.
You were only fifteen and very open and trusting. I am
aware now that they were not fit company for you or
my sister." He drew in a deep breath. "I suppose I
knew it then, but my father wished them to come. He
said he wished to meet the sparky young fellows who
had managed to get me sent down." He gave a bitter
laugh. "You would think he would have been angry
rather than pleased, but he said it showed I was devel-
oping some backbone at last. I have always suspected
that one of them must have deeply offended you, for
you never came to stay after that and have seemed to
avoid me ever since."

For a moment she could not breathe, and resentment flared within her that he should probe a wound
that if not completely healed, was protected by several
layers of scar tissue.

"I hope we can be friends again, Selena. That you
will remember the boy who brought you posies of
flowers from the garden and played charades with you
and Jane, rather than the boorish young man I turned
into when I was at university."

Her resentment evaporated as she remembered
these episodes and other instances of his kindness. She
had not allowed herself to think of them for a long
time. She finally raised her eyes. His begged for her
forgiveness more eloquently than any words could
have, and she felt pity stir in her breast. Cedric had
always wished for approval from his father, his mother,
his sister and his friends. There had been a time when
he had tried very hard to please them all. How diffi-

cult it must have been for him to try to achieve it when they each demanded something quite different from him.

"Let us not talk of it again," she said. "You are forgiven, Cedric." She felt her heart lighten with the words.

CHAPTER 15

Selena turned her head as she heard the sound of horses' hooves thundering against the hard-baked surface of the road behind them and saw Adolphus and Charles cantering down the hill. If they had not both been excellent horsemen, it would have been extremely foolish to descend so steep an incline at such a pace. Charles led the way and as he closed the distance between them, he waved his hat in the air and called a greeting.

"By God! I wish I could ride like that," Cedric murmured.

Charles appeared to best advantage in the saddle, Selena reflected. When Lord Carteret had ridden Spirit, he had handled him well, but the effort it took him had been obvious, from his firm hold on the reins to the way he had gripped him with his legs. Charles seemed to communicate his wishes to the horse with the lightest of touches. She felt a blush creep into her cheeks as she remembered that light touch on her own skin, and how she had completely misconstrued his wishes.

The party pulled up to wait for them, and when greetings and a brief résumé of their respective activities had been exchanged, Charles fell in next to Selena. There was a pent-up excitement about him, and the smile he flashed at her was even gayer than usual. It was infectious and she laughed.

"You enjoyed your visit to Horton, I think."

His eyes glowed with enthusiasm. "I did. I have always liked the house, but I have never before surveyed the estate. I find I am more interested in such matters than I had ever thought possible."

"I don't suppose you have had much leisure to pay such matters any attention."

"No, or the desire to do so. There seemed little point when… well, never mind that."

"When you would be going away again so soon?" Selena finished for him. "When your father's estate would never be yours?"

He looked at her in some surprise, his eyes rueful. "You have given voice to my thoughts with insightful accuracy, Selena. When did you grow so wise?"

She averted her glance, fully aware that she did not deserve the soft glow of admiration with which he regarded her. She had not been wise on any number of matters, although she hoped she was becoming more so. Her insight had not been the product of wisdom or even her long acquaintance with him but had been inspired by her own feelings. She had often thought of both of these things; hoping that he would not go away again so soon, and without ever having wished any harm to Adolphus, regretting that he was not the first-born son, and so might never have left in the first place. She could hardly tell him so, however, and turned the subject.

"I also like Horton. It is a fine house. I am glad Caroline is going to lavish some care upon it."

"Yes, Father told me you visited my great aunt with my mother. What did you make of her?"

"I found her very sympathetic," Selena said softly. "She understood what it was like to lose someone close to her, and she treated me very kindly."

"I am glad she brought you some comfort." His words were gently spoken and heartfelt, however, he lightened the moment by raising a questioning eyebrow and saying with a look of amusement, "But what did you find to talk about? You are no more bookish than I am, Selena."

A gurgle of laughter escaped her. "Your great aunt soon discovered that. She talked to her sister's portrait and told her that although I was shockingly ignorant, she should not hold it against me. She took a liking to me, you see. I think because there was a passing resemblance between your Great Aunt Margaret and I and because she discovered you and I had always been the best of friends. She liked me to talk about you. You were a prime favourite with her."

Charles grinned. "She was not such a blue-stocking as she pretended, you know. She used to make me tell her tales of my adventures, and the more reprehensible they were, the more she enjoyed them. She used to say that all men were fools, and I more than most, but that she could not deny that we were entertaining. Then she would glance at the portrait and look guilty."

Selena considered this. "She must have been very beautiful in her time. Do you think she did not marry because her sister didn't wish her to?"

"I have no idea. I don't remember Great Aunt Margaret, but I hope that wasn't the case. When she died, Cecelia had no children to look after her, no jointure as she would have had if she had been widowed, and worst of all, she was horribly lonely. It is no wonder she talked to her sister's portrait. Father invited her to live with us, but she wouldn't countenance the idea."

"I imagine after living life on her own terms for so many years, it would have been difficult to adapt to being part of someone else's household."

"Indeed it would," Charles said, a wry smile twisting his lips.

Selena had been thinking of not only his great aunt but her stepmother, however, she instinctively knew that he was thinking of his own circumstances. Despite his fondness for his family, she knew he would never be content to live at Bassington Hall. To be dependent on his family after so many years of making his own way in the world would not suit him at all. To her surprise, she realised she was glad of it. To have him always so close would be an exquisite agony that she doubted she could endure. But she could not help but be glad that he was here now, that he was speaking to her not as a child to be indulged or reprimanded, but as a friend he could talk to. She would enjoy the time left to them before he returned to his regiment, store up the memories from this visit, and then carefully wrap them and put them away, as her maid stored her summer dresses when winter came.

They had come to a crossroads and the Mawsleys and Rowlands took their leave, going in opposite directions. Soon afterwards they came to Eglingham, and Selena looked enquiringly at Charles when he did not turn down the track that would take him most directly to Bassington Hall.

"We thought we might see if your father is at home. We would like to know what he has discovered, if anything."

They found Lord and Lady Bassington with Lord Carteret in the drawing room. Selena went quickly forwards, an apologetic smile on her lips. "I do hope you have not been waiting long. It is too bad that no one was at home to receive you. Trinklow has taken good care of you, I trust?"

Lady Bassington reached for a wine glass set on the table beside her and raised it. "He has, as you see." She looked at Selena with approval as she took a small sip. "That was very prettily done, my dear. You will make a fine hostess when you marry."

"Indeed she will," Lord Carteret agreed.

Selena looked from one to the other and laughed. "Never have I received such praise with so little effort."

Lord Bassington chuckled. "We would hardly be sitting here drinking your papa's excellent claret if no one was at home, Selena. Your papa came in a few minutes ago and your stepmother wished for a private word with him."

"Which I have now had," Lady Sheringham said, coming into the room. "He wishes to change before greeting our guests and I suggest you and Albina do the same but do not be long."

As Selena passed her, she laid a hand on her arm, and said quietly, "Albina is to be admitted into my lord's confidence, so perhaps you will explain to her the nature of his investigation but try not to alarm her."

"I doubt I could," Selena said dryly. "She was the only one of us who was not afraid when we thought we saw evidence of a ghost at the castle."

"Yes, well, this concerns something that is real and not imaginary."

As Selena had predicted, Albina was not at all alarmed, but intrigued.

"I admit that I was a little startled when I saw that skull," she said in hushed tones, "although I do not think I would be if I saw another. But now that I know it belonged to that poor girl, I am determined that we must aid Papa in his investigation. This Selena, is far more interesting than Lady Bassington's novel because it is a true story." She opened her bedroom door on the words. "We must hurry, for I do not wish to miss a thing."

Selena found her waiting when she came along the landing some fifteen minutes later, notebook in hand.

"What is that for?" she asked.

"I thought I might jot down my thoughts in case I can be of help."

The murmur of voices that filled the drawing room stopped as they entered it. Lord Sheringham was already there, and he came to them, his expression serious.

"What I am about to relate might upset you. But

as these things have a way of getting out, I thought it best you heard my discoveries from my own lips, and in the presence of family and friends."

"Thank you for your consideration," Albina said. "But we will not be overcome, I am sure."

Lady Sheringham sat on a long mahogany sofa, upholstered in green silk brocade. She patted the place to either side of her and the girls obediently took their seats. Lord Sheringham stood in front of the fireplace around which everyone was gathered. He clasped his hands behind his back and rocked up and down on his feet, his lips pursed, as if considering where to start.

"I shall begin by summarising the evidence. In my possession are a skull and a necklace found in close proximity to each other. There appears to be no doubt that the necklace belonged to Ellie Crake. The skull had a chipped front tooth, as did Ellie, so we must assume that it was indeed her. I also have a letter which says little more than she was going to a place where she hoped she would be less miserable. We know then that she was unhappy. The apparent cause of her unhappiness was her feelings for a Mr James Rowe, a seasonal worker, who left some five weeks before Ellie disappeared. It was in the hope of discovering his whereabouts that I went to Newcastle."

He paused and nodded at Charles. "Your suggestion that I enquire for him at the farmers' market proved to be sound advice. I was directed to his parents' farm some five miles outside of the town. I found him there."

"Why would he choose to work for Mr Crake at a time when he must have been sorely needed on his own farm?" Charles asked.

"A good question, and one that is easily answered. He had fallen out with his father over his unwillingness to listen to his advice. Mr Rowe is very set in his ways, and things came to a head when he told his son that he would do things his way or get out of his house. James decided on the latter option. He claims he wished to see how other people ran their farms, hoping to have more tangible evidence that his ideas worked when next he saw his father."

"A very sensible thing to do," Lord Bassington interpolated.

"As it turns out, it was," Lord Sheringham continued. "When he returned home his father had realised how much he depended on his son and was willing to listen to his ideas. Mrs Rowe bore out almost everything he said, and I only discovered one discrepancy in his story."

Albina sat forwards, her eyes intent.

"He informed Mr Crake that he had received news that his mother was ill, which is why he left a week earlier than expected. His mother is an honest woman and admitted that no such news could have been sent because not only was she not ill, but none of them knew of James' whereabouts." He glanced almost apologetically at the sofa where his wife and daughters sat. "James claims that he invented the story to protect Ellie Crake's modesty. Apparently, she went to the hayloft where he slept, lay down next to him, and declared her love for him. In other words, she threw herself at him. He let her down as gently as he could, and the following morning left the farm."

"It is possible, I suppose," Charles said doubtfully. "But it is equally possible that he took what was freely offered to him and left before Mr Crake or one of her brothers could take the pitchfork to him." His eyes narrowed. "Ellie disappeared five weeks later, that would be long enough for her to discover that she was with child, or at least suspect that she was. The shame of such a discovery, coupled with Rowe's rejection of her may have been enough to tip her over the edge, to make her throw herself in the lake."

Lord Sheringham looked grave. "Despite the lie he told, I am inclined to accept Mr Crake's assertion that James Rowe was an honest man. I think I am a good judge of character, Charles, and I believe his story. I think you will too when I have finished reporting my findings."

He was distracted by the sound of paper rustling as Albina turned over a page in her notebook. She nodded encouragingly at him, her pencil poised. "Go on, Papa."

He raised a brow but carried on. "Ellie tracked him down. She had chatted to him often and he had mentioned that his family had a farm near Newcastle."

Gregory gave a low whistle. "She was a deter-mined little thing."

"So it seems," agreed Lord Sheringham. "I think we have already established Mrs Rowe's honesty. She informed me that she received Ellie kindly, that she felt sorry for her. Ellie was convinced her father had warned James off and sent him away, and she had persuaded herself that he would not have done so if James had not returned her feelings." He gave a wry smile. "It seems that he let her down a little too gently."

"But how did she end up in the lough?" Selena asked.

Lord Sheringham sighed. "The only thing I know for certain is that after James persuaded her that she had mistaken his feelings, Mr and Mrs Rowe drove her into Newcastle and put her on the stagecoach to Alnwick. She was deeply mortified and extremely upset. The landlord of the inn the coach leaves from confirmed this. He remembered Mr and Mrs Rowe bringing a young lady in. He said she was sobbing as if her heart were broken, but that she certainly got on the coach. When she walked home, she would have passed close by Kimmer Lough if she had cut across the fields, and I am very much afraid that it is looking ever more likely that she put an end to her misery there." He glanced at Charles. "Unless you have found out anything that suggests otherwise?"

"I have not," Charles said heavily. "Sally Grant thought that she might have gone in search of James Rowe, but it was supposition and not fact that led her to this conclusion. She never heard from her."

Selena was saddened and shocked. None knew better than she the pangs of unrequited love, but she had never been driven to such a state of unhappiness as Ellie. It was unthinkable. Ellie had been part of a close family, as Selena was. Whatever humiliation she might have felt after being spurned by Mr Rowe, surely it would not have been enough to make her take her own life rather than seek solace from those that loved her? *But you did not seek solace after your humiliation.* She gritted her teeth. *The cases were very different, and the consequences would have been unbearable.* It was an old argument that she had not had with herself for some time.

"Selena?"

Charles' warm, concerned gaze acted as a soothing balm and she managed a small smile.

"It is such a sad tale," she said quietly.

"Indeed it is," Lord Sheringham said. "And one I must, unfortunately, take to her parents." He shook his head. "It will be a sad blow to them; they were adamant that she would never have done such a terrible thing."

Albina turned back to the first page in her notebook and ran a finger down the neat lines. "I don't think you should, at least not just yet."

Lady Sheringham looked at her, a mixture of surprise and disapproval in her charcoal eyes. "Albina! You may have been allowed to attend this meeting, but you have no right—"

"Do not worry, Elizabeth," Lord Sheringham said gently. "I have always encouraged thoughts and opinions to be shared in this house. Go ahead, Albina. I am interested to hear what you have to say."

Albina looked at her mama as if hesitant to speak without her approval. Lady Sheringham gave it with the slightest of nods.

"Well," she said, "I will admit that you have made a good case to support your conclusion, Papa, but your evidence is still largely circumstantial."

"Go on," he said, a slight smile in his eyes.

"Although it seems likely that the skull was Ellie's, we cannot be certain of that. I am sure there are many people who have chipped a tooth, after all. And then there is her character to consider. Newcastle must have seemed a great distance away to a girl I doubt had been further than Alnwick before. It seems to me that she must have been strong, resourceful, and brave to not only travel so far but to then discover James Rowe's precise location."

She crossed out some of the points in her notebook. "I am sure she must have been brought up respectably as she is the daughter of Lord Bassington's tenants, but her trip to the barn illustrates the boldness of her character. She was determined to get what she wanted, in short, Mr James Rowe. Whilst I imagine she must have felt a great deal of embarrassment, humiliation, and probably shame when she realised how mistaken she had been, I cannot imagine such a girl taking her own life."

She drew a circle around the last item on her list. "We know that she was put on the coach from Newcastle to Alnwick, but we cannot know where she alighted from it. Even if it happened as you say, and she walked near the lough on her way home, we still cannot be sure that she threw herself in. It is a hard thing indeed to tell someone that their child has committed suicide, and I cannot think it right to do so if there is still so much doubt of it."

As Lady Sheringham looked at her daughter with a mixture of respect and bemusement, Lord Sheringham said quietly, "You have posed more questions than you have answered, Albina, but I cannot find any fault with what you have said."

"I agree with Miss Tate," Lord Carteret said quietly.

"So do I," Charles agreed. "As I have said before, Ellie was robust."

"Then," Lord Bassington said, frowning, "we must consider the possibility of murder. There are many strangers in the area at the time of year she went missing, after all. Most farms hire extra help at harvest time."

"Even if I were to consider such a possibility," Lord Sheringham mused, "I fear that after so much time has elapsed, I have no hope of proving it. It seems that Ellie's fate will forever remain a mystery. One thing, however, is clear. Something must be done with her remains, for I do not think we can doubt that it is Ellie's skull sitting at present in the drawer of my desk. I think I shall have a word with Mr Harbottle before I do anything else. He has gone to visit his sister and will not be back until next week, but I don't suppose a few more days will make any difference to the poor girl."

CHAPTER 16

For once Charles took the doctor's advice. He walked every day, a little further each time, and was happy to feel his strength returning. He did not neglect his other duties but accompanied his father or Adolphus about the estate asking numerous questions. When he was not doing that, he closeted himself with the account books, learning what profited the estate most, and then asked more questions of the steward. He treated all of them with the respect he would show a superior officer with greater experience than him.

The more he learned, the more he realised how much he had to learn, but this did not dampen his ambition, only made him all the more determined to redouble his efforts. His home was no longer merely a playground where he could lose himself in self-indulgent pursuits but a means of securing him a future that he had never dared let himself imagine, and he applied himself with all the diligence and single-mindedness that he was famed for in the army. The small flame that had been lit within him at Horton now blazed to such an extent that his father, afraid that he would soon be burnt to the socket, called him to his study the day before the dinner that was to be given in his honour.

"When I suggested that you take an interest in estate matters, my boy, I did not intend you to let them consume you quite so much. A man must have balance in his life. Stay at home today. Entertain our visitors as they arrive, spend some time with your sisters, enjoy yourself." He gave a dry laugh. "I never thought I would see the day when I needed to give *you* that advice."

Charles realised what a scapegrace he must always have appeared to his father, and it was suddenly very important to him to make him realise that he was something more. "I wanted to prove myself worthy of all the support you have always given me. To give something back."

Lord Bassington grasped him firmly on the shoulder. "Don't be a fool. You have done that already. I could not be prouder of you. Like Sheringham, I prefer to be a good landlord than a politician, to serve our people with my actions rather than my words, but thanks to Brigham, I have contacts who have always ensured that I knew of your progress, your prowess in the field." He smiled wryly. "And it is just as well, or I would not know the half of it. You have never been one to boast and have only ever volunteered the vaguest details of your part in the campaigns you have fought."

Just as Charles had made friends with all and sundry regardless of status as a boy, so he had rated many of the rank and file soldiers of his acquaintance. Their only path to advancement was through their ability and courage, and he had been privileged to have served alongside them.

"To do otherwise would have been contemptible," he said. "Whatever part I may have played was only ever a reflection of the actions of countless other men who acquitted themselves just as well, many of whom died before their time, unheralded because they were no one in the eyes of the world. I cannot begin to count all the friends I have seen fall."

His fists clenched as he spoke, and his eyes shone with both the passion of his feelings and, to his mortification, tears. He gritted his teeth and willed them away as he had done many times before. However, his father did something Charles had not experienced since he was ten years old and his pony had had to be put down. He suddenly clasped him to his barrel of a chest, saying roughly, "And so it comes. Let it go, Charles. Let it go. You will be no less a man because you mourn your comrades."

When, some time later, they emerged from the study, the unmistakeable sounds of an arrival could be heard. They found the entrance hall in chaos. His sisters had arrived together, with the six children they had between them and their husbands in tow. They were very alike. Both had their father's luxuriant russet hair and their mother's grey eyes, and they also shared her height and voluptuous figure.

Always close, they had not only shared a marriage ceremony, but they had also produced each of their children within weeks of each other. However, whilst Judith, Lady Forth had produced only boys, Mrs

Victoria Hardy had produced only girls. This did not engender the disappointment often felt in aristocratic families, however, for although Mr Hardy had been raised a gentleman, his father had made his money in trade before buying a neat little estate in the country, and he could leave his property and money where he pleased.

"Charles!" the sisters said together, moving towards him, their hands outstretched.

As neither lady ever hurried, their offspring, who did not seem to have inherited their mothers' languor, were there before them. Charles was the handsome, dashing uncle that only rarely descended upon them, but was adored, nonetheless. The youngest of the children was six and the oldest only ten, and they had all enjoyed a very relaxed upbringing, so it was perhaps to be expected that they would launch themselves at their uncle without any thought to dignity or decorum.

Charles laughed as they charged and knelt on one knee, his arms outstretched to receive them. If they were to knock him over, at least he would not have too far to fall. When he had hugged all the girls, shaken hands with the boys, and the hall had stopped echoing with shouts of "Uncle Charlie!", he got to his feet and kissed his sisters. Lord Bassington had already done so before greeting his sons-in-law and now bore his grandchildren off to Lady Bassington's parlour.

Sir John Forth was not much taller than Judith, but he was broad and very well-built. He took Charles' hand in a strong grip. "Happy to see you in one piece, Charles."

Before he could reply, Mr Arthur Hardy, a tall, bespectacled, lean man, had stepped forwards to clap him on the back. "We all are. I hear it was a close-run thing. I hope you get a decent amount of prize money, for I'm sure you earned it."

"I must admit I have not given that any thought," Charles said.

He had always given his prize money into Arthur's keeping for him to invest. Arthur had talked him into it early in his career, telling him that if he died, he would not miss it, but if he outlived his army career, it might provide him with some much needed extra money. Arthur might be a landed gentleman, but he had inherited his father's sharp brain and liked to use it.

"Do not start talking business already, dear," Victoria said on a sigh.

"No, of course not," he said, his eyes twinkling. "I know how fatiguing you find it." He winked at Charles. "There will be time enough to bring you up to date with your investments before we leave."

Sir John smiled fondly at his wife. "We had better rescue your mother from the children."

Judith sent him a laughing glance. "How right you are." She took Charles' arm as they made their way to the parlour. "She adores them, of course, but perhaps not all at once. Now, tell me, brother, and no putting a brave face on it, how have you been?"

Lady Bassington might have been overwhelmed by the noise of six children all trying to talk to her at the same time if she had not quickly informed them that they must all be needing some fresh air after being locked up in a carriage for so long and opened the doors into the garden. Her offspring found their parents on the lawn, watching in fond amusement as the children charged about with no particular purpose in mind.

Judith and Victoria came to their mama, taking a place on either side of her. Lady Bassington smiled warmly at them, before looking over her shoulder at the gentlemen who stood conversing a little way behind them.

"Bring out some chairs, will you?"

As they disappeared into the parlour, Judith leaned a little closer. "Charles has made light of his illness, Mama, but I expected he would. Is he really better? He has lost a great deal of weight."

"He is not as thin as when he arrived," Lady Bassington said in a low voice. "The poor boy had quite lost his appetite."

Victoria exchanged a glance with her sister. "Then he must have been very ill indeed."

"I believe he was. But he is much improved and is now eating as well as he ever did. Doctor Shilbury has recommended that he walk to exercise his lungs and increase his stamina. Pooley informs me that he goes out almost as soon as the sun is up."

"I really think you should encourage him to sell out," Judith said.

Victoria nodded at her sister. "She is right, Mama. The war with Napoleon appears to be over, but then we thought that before, didn't we?"

As the gentlemen began to emerge from the house, Lady Bassington murmured, "The seed has already been planted and watered, but Charles must do it because he wishes to, not because we desire it."

Lord Bassington came behind Sir John and Arthur

carrying not a chair, but his wife's favourite chaise longue, replete with cushions.

"He is a dear," Judith said.

Once Sir John and Arthur had handed their ladies to their respective chairs, they disappeared inside again, only to reappear moments later carrying footstools.

"You have trained them well," Lady Bassington said softly.

Victoria gave a hushed laugh. "We had a very good teacher, Mama."

Charles strode next through the door, a wooden bat with a rounded end in one hand, and a ball in the other.

"Those children need some organisation," he said, glancing at the gentlemen. "We are going to have a game of rounders."

As they walked across the lawn, Charles whistled, and the children immediately ran to him.

Judith sighed. "If only they would respond to their tutor as readily. Charles would make a very good father."

When Lady Bassington's lips curled into a rather secretive smile, her daughters gasped in delight and then spoke in unison.

"Who is she?"

Lady Bassington shook her head. "I may be wrong. We will discuss it after the dinner party."

"Oh, Mama!" they protested, but they were forced to subside as Sam came out of the parlour carrying a table, and Jonathan followed him with a heavily laden tray, the butler following in their wake.

"I thought a glass of Mrs Chivers' elder wine and

some of cook's freshly made strawberry tarts might be welcome after your journey, Lady Forth, Mrs Hardy."

Judith sighed. "What a treasure you are, Pooley."

"Past price," agreed Victoria.

The butler offered them a small bow and withdrew, only the slight spring in his step hinting at his pleasure in their compliments.

Judith took an appreciative sip of her wine. "Where are Adolphus and Caroline? I must say she has refurbished your parlour very prettily, Mama."

Lady Bassington caught a drop of strawberry juice that had fallen on her chin with the tip of her finger. "Adolphus has gone with Lord Carteret into Alnwick. There is a cattle market there today that they were interested in." She sucked the juice from her fingertip before continuing. "Caroline retired early with a headache last night, and she is still not feeling quite the thing this morning, so I insisted she kept to her bed. She has been very busy organising the dinner, and it would be such a shame if she were to miss it. I told her that there was no need for her to go to so much trouble, that none of our friends required anything out of the ordinary, but she does like everything to be just so."

"Poor Caroline," Victoria said. "I shall go up and see her later. I expect she is looking forward to going to Horton."

"She couldn't be happier," Lady Bassington confirmed.

Judith gave a gurgle of laughter. "And neither can you, I'll be bound."

Lady Bassington's eyes reflected her daughter's amusement. "I have grown very fond of Caroline, but she must always be doing something or other. I find her quite exhausting."

"Oh, well done, Mary," Victoria said, as her eldest daughter swung the bat, and the ball flew between her grandfather's outstretched legs.

Lord Bassington ran after it. He picked it up but did not turn and throw it.

"He should not make it so obvious that he is giving her extra time," Victoria said, "she is very competitive and will not like it if she thinks he has helped her."

When he still did not turn but put a hand up to his shade his eyes, his gaze fixed on some point in the distance, it became apparent that something had caught his interest. The ladies stood, the better to see what it might be.

Parts of the long, winding driveway that led to the house were visible from the east lawn and two curricles could be seen bowling along it, side by side. Three horsemen kept pace with them, galloping along the grass to one side of the carriageway. This was not an unusual event in itself, but the pace with which they were approaching, most certainly was.

The rounders game had now been abandoned, and the ladies strolled across the grass and joined the small group that had moved closer to the drive. Judith squinted in an effort to see more clearly. "I hope there is not some sort of emergency."

Charles' excellent vision had earned him the nickname Hawkeye in his regiment, and he grinned down at her as the approaching vehicles were obscured by a stand of trees where the road gently curved towards the house. "That is Gregory's curricle and if I am not much mistaken, the other belongs to our cousin,

Allerdale. I recognise the horses. I think you will find they are merely enjoying a race." He cocked a brow at his mother. "You did not tell me to expect him."

Lady Bassington's smile was rather smug. "I thought you might enjoy the surprise."

"How typical of Miles to arrive in such a fashion," Judith said dryly.

Victoria rolled her eyes. "It is too bad of him. I hope he does not terrify his new bride."

Lady Bassington chuckled. "I don't think he will. Eleanor is an extraordinary young woman."

The veracity of this statement became clear as the vehicles drew nearer. Charles began to laugh. "I think, Victoria, that it is Miles' bride who is most likely putting the fear of God into him! It is she who is driving!"

"So it is! And is that Lady Selena driving the other one?"

Charles' eyes snapped back to the approaching curricles. Gregory's had been half a length behind his cousin's, but it now drew abreast again and there was Selena, throwing a quick, laughing glance across at her opponents, before cracking her whip with the neatest flick of her wrist and gaining a slight lead.

A fond, admiring smile curved Charles' well-moulded lips. "It most certainly is. I did not know that she had become such a fine whip."

Something in his tone made the sisters exchange an arrested glance.

"I assume that is Lord Carteret riding next to Adolphus?" Judith said casually. "He is very handsome."

"Isn't he just," Victoria readily agreed. "But I

think the other gentleman even more worthy of the epithet. Who is he?"

"Lord Ormsley," Charles said, his voice rather flat. "Who Selena has reliably informed me, is a very respectable gentleman."

Lady Bassington's eyes flicked from one daughter to the other. "He is also a very eligible gentleman, and he seems to have taken a shine to Selena."

"He is almost old enough to be her father," Charles snapped.

Ignoring this, she continued, "Lord Carteret also seems to favour her."

"He is a much better choice," Charles conceded. "But he is probably too sensible for her. I cannot imagine him allowing his wife to take part in curricle races."

As the vehicles approached the house, Pooley, Sam and Jonathan came out to greet the guests. Jonathan's mouth dropped open as they raced by, Sam tried but failed to repress a grin, and Pooley merely raised his brow the merest fraction and indicated that they should follow him back into the house, no doubt with the intention of taking the shortest route to the stables.

Selena remained fractionally ahead, and the onlookers held their breath as they neared the last bend in the drive. It was very sharp as it turned towards the stables, and neither lady seemed inclined to check their pace. Selena was now at a disadvantage as she was on the outside, and she drove so close to the other curricle that it seemed their wheels must touch. Lady Allerdale, however, was handicapped by the difficulty of trying to hold her horses tight against the inside of the bend and must surely slow her pace or risk disaster. As the dark-haired man beside her raised his hand as if to take the reins from her, she finally checked her pace and Selena shot by.

As the audience gave a collective sigh of relief, Lord Allerdale raised his hat and grinned. The children, who had naturally been quite oblivious to the danger, now chased after the curricle with cries of, "Cousin Miles!"

The horsemen had been more circumspect and now followed at a dignified trot.

"I had better go and greet them," Charles said, striding towards the stables.

Judith and Victoria each looped an arm through their mother's and began walking slowly back towards their chairs.

"I do not think I have ever seen Selena behave in so bold a fashion," Victoria said contemplatively.

"No, indeed," replied her sister. "And I have never seen her look so animated. Did you notice the delicate pink flush in her cheeks and the excited sparkle in her eyes? It rendered her quite beautiful."

Judith glanced sideways at her parent. "I cannot see why it was necessary for Charles to go and greet them when we have two footmen and a butler to either show them to their rooms or bring them out to us."

"That is true, dear, but do not forget that Charles is eager to see his cousin. They have always been close."

They paused by a rose bush, and Victoria bent to inhale its sweet scent. "And from all you have told us, Mama, he has always been fond of Selena as well. I believe you said that he felt very *brotherly* towards her?"

Lady Bassington ran her finger over the delicate petal of a red rose. "Yes, I had always thought so."

"Interesting," Judith murmured.

"Very," agreed Victoria.

Charles would have gone further than either of his sisters; he had thought Selena had looked magnificent and would have liked the privilege of helping her down from the curricle and telling her as much. However, although he set a quick pace that left him rather breathless, he was too late to do so. The gentlemen were gathered together in the centre of the yard, laughing and offering Selena their congratulations, whilst the children were milling about their uncle and their new aunt.

Miles Gilham, Earl of Allerdale, was a dark handsome man, whose face was sculpted with high cheekbones, a strong jaw, and a determined chin. His eyes were of a deep chocolate brown, but there was an intensity about them which robbed them of any degree of softness. Only a year earlier they had generally held a haunted, bitter look, but as he glanced up from the laughing face of his petite wife, they glowed with a warmth that did not lessen as his glance fell upon his cousin. He said something to the children, and they raced past Charles, crying, "Cousin Miles has promised to play rounders. Don't be long, Uncle Charlie."

Miles crossed the short distance between them with long, powerful strides.

Charles shook his hand and grinned. "I can see

the married state suits you, Miles, but you are clearly under the cat's paw; I never thought I would see the day when you allowed a woman to race your greys!"

"No more did I," his cousin said, grinning ruefully. "But since we last met, I have discovered life is full of surprises. Not the least of which occurred today when we came across Lady Selena driving her brother's chestnuts so competently. Eleanor could not resist challenging her to a race." He shook his head. "It is all my mother's fault, of course. Almost the first thing she did after arriving at Brigham was to demand the race they had agreed to before we left Town."

"And who was the victor?" Charles asked.

"Eleanor, but it was a close-run thing as it was today."

They glanced at his wife who now stood a little distance from the others, her hand on Lord Ormsley's sleeve. He was smiling down at her and now covered her hand with his own.

"If it isn't enough that he is making up to Selena, he must now flirt with your wife," Charles said irritably.

Miles raised a brow. "Pot kettle black, are the three words that spring to mind, Charles. You must still be feeling a trifle out of sorts."

"Perhaps, but don't you mind? I did not think you the man to let another trifle with your wife. In fact, I would have thought if anything were likely to provoke your ever-ready temper, it would be that."

Miles laughed. "I have every faith in Eleanor. Besides, have you forgotten that Ormsley asked her to be his wife before I met her. I wonder if my aunt had forgotten it, or if she hoped his presence might cause her some amusement? If it is the latter, then I think she will be disappointed. His presence does not concern me at all. I imagine this first meeting might have been a trifle awkward and am pleased that they are clearing the air."

Charles looked astounded. "You *have* changed, Miles."

His cousin smiled enigmatically. "So have you, I think, Charles."

Before he could consider what he meant by this, Gregory came up to them, a grin on his face. "What a capital race! Have I not taught Selena well, Charlie?"

"Very," Charles agreed, "but I must admit I am glad it was your curricle and not your phaeton she was driving."

"Oh, I would not have let her race that," he said cheerfully, "she would have overturned it for sure."

The party began to move towards the house as a carriage laden with baggage drove into the yard.

"Good grief," Charles said, laughing. "Have you come for a month, Miles?"

"No, we have sent out carriage on to Murton. We are only staying for two nights. That must be Ormsley's carriage." His lips twitched. "Perhaps he is staying for a month."

Realising he was being baited, Charles laughed. "He has been staying at the castle for the last fortnight, so that would explain it."

Pooley led the guests through the house to Lady Bassington's parlour, which was now completely denuded of chairs.

"If you would come outside, you will find refreshments awaiting you."

Once introductions and greetings had been exchanged, the children ran up insisting that the game of rounders was resumed. Charles grinned and raised a brow when Carteret allowed himself to be persuaded by Julian, Judith's oldest boy.

"I have nephews, Charles," he said, by way of explaining his lapse in dignity.

Selena, he knew, would need no persuasion, and she gladly took ten-year-old Mary's hand, as Eleanor was claimed by Victoria's middle child, Susan.

As he expected, Lord Ormsley did not follow the other gentlemen but accepted a glass of wine from Pooley. He was pleased. Selena would surely think less of him for behaving in such a stuffy way. He had not counted on Sarah, Victoria's youngest girl, a waif with long auburn hair and huge green eyes, running up to him, however. She tucked her hand confidingly into Lord Ormsley's saying, "Do come and play, sir. I would not wish you to feel left out."

For a moment, the man looked quite taken aback, but then he bowed saying, "Certainly, young lady, lead on."

Selena looked over her shoulder at him, her eyes brimming with amusement. "You have escaped archery competitions, charades, and who knows what else only to be roped in to playing rounders."

"Ah, but none of those activities were graced by your presence, my lady," he said smoothly.

Charles suddenly found himself grinding his teeth.

CHAPTER 17

Although there were only two miles between Bassington Hall and Sheringham Court as the crow flew, it was four by road. Selena declined Gregory's generous offer to allow her to drive home, content to sit back and let the late afternoon breeze cool her. She had enjoyed a wonderfully relaxed afternoon, surrounded by friends old and new.

She smiled softly as a host of pleasant memories filled her mind. Mary, her determined chin thrust forward as she swung at the ball, her screeches of delight as she ran around the neatly folded coats that had marked the course. Lord Carteret taking a downcast Julian aside during a refreshment break after Mary had teased him that she had hit the ball further than him. An excellent boxer, he had obligingly taught the young boy to throw a few punches and had restored his pride by allowing one of them to connect with his chin, staggering backwards and clutching his jaw as if he had received a formidable blow. Lord Ormsley coming to a disconsolate Sarah when she could not hit the ball at all, bending down and placing his hands over hers so that she could hit the next one. She had trailed after him for the rest of the afternoon and he had not seemed to mind at all. That might have been due to his excellent manners of course, but Selena did not think so.

Charles with his sleeves rolled up and his shirt open at the neck, revealing the strong column of his throat and a tantalising glimpse of the red-gold curls that covered his chest. Her breath caught a little at this memory. Charles lifting six-year-old Simon onto his shoulders as Miles did the same with his brother Philip, and then racing the short distance to the house with the boys laughing in delight. Adolphus kindly lifting Simon quickly from his shoulders as he staggered the last few steps, clearly spent.

Eleanor walking arm in arm with her, telling her how happy she was, how blissfully, wonderfully happy and confiding that she hoped it would not be too long before she was with child. Selena had rejoiced in her friend's happiness but had been aware of a small pang of envy. She had realised that she too wanted children. Lots of them.

Her eyes had naturally wandered towards Charles and had rested on him regretfully for a moment before passing on to the other gentlemen. She might not feel the same degree of affection for Lord Ormsley or Lord Carteret, but she liked them both. Particularly Lord Carteret as she knew him better and had come to realise that he was not as cool and aloof as he had first appeared. Surely love could grow from liking and respect?

It appeared to have done so for Lady Bassington's

daughters. She had witnessed many laughing looks and fond smiles between Sir John and Lady Forth and Mr and Mrs Hardy that pointed to a strong bond between them. She would turn twenty next week and must look to her future. She had never been a calculating sort of girl, but perhaps her stepmother had been right when she had said reason must trump impulse, and perhaps Lady Forth and Mrs Hardy had been right when they had taken their fate into their own hands rather than wait and hope for their gentlemen to offer for them.

Gregory set Selena down by the front steps. She ran lightly up them and smiled at Trinklow as he opened the door to her.

"Thank you. Is Albina back from her visit to the Mawsleys?"

"No, milady. It seems that everyone is running a little late today, so I have asked cook to put back dinner by an hour. Even Lady Sheringham has not yet gone up to change."

It was not like her stepmother to be so tardy.

"Oh? Where may I find her?"

"In the little parlour, Lady Selena."

This room had been a favourite of her mother's. It was located in the west wing, opposite her father's study, and benefited from the afternoon sunshine. Even though it was small, her father had put in two glass doors for easy access to the walled garden that the first Lady Sheringham had lovingly created. At this time of year, it was a riot of colour, with the last of the cream, pink, and crimson roses flowering, intermingled with hydrangeas, marigolds, delphiniums, sweet peas and cornflowers. The room had escaped her stepmother's changes, perhaps because she had deemed it too insignificant, but recently she had adopted it as her own.

She found Lady Sheringham staring out at the garden, but her eyes had a rather blind look about them. A letter lay abandoned in her lap, and her tightly clasped hands rested on it. The doors to the garden were open and swinging slightly in the cool, brisk breeze. Selena crossed the room and pulled them to, the dull thud of them closing rousing Lady Sheringham.

"Oh, Selena, you are back. Did you have a pleasant afternoon?" Her eyes found the clock on the mantle as she spoke, and a soft gasp escaped her. "Goodness me, I had not realised it was so late."

"Do not worry, my dear," Lord Sheringham said, appearing in the doorway with Gregory behind him. "Dinner has been put back. Albina has not yet come in."

"Oh, I see," she said distractedly.

Lord Sheringham came a little further into the room. "My dear, is something amiss?"

"I have received a letter from my parents," she said, her voice tight. "They are coming to visit us and are bringing Viscount Rensley with them."

"Rensley?" Lord Sheringham's brow creased in thought. "I do not believe I am acquainted with him."

"He is a friend of my father's. An old bachelor who has not left his estate for years. I cannot imagine why he has decided to do so now."

"Well, we will discover that soon enough. Lord and Lady Camberley must always be welcome in my home. Do they mention the purpose of their visit or how long we may have the pleasure of their company?"

This was said rather dryly as if he did not expect it to be a pleasure at all.

"They accuse me of keeping Albina from them; they complain that they have only seen her a handful of times over the last several years." Her voice was bitter, and her eyes had a rather wild look about them. She seemed to have forgotten the presence of her stepchildren, her gaze clinging to her lord's face as if there she would find the answer to her prayers. "I do not want them here, but they will already be on their way, and I cannot stop them. They will arrive tomorrow." She rose, the hand that still held the letter trembling. "They never wanted me, but they have always wanted to take Albina from me. They said that I was not fit to bring her up."

Selena and Gregory exchanged a shocked glance. Lord Sheringham took the letter from her and dropped it in the empty fire grate, before taking her hands in his.

"Calm yourself, my dear. They cannot take Albina from you and neither will they abuse you under my roof." He smiled gently. "You are not without a protector now. If they prove insupportable you may ask cook to burn the dinner, and I shall request Trinklow to water down the wine. That should get rid of them."

A sound half sob, half laugh escaped her. "I admit that might prove amusing if it would not provide them with the perfect opportunity to criticise me further."

"They will not criticise you in my presence,"

Gregory said, stepping forward to stand beside his father.

"Nor mine," Selena said, coming to her stepmother's side. "Or Albina's, I think. She has already told us how angry they make her for doing so."

A flush of embarrassment stained Lady Sheringham's cheeks. "Has she? I did not realise. Thank you, both. I should not have said as much——"

"Nonsense," Lord Sheringham said. "We have always shared our problems in this house. Mostly, anyway."

He glanced at Selena as he said this. She let out the breath she had not been aware she was holding as a discreet cough from the doorway announced Trinklow's presence.

"I am sorry to intrude, but a footman has come from Mawsley Grange and is awaiting a reply."

He handed Lady Sheringham a letter. "I believe it is from Miss Tate."

Lady Sheringham read it aloud to save time paraphrasing it afterwards.

Dear Mama,

I have had such a splendid day. Sarah and Ralf's cousins, Mr and Miss Asquith are visiting, although it is unfortunate that they can only stay for one night, for they are both extremely amiable and all that is polite. We played battledore and shuttlecock on the lawn this afternoon, and I discovered an unexpected aptitude for the game. We then took a walk and saw otters in the river. I thought them delightful.

Although Ralf and I agree upon most things, I could not share his opinion that they were a pest who denuded the fish stocks. They need them as much as we do, in fact, more so, as they appear to be the main staple of their diet, and so, as I told him, it is people who are the pests.

Lord Sheringham chuckled at his. "Albina is a girl of very decided opinions backed up by unquestionable logic, and I like her the better for it."

I am afraid we lost track of time and were late back. Mrs Mawsley has kindly invited me to stay for dinner and if you will permit it, the night. When Sarah told Miss Asquith there was to be dancing at Lady Bassington's dinner, they asked me how I liked the waltz, and when I admitted that I do not know the steps, she suggested they all teach me after dinner.

I would not like to do anything you might dislike, Mama, but it occurred to me that I really should learn the dance in preparation for my season. I know it would not do for me to dance it publicly before then, but Mrs Mawsley said that if girls did not practice first at private parties, they could hardly be expected to appear to advantage at public ones.

"Very true," Gregory said feelingly. "If you knew how many ill-tutored girls had crushed my toes whilst attempting it, you would understand why I am quite happy to give the assemblies a miss."

I do not know if there will be waltzing tomorrow evening, but I would like to be prepared just in case. If you do not approve, I will quite understand, and Mrs Mawsley will send me back in her carriage after dinner. If you do, would you please send my nightgown and a change of clothes?

Your loving daughter,

Albina

Lady Sheringham glanced over at the butler. "Please tell the messenger that I am perfectly happy for Albina to stay the night and ask him to wait whilst her maid packs a bag for her."

"I was not sure you would agree to it, especially

the waltzing," Lord Sheringham said approvingly, taking her hand and dropping a light kiss upon it.

To Selena's surprise, her stepmother showed none of her usual embarrassment at such an open display of affection but curled her fingers around his hand for a moment.

"As you say, her logic is faultless, and I am pleased she is making friends. Besides, it will give me time to regain my equilibrium."

Selena smiled. It seemed her stepmother was being drawn inexorably into the web that had always held her family together, woven from good intentions, its delicate threads bound together by affection and love.

The family were still at breakfast when Trinklow brought them the news that a carriage was approaching the house, and as he did not recognise the equipage, he suspected it was Lord and Lady Camberley.

Lady Sheringham had just brought her coffee cup to her lips, but she jerked to her feet at this news, spilling a good quantity of the muddy coloured liquid over her gown. As she gave a groan of dismay, Lord Sheringham calmy passed her a napkin and told her to sit down.

"You will finish your meal, my dear."

He glanced at Trinklow, "See our guests are taken to their rooms and bring them to the drawing room in half an hour."

"Certainly, sir."

The butler indicated that the footmen should follow him with a slight nod of his head.

"But, my lord," Lady Sheringham protested, "they will take it as a sign of disrespect if we do not greet them."

"They may take it as anything they like," he said gently, pouring her another cup of coffee. "As they did not see fit to warn us at what time we should expect them, they can hardly cavil at the fact that we are not ready to receive them. Besides, my dear, you would not like to greet them with a coffee stain on your dress."

"No, of course not. I must go and change at once if I am to be ready in time, as well as send a note to Mawsley Grange requesting that Albina return immediately."

Lord Sheringham glanced at the half-eaten slice of toast on her plate. "You will eat your breakfast, drink your coffee, and only then change. The children and I will entertain Lord and Lady Camberley until you are ready. And no note will be sent to the Grange. I expect they will still be breaking their fast too."

"Should I change out of my riding dress, Papa?" Selena asked.

"There is no need for you to do so," he assured her. "You and Gregory may go for your ride once Elizabeth joins us." His glance swept over everyone present. "I do not expect the tone of my house or the manner of its occupants to alter to suit our guests. They will take us as they find us, and if they do not like it, they may leave. I am master here."

Gregory grinned. "Puffing off your consequence, father?"

Lord Sheringham's lips twitched. "Not at all, just making my expectations clear."

They found two white-haired people somewhere in their sixties, sitting stiffly on the green silk sofa, an untouched tea tray on the table beside them. Selena saw immediately that her stepmother had her nose from her father and her dark eyes from her mother. They wore identical expressions of disapproval, their mouths pinched tightly shut, and their eyes cold.

"Please do not get up," Lord Sheringham said cheerfully, overlooking the fact that neither of them had attempted to do so. "May I introduce my eldest son, Gregory, Viscount Perdew, and my daughter, Lady Selena."

Gregory performed an elegant bow, and Selena dipped into a shallow curtsy.

"It was not the habit in my day," Lady Camberley said, inclining her head the smallest degree, "to greet visitors in riding dress, nor to wear one as tight-fitting. I am surprised you can breathe, Lady Selena. It is quite extraordinary."

"I am glad you think so," Selena said, smiling brightly. "It is quite my favourite."

Selena would not have thought it possible, but Lady Camberley's mouth grew even more pinched, like a purse whose strings had been pulled too tight.

"Please, forgive us," Gregory said in a conciliatory tone, "but we were on the point of going for our morning ride when you arrived."

"Couldn't get out of bed to do it before breakfast, I suppose," Lord Camberley said, frowning. "Where is my daughter, Sheringham? When you asked for my permission to marry her, I thought you a man who would know how to keep his house in order. I hope that I was not mistaken and that becoming a countess has not filled Elizabeth's head with ideas of her own self-importance."

Lord Sheringham sat down and crossed one leg over the other. "I did not ask your permission to do anything, Lord Camberley," he said quietly, "but merely showed you the courtesy of informing you of my intentions. Elizabeth suffered a slight accident at breakfast and will be down when she has changed her dress. And although I fear she was sadly lacking in any idea of her own importance when I met her, I am happy to report that she is slowly coming to realise how important she is to all of us."

"She's turning into a great gun!" Gregory exclaimed.

"And has shown me more patience than I deserve," Selena said.

Lady Camberley raised her pencil-thin eyebrows. "That, I can well believe."

For some strange reason, rather than angering her, this snide remark made Selena want to giggle. She caught Gregory's eye and her resolve not to, was sorely tested.

"When might we expect Viscount Rensley?" Lord Sheringham enquired.

"Tomorrow," Lord Camberley said stiffly. "He suffered an indisposition on the road; he used to live in India, and occasionally suffers from a liver complaint."

Lady Sheringham came a little breathlessly into the room. "I am sorry to have kept—"

"Elizabeth!" Lady Camberley snapped. "Why are you not wearing a cap?"

As she flushed, Lord Sheringham stood and came to her, taking her hand and leading her to a chair next to his own.

"Elizabeth is not wearing a cap because she is a very obedient wife. I asked her not to when we are at home," Lord Sheringham said coolly. "She has such beautiful hair that I think it a shame to cover it up."

"It is not seemly," Lady Camberley said sourly.

"I must be the judge of what is seemly in my own home," Lord Sheringham said, his voice hardening for the first time.

Lord Camberley bristled at his tone. "Do not think your title gives you the right to ride roughshod over us, sir. We are all equal in the eyes of the Lord."

"I quite agree," Lord Sheringham said more gently. "And He will render to every man according to his deeds."

Lord Camberley held his gaze for a moment longer and then dropped his eyes.

"Where is Albina?" Lady Camberley said querulously. "I long to see my only grandchild."

Her wish was granted, for she came into the room on Ralf Mawsley's arm, exclaiming, "No, I will not have it, Ralf, it was you who trod upon my toes."

The laughter in her eyes was extinguished when she saw her grandparents. She curtsied, saying calmly, "Grandpapa, Grandmama, I did not expect you to arrive so soon. Allow me to introduce Mr Mawsley."

Ralf bowed and smiled in his easy-going way, "I am happy to make your acquaintance, sir, ma'am."

When he found himself on the end of two hostile stares, his smile did not waver, but he said, "I see I am interrupting and will take my leave." He bowed to

Albina and winked in a friendly fashion. "I shall see you this evening, and then we shall see who stands on the other's toes."

"I shall come with you," Gregory said.

He sent a look of enquiry at Selena, but she shook her head.

As they left the room, Lord Camberley said sharply, "Who was that young man?"

"I told you who he was, grandfather," Albina said, taking the seat Gregory had vacated. "The Mawsleys are our neighbours."

"Don't be obtuse, girl," he snapped. "I meant who are his people?"

"Oh, I see," Albina said, completely unmoved by his irritability. "He is the nephew of Viscount Grooby."

"In other words, he is a nobody!"

"Do not forget," Lord Sheringham said softly, "that we are all equal in the eyes of the Lord."

Selena bit her lip.

"Elizabeth," Lady Camberley said, "why have you allowed Albina to be alone with a *man?*"

"Oh, I was not alone with him," Albina said. "His sister is a friend and I stayed at Mawsley Grange last night. Mr Mawsley brought me home in his curricle, but his groom was up behind him."

Lady Camberley's eyes narrowed. "And what is this about seeing him this evening and stepping on his toes?"

"We have been practising the waltz in case it is to be danced at Lady Bassington's party this evening."

"It is a shame you gave us such short notice," Lady

Sheringham said quickly. "We had already accepted the invitation."

Lord Camberley recovered his tongue. "You must cancel, Elizabeth. Dancing is the work of the devil!"

"That will not be possible," Lord Sheringham said. "Nor would it be appropriate to ask if the invitation could be extended as it is for close friends and family only, to celebrate the return of Captain Charles Bassington from Waterloo. I will, however, ensure that a fine dinner is set before you."

Lord Camberley's chest swelled with indignation. "It seems to me that I have been grossly deceived as to your character, sir. You seem to be leading a life of dissipation, and what is worse you are exposing our granddaughter to it."

Albina laughed. "No, Grandpapa, you cannot be serious. We live a very respectable life."

"Albina, you know nothing about it," Lady Camberley said. "When you were living a life of quiet study, we were willing to leave you be. But now it is time you were married to a serious man who has a healthy respect for the Lord. That is why Viscount Rensley is coming. We are willing to give you a very respectable dowry if you marry him."

Lady Sheringham had paled, but her voice when she spoke was strong. "You will not choose a husband for Albina, and certainly not one who has one foot in the grave."

"Our good friend Viscount Rensley died last year, Elizabeth," Lord Camberley said sternly. "Something you would know if you had visited us more frequently. It is a young relative who is the new viscount. I admit that he strayed from the path for a time, but he has seen the light and has repented."

"And if you marry him, Albina," Lady Camberley said in a coaxing tone, "you would be near to us and we could guide you, just as we have guided him."

"No!" Lady Sheringham surged to her feet. "Your God is not mine! He allows tyranny and cruelty! I will not have Albina subjected to His ways!"

"Do not blame the Almighty for your shortcomings, Elizabeth. You were always wicked, and we had no choice but to punish you and neither did Tate," Lord Camberley said. "It was for your own good. Proverbs 11:21 – ...*the wicked shall not be unpunished*."

Selena and Albina stood, taking a stance to either side of their mama. Lord Sheringham placed himself behind his wife and rested one hand lightly on her waist.

"Mama is not one the one who is wicked," Albina said in a voice of quiet fury. "It is you who are wicked. I have studied the Bible closely and know that you pick and choose the parts that seem to justify your actions. You would be better paying attention to John 3:18 – *My little children, let us not love in word, neither in tongue; but in deed and in truth.*"

Lord and Lady Camberley's mouths dropped open. They looked at their granddaughter as if she had grown two heads.

"I see you are past praying for," Lord Camberley finally said. "We are too late."

His lady nodded sombrely. "We shall leave this house of sin immediately."

"Yes, I think that would be for the best," Lord

Sheringham said, going to the door and holding it open.

Trinklow came through it, carrying a tray holding a bottle of wine and several glasses.

"I thought our guests might like something stronger than tea," he said.

Lord and Lady Camberley swept past him, glancing at the bottle as if it were a snake about to strike.

"Thank you, Trinklow, but Lord and Lady Camberley have decided not to stay after all. Call for their carriage, will you?"

Selena thought she saw a hint of relief in the butler's eyes, but his voice was impassive as he said, "Immediately, sir."

Lord Sheringham closed the door behind them and said with a gentle smile, "I suspect we shall not receive a second visit."

Lady Sheringham put her hand to her eyes, and he went quickly to her. "I am sorry if you find the thought of being permanently estranged from your parents distressing, my dear, but——"

Lady Sheringham raised her head. "No, it is not that. I am happy for it to be so. I am moved," she said, "because of the good will and support I have received this day."

"I hope you did not expect anything less, my love," Lord Sheringham said. "I did not speak up for you more, because in order to be rid of them for good, I knew they would have to hear from Albina herself what she thought of them." He smiled fondly at his stepdaughter. "I felt sure you would not mince your words."

Selena chuckled and put an arm around Albina's waist. "I am in awe of you, sister. If ever I need someone to fight my battles, I shall come to you."

Albina smiled. "I think you are quite capable of fighting your own battles, Selena."

Lady Sheringham clasped her daughter to her for a moment and laughed softly. "I am so very proud of you. You dealt with them far more effectively than I ever could."

"Perhaps, Mama," Albina said, her voice grave. "You said to me once that you would not allow me to be subjected to the upbringing that you had suffered, and I thank you for it." Her eyes shone with unshed tears. "I had not fully realised the import of those words, but I think I do now."

"Yes, well, it is all in the past," Lady Sheringham said. "Let us not dwell on it." A look of dismay crossed her face. "Edward! What are we going to do about Viscount Rensley?"

"*We* are going to do nothing," Lord Sheringham said firmly. "You may leave him to me. I shall give him some refreshment in my study, explain that his journey was for nothing, and send him on his way."

CHAPTER 18

The entrance porch of Bassington Hall gave directly onto the great hall, although the family more often than not referred to it simply as the hall. Perhaps because it lacked the elaborate plasterwork, carvings, or marble tiled floors that some of the grander houses of a similar age often displayed. The large, rectangular room was dominated by huge, small-paned windows along one wall. The opposite was hung with tapestries that may have at one time been colourful but were now rather faded from years of exposure to the sun. A massive fireplace dominated the south end of the hall but was rarely lit as, in general, the room was only used as a corridor to reach the other apartments on this floor or access the staircase which led to the long gallery and bed chambers.

Today was an exception, however. The dining room might have managed to hold up to twenty guests at a squeeze, but there was no hope of it managing to accommodate thirty, which was the number sitting down to dine this evening. Two long tables had been unearthed in one of the barns, where they had been languishing since Judith and Victoria's joint wedding breakfast, and had been scrubbed and covered with crisp, white linen. Branching candelabras were set at intervals along them, their flickering candlelight glinting off the gilt-edged plates and cutlery already assiduously polished to a sheen by Sam and Jonathan. And for the first time in many years, a fire blazed in the hearth, more to give the room a cheerful focus than in any expectation that it would warm it to any great degree.

No one was surprised when Lady Bassington, famed for her informality, told the guests gathered in the gallery as dinner was announced, that as most of them were such very old friends, they might sit where they pleased. Caroline, who had spent a considerable amount of time considering the seating arrangements blanched a little at this, but soon found her cheeks restored to blooming colour when Adolphus surreptitiously patted her bottom and grinned.

Charles was pleased the guests had begun to make their way down to the hall; he was tired of their repeated references to his health and the seemingly unending stream of questions about the battle, Wellington, or Napoleon.

He had caught only the merest glimpse of Selena, his view having been obscured by Ormsley and Carteret, who had buzzed about her like bees flitting about a rose. But they now moved a little to one side to exchange a few private words, and she turned her head and smiled at him. His heart lurched, and then seemed to stall.

Her gown of soft, white satin, whilst perfectly respectable, was cut lower at both the back and front than any he could recall her wearing before, revealing a tantalising expanse of creamy skin, which swelled a little as it met the V-shaped neckline, hinting at the plump bosom beneath. Her thick, chestnut hair had been loosely arranged at the back of her head in a style that appeared to defy gravity, the heavy mass only seeming to be secured by a white ribbon threaded through it. Two long curling strands had escaped, whether by accident or artful design, he was not sure, but they provoked in him a desire to pull at the length of ribbon, and release the remainder of her luxuriant locks, to watch them tumble about her softly rounded shoulders. He frowned. It did not seem right to be thinking of Selena in this way.

"She is a vision, isn't she?"

He blinked and found the warm, faintly amused voice belonged to his cousin Eleanor. She took his arm, mischief dancing in her eyes. "Whilst I will allow that it is perfectly understandable that you should stand gazing at Selena in admiration, I cannot help but feel that it shows a shocking lack of strategy on your part. Lord Ormsley has now gained the advantage and is leading her down to dinner."

He glanced up and saw Selena's hand resting lightly on Lord Ormsley's arm, her laughing face turned towards him as if he had just said something vastly amusing. He at last recognised the spurt of irritation that pricked him at the sight for what it was, jealousy. He pushed the unpalatable thought away, saying lightly, "It is only fitting that someone of his rank should take her down to dinner."

"Perhaps in the normal course of events," Eleanor conceded, "but, as usual, there is nothing normal about your dear mama's arrangements." When he said nothing, she added gently, "I became quite well acquainted with Selena before we left Town, Charles, and I know that she does not care for rank, even if you do. I hope you would not allow such a consideration to make her unhappy. She adores you."

"When she was a child perhaps—"

"It may have escaped your notice," she murmured dryly, "but she has not been a child for some years."

His irritation now turned on the diminutive, elfin-faced lady beside him. He had enjoyed her frankness when they had met briefly in Town, had even told her that he regretted he would not have time to know her better, but now her words rankled, the more so because they held more than a smidgeon of truth. It had indeed escaped his notice that Selena had made the transition from child to woman until very recently.

"It does not appear to me that her adoration is solely mine," he snapped out.

He could not see what he had said to warrant the wide smile that crossed Eleanor's face.

"A girl can only wait so long, you know. Selena is fully aware that she is nearly on the shelf, and she wishes for a family of her own."

"Then she had better choose one of her suitors," he growled, "either of which can provide for her far better than I."

"Well, do you know, if you are going to submit quite so tamely, I think it highly probable that she will. Of course, if she understood that your feelings towards her had changed, they wouldn't be in the running."

She left him on the words and went to her husband, who had been waiting for her at the bottom of the stairs. Charles noticed Miles raise his brow in enquiry and Eleanor shrug, and realised that he knew what she had been about.

Even as Charles frowned, the words of advice he had proffered his cousin when he had been about to be paraded before the season's hopefuls at his mother's ball came back to haunt him …*for heaven's sake wipe that scowl from your face… You don't have to make a decision tonight, after all, and I hope you won't; it don't do to rush into these things. Flirt with every pretty girl in the room and enjoy yourself; it's what I intend to do.*

Their situations were vastly different, of course; he was not heir to a marquess, and he had known Selena forever, although the feelings she now stirred in him were new, and then he had no decision to make, or did he? No, he did not. It was not his decision to make; even if Selena did still adore him, and that was by no means clear, he would need Lord Sheringham's permission. And why would he agree to such a thing when there was such a discrepancy in their fortunes and two better prospects who were clearly interested in her? On top of all this, his pride still baulked at the idea of knowing that his money would come from her, and how could he expect her to live in the lodge at Horton, wedded to a mere steward?

The spread was lavish, the wine, first class, but for once it was wasted on Charles. Years of practice ensured that a smile remained pinned to his face and a stream of cheerful nothings issued from his mouth, and he laughed at the appropriate moments when his father gave a speech both touching and comical, as he spoke of his pride in both of his sons. But inside he felt muddled, and his excitement at the prospect of perhaps one day running Horton had dimmed a little.

After dinner, the ladies went back up to the long gallery and the gentlemen passed the port around. Charles had drunk very little since his illness but quickly drained two glasses with no respect to the quality of the fortified wine, which did not relieve his feelings but only served to muddle his thinking further. It was perhaps just as well that it had been agreed that the gentlemen would not linger in the hall as the musicians would only play until nine o'clock, leaving them enough time to return to Alnwick before dark. As they began to head for the stairs, Lord Allerdale put a hand on his shoulder.

"Stay a moment, Charles."

"Why?" he muttered, his voice low as he whirled around. "Has your wife not taunted me enough with suggestions that can never be?"

He tried to move away, but Allerdale's strong hand only tightened on his shoulder. Charles' words had not been complimentary in either content or inflexion, and he was not surprised to see anger simmering in the dark eyes that regarded him.

"I shall, just this once, let that pass," his cousin said softly, "but only because you are in no condition to pick a fight and are clearly in trouble."

Charles suddenly clasped the hand that still lay on his shoulder. "Forgive me. I am not myself." He gave a shaky laugh. "Too much wine with dinner, and port afterwards."

"Do not make excuses, Charles," Miles said, a faint smile touching his lips. "I think, for once, you are completely yourself, and none know better than I the torture a man can feel when he finally realises the one woman he wishes to make his might be beyond his reach."

Any reserve Charles felt, fled before this admission. "But that is just it; she is beyond my reach."

His reasons for this statement suddenly flooded from him like steam escaping a boiling kettle. He felt a sudden wash of embarrassment overtake him when he came to a stop.

"Now I have explained, I beg you will let things be. We had better join the others. I can hear the musicians tuning up, and the first dance will begin shortly."

"Not so fast," Miles said, pouring them both another drink, and sitting back at the table. "No one will wonder at it if you do not dance tonight, Charles. They will put it down to your recent illness, and perhaps it is just as well that you don't, or at least only dance once; half an hour of sustained exercise whilst talking, is no easy feat for someone who is still recovering from an inflammation of the lungs."

"Now, wait a minute—"

Miles held up his hand. "Do not waste your breath, my favourite cousin; I saw how much you were blowing after we ran the short distance back to the house after the rounders match."

Charles gave a rueful grin. "Yes, damn you, but you do not have to remind me, or watch over me as Carteret has insisted on doing." He suddenly frowned. "I would have thought you might be more interested in promoting his match with Selena. He is your closest friend, after all."

Miles crossed his legs, and his fingers tapped idly against the glass he held. "Which is precisely why I am not tempted to do so. He is a man of two halves, Charles. One side is sensible of his obligations and that might tempt him to offer for Selena."

"And the other side?" Charles prompted.

"The other side he firmly represses, but is there, nonetheless. He is the most honourable, man of my acquaintance, an excellent sportsman, and he possesses a formidable intellect, but he is also kind, considerate, and… creative. If he had been born without a penny, he might have made his way in the world as an artist. His sculptures are breathtaking, his paintings, sublime, but only his mother and sisters have ever seen them. His father was not a warm man and thought that side of him contemptible. He brought Carteret up to be as reserved as he. It would be an extraordinary woman who would be able to engage with him on every level. They would have to be able to discuss politics, poetry, art, and above all, love him in his entirety. I like, Selena, and am pleased to see how far she has come out of her shell, but I cannot think her the woman for him."

Despite his turbulent feelings, Charles chuckled. "No, by God! Her painting is atrocious and her interest in politics, non-existent." He sighed. "She was always used to be more interested in people than things and in nature too. She loves the countryside, horses, visiting her tenants. She always had a free spirit that resisted being tamed, an impatience with pomp or ceremony or the restrictions so often foisted on girls."

"She sounds an ideal match for you, Charles," Miles said gently. "And before you remind me of all the reasons why she is not, let me suggest that the obstacles you have quite rightly considered, may not be insurmountable."

"Go on," Charles said cautiously, unwilling to allow his hopes to rise.

"She is the daughter of an earl," Miles conceded, "but not one who is at all high in the instep. His first wife was the daughter of a baronet, his second daughter of a baron and the widow of a viscount. He could have looked much higher if status had been important to him."

"But I have no title at all," Charles reminded him.

"Not true, you have the title of captain. One earned through putting your life on the line numerous times for your country rather than a happy circumstance of fate." Miles put down his glass and leant forwards, the aura of leashed power that had always surrounded him, palpable. "You have no fortune, but she has. You told me only yesterday that you wish to run Horton, to plough something back into the land that you love, and I have no doubt that you will succeed. Consider this; if your father permits you to manage the property and you marry Selena, you will not need to live in the lodge, you could move into the main house."

"I would not wish to live upon my father's or my wife's charity," he said stubbornly.

Miles sat up and assumed a haughty demeanour, suddenly looking every inch a marquess' son. "I had not thought you so short-sighted, Charles. Although I would not be surprised if your father allowed you to live in the house, gratis, you would be able to afford to lease it and the land."

"No," Charles bit out, "my wife would be able to afford to lease them."

Miles raised a rigid finger and all but poked Charles in the chest. "Again, I say you are short-sighted. Although you might have to rely on your wife's funds at first, if you made the estate profitable enough, you would be able to pay your own way, and when you had done so, if her fortune is still unpalatable to you, you could insist that only she use it, or have it tied up in your children."

Charles' breath caught in his throat. He remembered the rocking horse in the nursery at Horton, and how he had thought the house would come alive with the presence of children. He was gripped with a strong desire that those children should be his and Selena's.

"But what about Ormsley?" he muttered.

Miles sat back. "I do not think you need worry about him. I have discovered from my father that he is an admirable man, even more interested in politics than Carteret. He was captivated by my wife, which is completely understandable; she is both engaging and intelligent—"

Charles' lips twitched at the warm admiration that laced his cousin's words.

"But he is nigh on thirty-seven, and although it seems he has found some amusement here and is not at all as starched up as my mother implied, I think you will find he is merely passing time whilst parliament is prorogued."

"But even if what you say is true, I would have to persuade Lord Sheringham of my suitability."

"That is true, but you cannot know what is in his mind. I suggest that you request a meeting with your father, tomorrow. Tell him your heart's desire and ask him if he would be willing to accede to the scheme I have proposed." His lips twisted wryly. "If he is anything like my father, he will be a step ahead of you. If he agrees, go to Sheringham and put your case before him. Only then will you know where you stand."

Charles was so used to being in firm control of his emotions, that he could hardly bear the strange fluctuations between hope and despair that he was now experiencing. "But there is still Selena," he murmured. "She has appeared quite content to share her attentions since I came home. I no longer know where I stand with her."

Miles leant forwards, his eyes boring into Charles' with an intensity that could not be ignored. "Then stand up to the competition, you idiot. Get yourself up to the gallery and demand the orchestra play a waltz. If you do not know how she feels after that, you are a lost cause."

They both glanced up as a cough, hastily smothered, sounded somewhere high above them. Charles' eyes came to rest on a small grille set high in the wall. He groaned as Miles chuckled.

"Your mother, I presume."

"In the priest hole," Charles confirmed in a low

voice. He shook his head ruefully. "I had better not disappoint her."

Selena had made the Sheringham party late. Although her maid had assured her of the elegance and propriety of her dress, she had not been sure she could present herself feeling so exposed. But when she had suggested that the maid bring her a chemisette or a fichu, she had wrung her hands but determinedly refused, saying that her mistress may dismiss her if she wished, but that she would not do so; it might be acceptable for daywear, but it would be a crime to ruin the line and simplicity of her dress by such an unnecessary addition to her raiment.

Lady Sheringham did not berate her for dragging her heels as she had in Town, but seeing the uncertainty in Selena's eyes, smiled and said with some satisfaction, "You look wonderful in that gown, just as I knew you would."

"Like a Greek Goddess," Albina said.

Gregory choked. "That's coming it a bit too strong, but I will say this for you, Selena, I've never seen you look so… so fine."

When she turned to her father, his eyes were glistening with emotion and a smile that fell somewhere between bemusement and admiration hovered on his lips.

"You look quite beautiful," he said gently, before glancing at his wife and stepdaughter, "as do you all."

Albina and her mama exchanged a knowing glance. Both of them were striking in appearance, their dark hair and eyes highlighting their alabaster skin, however, their noses were too large, and their chins too determined to earn them the accolade of beauty.

"Papa has such lovely manners," Albina said, amusement dancing in her eyes.

Lady Sheringham laughed softly. "He saved the situation admirably."

"Nonsense, I meant every word," he said hastily, but then burst out laughing. "You are joking me! You did it very well, too."

By the time they arrived at the hall, the long gallery hummed with the conversation and laughter to be expected when a large group of friends and family gather together. Selena's eyes automatically scanned the crowd and inevitably alighted on Charles, surrounded by a host of people who appeared to be hanging on his every word.

She was pleased to discover that she was able to resist the temptation to join them, and she was aided in this endeavour by the attentions of Lords Ormsley and Carteret. Both of them appeared unusually relaxed and made her laugh with their compliments, which grew steadily more extravagant as each tried to outdo the other as if it were a very good game. When Lady Bassington announced that they might sit where they pleased at dinner, they both held out their arm for her, and when she looked from one to the other in laughing dismay, they bade her wait whilst they went a little aside to settle the matter as gentlemen.

She turned her head and saw Charles standing at the far end of the room, momentarily alone. And all her good work was undone. She could no more have prevented herself smiling than she could have stopped the moon waxing and waning. Her lips parted slightly as she drew in a deep breath in an effort to slow the rapid beat of her heart, and her yearning eyes drank in every detail of his face as if she was seeing it for the last time.

She stiffened as she realised that his glance had strayed to the neckline of her dress and he was frowning as if he did not share the admiration it had provoked in so many others. The spell was broken, and she turned to Lord Ormsley who was now by her side, laughing up at him as he made some reference to a duel being averted, hoping that she had not given herself away.

She hardly tasted a mouthful of the various dishes he served her, and her conversation was desultory. Fortunately, the informality of the seating arrangements encouraged many of the diners to ignore etiquette and speak to whom they wished rather than just the people sitting to either side of them, and so she hoped that her lack of attention had gone unnoticed. She resolutely refused her eyes their persistent wish to stray in the direction of Charles and was surprised when the thought that she wished he would go away, crossed her mind.

His visits home had always been a bittersweet pleasure for her; the joy of his company accompanied by the knowledge that it would be fleeting, but she had always had the next one to look forward to and the half-acknowledged hope that he would one day return her feelings to sustain her. But now, his presence was a bittersweet torture. She no longer had that hope and knew that whatever the future had in store for her, it would not include him.

Her regard for both Lord Carteret and Lord Ormsley had deepened over the last few days. Their behaviour both at the rounders match and this evening had been kind, charming, and amusing, all excellent qualities in a husband. It might be a long time before she had the opportunity to develop her acquaintance with any gentleman of their undoubted quality again. She would be a fool if she let such an opportunity slip her by.

Lady Bassington stood, signalling that the ladies should withdraw. Lord Ormsley also rose to his feet. He took her hand, gently pulling her up and dropped a light kiss upon it.

"I hope you will reserve a dance for me, Lady Selena."

She smiled warmly at him. "You may be certain of it, sir."

Jane Rowland took her arm as they mounted the stairs to the gallery and, avoiding the clusters of chairs that had been set at intervals along one wall, led her to a window seat.

"I wanted a private moment with you, Selena, to thank you for setting Cedric at his ease at Chillingham."

"It was nothing," Selena murmured.

Jane's smile held a hint of sadness. "I do not know what caused you to set him at a distance, and to a lesser extent me also—"

Selena didn't want to have this conversation; she had enough to contend with this evening, but she could not ignore the hurt look in her friend's eyes.

"Jane, I have always held you very much my friend."

"Then why have you held yourself off from us? You never visit me at Rowland House anymore; I must always come to you. Did one of Cedric's stupid friends offend you as he suspects?"

She had asked her this question before and Selena had always turned it off with a denial, but her emotions were very close to the surface this evening.

"Yes," she murmured. "But it was all so long ago, and I do not wish to rake up old resentments. I am no longer dwelling in the past but looking to the future."

Jane took her hand. "Very well. I will not press you further."

"Thank you."

Her friend raised one finely drawn brow, and said with a knowing smile, "And does this future include Lord Carteret or Lord Ormsley?"

Selena flushed and gave a low laugh. "I am not sure, perhaps."

"I am glad of it," Jane said. "I spoke with Lord Ormsley before you arrived and thought him both intelligent and amusing." She leaned a little closer. "But I think his charm has been honed to a fine art. There is something very practised about it."

Selena passed their various encounters under review and realised her friend was right.

"Lord Carteret, however," Jane continued, "is much nearer to you in age, and although he is a little reserved, there is something about him that speaks of constancy and hidden depths."

Selena suddenly realised that she was not the only young lady that might never have the opportunity to meet such distinguished gentlemen again, and although it went against her own interests, said softly, "Perhaps, Jane, you should make a push to engage his interest."

Her friend smiled ruefully. "I might, if I thought I stood a chance of doing so."

Their confidences came to an end as Judith, Victoria, and Eleanor came up to them.

"Selena," Judith said, "walk with me and my sister. We hardly had an opportunity to speak when last you were here."

"I shall keep Miss Rowland company," Eleanor said, taking her place in the window seat.

The sisters positioned themselves on either side of her and they began to stroll slowly along the gallery.

"We must thank you for being so patient with our unruly children," Judith said, slipping her arm through Selena's.

Victoria took her other one. "You always are, whenever we visit. Mary reminds me very much of you at that age." She sighed. "It is hard to credit that you are all grown up."

"Yes," her sister agreed, "it ages us so dreadfully."

Selena laughed. "You have hardly changed at all, and as for the children, I like playing with them."

"You are quite the favourite with my girls," Victoria said. "They consider you almost one of the family and have even taken to calling you Aunt Selena."

"I am happy to be an honorary aunt."

Judith patted her arm. "Yes, dear, but you were not destined to only be an aunt as some unfortunate ladies are. You will want children of you own."

"Yes," Selena said softly. "And I shall want them to enjoy the freedom that I enjoyed as a child."

"Quite right," Victoria approved. "But you must choose your husband carefully; your happiness and that of your children will depend on it. I knew almost immediately that dear Arthur and I would suit, that he would allow me to be myself and be considerate of my wishes, which was far more important to me than a title."

"As I knew that Sir John would respect mine," Judith said. "But not every man is so accommodating, particularly those higher up in society."

"Papa always showed such consideration to my mama," Selena said quietly.

Victoria squeezed her arm. "He is an extraordinary man like my dear papa, and would always put your happiness first, I am sure. But there are others who are charm itself until they bring their brides home, and then expect them to bow to their wishes in all things."

"Yes," Judith agreed. "Particularly if they marry when they are older."

Victoria looked much struck by this. "How right you are, sister. Such gentlemen have had their own way for so long that it could hardly be otherwise. I have noticed that they often choose young brides with very little experience of the world who are unlikely to challenge them."

Selena's neck had begun to ache from turning one way and then the other as she tried to keep up with the words they batted back and forth with increasing rapidity. Her intellect might not be above the ordinary, but she realised they were warning her about Lord Ormsley as Jane had tried to do.

"We also wished to be within reach of our old home," Judith said. "It is so pleasant to be able to exchange family visits and for the children to know their grandparents so very well."

Selena barely registered these words as she was contemplating the fact that she now only had one potential suitor and was considering how best to proceed.

"I appreciate your advice," she said as they turned and began to make their way back down the long room. "Would you mind if I asked you for some more?"

"Of course not," Victoria said.

Judith smiled. "Ask us anything you please."

"Lady Bassington intimated that you may have… er… encouraged your suitors to come to the point. How did you do so?"

The sisters exchanged a triumphant look that was quite lost on Selena, whose cheeks were flushed with embarrassment and her eyes fixed firmly on the floor.

"Mama was quite right," Judith began, "some gentlemen need encouragement, you see."

Victoria leaned a little closer. "Indeed they do. Especially if the gentleman is of lower rank than the lady. Is that not so, sister?"

"As usual, I am in complete agreement with you, Victoria. Such gentlemen need to be left in no doubt of the lady's regard for him."

"But what if she is not completely sure of his regard?"

"Oh, that will become apparent when her own feelings are made clear, I am sure."

"And," Victoria interpolated, "he needs to understand that the lady in question is very determined to have him, that no one else will do."

Selena quailed a little this. "And what if he still does not propose?"

Judith sighed. "If he remains stubborn, then I am afraid more drastic action may be required."

Selena gulped. "What sort of drastic action?"

Victoria waved one hand airily in front of her. "Oh, nothing too alarming. A private kiss should bring him to his senses."

"And if that does not succeed, a public one certainly would," Judith murmured.

Selena gasped. "But that would be to force his hand."

Victoria laughed softly. "My dear, all of it is to force his hand, but it is only for his own good, after all."

The gentlemen had begun to come back upstairs, and Selena did not know if she was glad or sorry. The methods the sisters had espoused, might have worked for them, but Selena was not bold enough to put them into action she felt sure. Not feeling ready yet to resume the light-hearted raillery that had marked the evening before dinner, she went and sat near her step-mother, who was in close conversation with Mrs Mawsley.

That lady looked up and smiled warmly at Selena. "I have not had the opportunity to tell you how splendid you look this evening, Lady Selena. I expect you would like a quiet moment with your step-mama before the hurly-burly begins, and I have run on long enough."

As she stood, Selena said, "Please do not go on my account. I did not mean to interrupt."

"Bless you, child, there will be plenty more opportunities for Lady Sheringham and me to enjoy a cosy chat, I am sure. Besides, I wish to drop a word in Sarah's ear. These private parties where everyone knows everyone else can sometimes turn into a sad romp if the high spirits of the youngsters are not checked."

Lady Sheringham looked up and smiled, her gaze drifting over Selena's shoulder. She swivelled in her chair and saw her father approaching, but he was detained by Lord Bassington.

"Mama," she said quickly, "do you think Lord Carteret shows a particular preference for me?"

She was seeking reassurance and felt that if anyone could give it to her, it would be her step-mother; she had suggested in London that Selena tried to bring him to the point, after all, as well as telling her that by going to find Charles, he had proved he held her in high esteem.

"I thought so when we were in Town, but now it is difficult to tell," she said. "His manners are so good that he does not seem to favour any one girl above another. He certainly gave the impression he was enjoying your company earlier, but he is now talking with Jane Rowland and seems just as content. Lord Ormsley's attentions are too particular for my liking, however. I begin to think him a practised flirt."

"Yes, I think you are right, Mama. I do not think he means to offer for me but is just amusing himself."

There was no time for more, as Lord Sheringham came to claim his wife for the first country dance.

"I would have requested a waltz," he said, smiling. "But I do not know the steps."

The smile Lady Sheringham gave him in return was almost girlish. "No more do I, although I have seen it performed, of course. I thank you for your offer, but I am past the age of dancing, sir."

"Nonsense," he said, holding out his hand and saying with mock severity, "I am your husband, and you must obey me."

Lady Sheringham placed her hand in his and allowed him to draw her to her feet. "Very well, but it is many years since I danced even a country dance and it will serve you right if I make a mull of it."

Selena barely had time to recover from her surprise before Lord Ormsley claimed her for the dance she had promised him.

"I am to leave tomorrow," he said, "but I wish to tell you how very much I have enjoyed your company, Lady Selena."

"And I yours," she said truthfully.

"I accepted the Bassingtons' invitation so I could see you again, of course." A rueful smile lurked in his eyes. "I did wonder if we might suit, but I think I must make way for someone who is not only an older friend than I but more deserving of your affections and closer to you in age."

She was glad that the movement of the dance took her away from him at that moment, for she did not know what to say to this. She wondered why he thought Lord Carteret more deserving of her affections. Was he hinting that his feelings ran deeper than his own?

When Lord Carteret led her into the next dance, she determined that she would try to discover some sign of this.

"I do not know if I have made it clear, sir, how much I value your friendship."

"It has been my honour to serve you, my lady."

His expression gave nothing away, and he might have uttered those words to anyone, she realised. Even though she felt extremely awkward she forced herself to say lightly, "You are such a gentleman that I am sure you would deem it an honour to serve any lady of your acquaintance."

She thought she saw a gleam of amusement in his eyes, which was not quite the response she had hoped for.

"I certainly hope I would have the fortitude to do so."

Fortitude? Had it been so difficult being her friend? She took a deep breath.

"You once told me that you had been disappointed in love, Lord Carteret. I hope that this circumstance will not prevent you seeking happiness with another. Perhaps someone who has also suffered in such a way and would therefore be willing to settle for liking and respect."

There, she could not speak any plainer and she had not tried to deceive him. He bowed to her as the dance came to an end and took her hand, holding it for a moment, his gaze enigmatic.

"I begin to think I might be happy with such an arrangement," he said, smiling gently. "But I do not believe that you should 'settle' as you put it, at least, not yet."

He put her hand on his arm and escorted her to her stepmother. *Tell him you are determined on this course, that it is the only one open to you. That you are quite sure you would be happy.* She could not. She had done all that she could to encourage him apart from beg and she would not embarrass either of them by doing that.

She sat with her eyes downcast for a few moments. A small, bitter laugh escaped her. If she had needed a lesson in humility, she had certainly received one this evening. Neither gentleman she had thought might be interested in marrying her, actually were, and Charles had not even spoken to her this evening or indeed deigned to dance at his own party. She straightened her spine and gave herself a stern talking to. She should count her blessings rather than waste time in self-pity. She had a loving family, a home, and friends. Perhaps Lord Carteret was right, and it was too soon for her to settle. If she was still of the same mind next year, she would go to Town with Albina and this time make an effort to be amenable.

"Is this not a splendid party, Selena?"

She had not heard Albina take the seat beside her but now looked up, a genuine smile curving her lips as she saw the delicate flush in her sister's cheeks, the glow of pleasure in her eyes.

"Indeed it is. I am glad you are enjoying yourself."

"Oh, I am," Albina said. "I much prefer private parties to public assemblies."

"As do I," Selena said. "But I am determined we will enjoy your season next year."

Albina pulled a face. "I have no more desire for a

London season than you did. I have never been happier than I am now, and I do not wish to leave all my friends."

Her eyes turned in Ralf Mawsley's direction, and Selena felt a moment's disquiet. Her stepmother had changed considerably; she had softened and even acquired a sense of humour, but she doubted very much that she had altered to such a degree that she would countenance her only daughter marrying a nobody. She chose her words carefully.

"That is understandable, Albina. You lived a very quiet life before you came to the court, and everything and everyone is still new to you. But by next year you may wish for new adventures."

Albina gave her a very direct look. "Perhaps I will, but I intend to ensure that they will happen closer to home. I have great determination, you see. I have hitherto used it to excel at my lessons, to learn how to ride, to overcome my awkwardness in company, but now I think I might use it in the pursuit of my own happiness."

The thought that Judith and Victoria would have found a much more apt pupil in Albina crossed Selena's mind.

"I do not say I will make myself happy at Mama's expense, that would not be right, but I think, given time, she will come to see things my way. I am prepared to wait."

"Albina," Selena said, grasping her hands. "I think you are a remarkable young woman, and I very much hope that you will be proven right." She laughed. "And you are also very sly. You learned to waltz so you could dance with Ralf, not in preparation for the season you don't mean to have."

On cue, the opening strains of that dance sounded and Ralf Mawsley approached. He did not come to Albina, however, but went to her mama and asked permission to lead Albina onto the floor.

Lady Sheringham inclined her head graciously. "Very well, Mr Mawsley. As it is you my daughter has practised with, it will perhaps be as well that you should perform the dance with her."

Selena realised that Cedric Rowland was hovering by her elbow and glanced up.

He smiled and shuffled awkwardly. "I have brought you a glass of lemonade, Lady Selena. I will not ask you to dance, for my sister informs me that you never waltz."

"She will waltz this evening, however."

Selena's eyes widened as she saw Charles standing before her, and the hand that she had held out to receive the lemonade trembled as he took it in a firm grasp and pulled her so forcibly to her feet that she stumbled against him. A blend of anger and longing coursed through her.

"Unhand me, Charles," she said, her eyes blazing. "I am not one of your subordinates who need obey your commands. I will not dance with you."

But his arm was already about her waist and he swept her into the dance. Her feet seemed to have a mind of their own and automatically followed his steps.

"I am quite determined to dance with you, however," he said, grinning. "Even if I have to carry you about the floor."

The image this conjured drew a ragged laugh from her. "You arrogant… annoying… ridiculous man!"

"The first charge I deny, the second I will allow is a possibility."

Her breath caught in her throat as he held her a little closer than was decent, the glow in his eyes no longer caused by laughter but something softer, more intimate.

"The third, Selena, is undoubtedly true. I am completely ridiculous."

"Why are you ridiculous?" she asked, her voice a little unsteady.

"Because, my sweet girl…"

Her lips parted on a sigh at this form of address. His twisted in a wry smile.

"Because I find I do not have the breath to talk and dance at the same time. May we postpone this conversation until tomorrow?"

She somehow knew that was not what he intended to say, but her disappointment was ameliorated by the wonderful realisation that he was looking at her in a way he never had before, his eyes burning with a heat that was not at all brotherly. She suddenly felt weightless, as if she were floating. A tender smiled curved her lips and she nodded, giving herself up to the pleasure of being in his arms.

CHAPTER 19

When Selena had gazed up at him, her eyes full of hope, longing, and love, it had taken every ounce of Charles' not inconsiderable willpower, to refrain from declaring himself there and then. He had badly wanted to reassure her that he loved her, tell her that he was sorry it had taken him so long to realise it and apologise for any pain he had unwittingly caused her. But he could not do so before he had spoken to both his own father and hers.

He was fully aware, as perhaps Selena was not, that by the time he had led her from the floor, their feelings for each other must have been made clear to anyone who had observed them. The party had broken up shortly afterwards, and he had almost begged his father for an interview before he retired but had realised that to present his case with a heady mix of wine and love coursing through his veins would be foolish.

He rose as usual with the sun and went for his

morning walk. His steps led him onto Sheringham lands, and when he came to the old oak tree in the middle of the park, he sat on the grass, still damp with dew, and rested his back against its broad trunk. He closed his eyes, the sun bright behind his eyelids, and listened to the birdsong. He felt more at peace, more content, than he had for years. A long, low sigh escaped him, and he drifted into a light sleep.

A faint squeak awoke him not many minutes later, and a slow smile spread across his face as he saw a squirrel regarding him, its eyes bright with interest.

"Good morning, Little Squirrel," he said softly, holding out his hand.

The little creature scampered a bit closer but then shot up the trunk and disappeared into the branches above, as a little girl had nearly ten years before. She had trusted him with her child's heart that day, and he hoped very much that she would trust him with her woman's one today. He glanced at the upper windows of the house, raised two fingers to his lips, and sent a kiss winging through the cool, morning air.

He pushed himself to his feet and strode with long, purposeful strides towards his home, eager to face his fate head-on. His father was waiting for him in his study, a small pile of papers set neatly before him.

"I assume Mama has reported my conversation with Miles to you, sir?" he said quietly, his fingers going to his cravat, which suddenly felt too tight.

"She has indeed, Charles. Please sit." He waved his hand at a chair.

Charles sat, crossing his legs one way and then the other as he saw the stern look in his father's eyes. His heart sank as he realised that he might not even clear his first fence.

"I know I still have much to learn, but I assure you—"

Lord Bassington held up his hand, and Charles released a slow breath as he saw a faint smile touch his father's lips.

"Are you quite sure you wish to sell out, Charles?"

"Perfectly, sir."

"And have you made that decision of your own free will, and not because you think your mother or I wish it?"

"Yes, sir. I will admit that Adolphus and Mr Harbottle may have made me consider the possibility more closely than I had before. But it was not until you sent me with my brother to Horton that I realised that it might be possible for me to live a different life without being a burden to you and that I very much wanted that life."

"I needed to be sure, as your mother…" Lord Bassington smiled gently, "may have prodded both the vicar and Adolphus to hint to you that it might be time you reconsidered your future."

A faint frown creased Charles' brow.

Lord Bassington chuckled. "Don't like the thought that you have been dancing to her tune, eh? Well, you haven't been. She may have ensured that you gave the matter some thought, but that is all."

"And was it at Mama's bidding that you encouraged me to learn how to manage the land?"

"Not at all. The reasons I gave you were valid enough, although I will admit that I had another."

Hope rose in Charles' breast. "Do you mean you wished me to manage Horton?"

"I was certainly preparing you for the day when you might take possession of the estate."

Charles felt a rush of blood to his head. "Take possession? What can you mean?"

"My father purchased Horton for Cecelia. The house and the income from the land were to be hers for the remainder of her lifetime, so that she could afford to maintain the house and the park, and fulfil her obligations to the tenants." He smiled wryly. "Farnaby managed it all for her, although first my father and then I kept an eye on him, and as you know, no one could persuade her to allow workmen into the house."

"And after her death?"

"Then the estate came to me until certain conditions were met."

Charles felt a stab of impatience as Pooley came in carrying a pot of coffee. However, he accepted the cup offered to him with a smile.

"The Bassingtons have always loved the land and taken pride in their management of it. We were haunted by the prospect of the line dying out when successive generations only gave birth to one son. However, we are a hardy breed and survived. My grandfather was the first Bassington to have two sons, and I believe the event was much celebrated. He bought his youngest son, my uncle Peter, a small estate in Leicestershire when he turned twenty-one, so that he might marry and live an independent life, and of course, hopefully, produce more Bassington sons."

"I never met my great uncle," Charles said. "I

have only ever known him to be the black sheep never to be spoken of."

Lord Bassington looked grave. "My grandfather and father were greatly ashamed of him. Not only did he not marry, but he did not take care of the land. Furthermore, he lived beyond his means and drank himself to an early grave. He had mortgaged the estate to the hilt, and it had to be sold."

"He really was a ramshackle fellow," Charles murmured.

"Yes. It coloured my father's view of how younger sons should be treated. He did not wholly blame Peter. He felt that his father had spoilt and indulged him, and so ruined his character. He was convinced that if he had been brought up with the expectation of having to make his own way in the world, been forced into a profession until he was older, then he would have done much better."

"I agree," Charles said.

"Yes, well, unfortunately, my father was not able to put his theory to the test as I was his only son. That brings me back to you. My father stipulated in his will, that if I had a second son, and he not only worked for ten years in a profession but brought honour to both himself and the family by his conduct, then he should inherit Horton providing two further conditions were met."

Charles leant forward, resting his elbows on his thighs, his eyes eager. "Go on."

"That he was not told of his prospects until at least ten years' service in whatever profession were up, and even then, only if I considered him capable and willing to run the estate properly, the other was that he married." He came around the desk and shook Charles' hand. "The anniversary of your ten years' service was yesterday, my boy. Time and chance have taken care of the first condition, it is up to you to take care of the second."

Charles shook his father's hand vigorously, "Thank you, and thank Grandfather!"

"Now go and badger Lord Sheringham," he said, turning to the desk and passing him a sheaf of papers. "You are not rich, Charles, but these papers will show that the estate will provide you and your wife with a comfortable income."

He decided not to present himself in his riding gear smelling of the stables, and so took the gig. He had just turned down a narrow lane when he saw a figure trudging along the middle of the road. She carried a rather battered portmanteau in one hand, and a bundle on her back. As he drew closer, he saw a small head covered in a tiny mob cap peeking out of it and realised the woman was carrying a baby. She moved to the side of the road and turned her head as he passed. Charles blinked and looked again, and the woman pushed a strand of brown hair from her face and smiled, revealing a chipped front tooth. Charles drew to a halt and jumped down from the gig, striding towards her, a disbelieving smile on his lips.

"Ellie Crake by all that's great."

She attempted a curtsy, but Charles grasped both of her hands.

"I can hardly credit it. Ellie, we thought you dead!"

"Why would you?" she said. "I left a note, telling Ma and Da not to worry."

He raised a sceptical brow. "Did you really think they would not?"

Ellie shook her head and sighed. "I wasn't thinking clearly, not then and not later. It was only when I had my own bairn that I realised the trouble I must have brought on them."

Charles took her bag and led her to the gig. "Will you be all right with the baby on your back?"

"If I sit a little forward. I don't want to wake him; he's only just dropped off."

She took the hand he offered and climbed up. "Thank you. It seems further than I remember."

He set the horse to a trot before saying, "Ellie, why didn't you come home after you were put on the stage-coach by the Rowes?"

The young woman looked quickly up at him. "So they did look for me."

"I'll explain how I know later, tell me what became of you."

"I couldn't come home. I felt so foolish, so stupid, so humiliated. I got off the coach before it left Newcastle and found work at an inn." She sighed. "I didn't know how fortunate I'd been living on the farm. I'd never worked so hard for so little. I moved from one thankless job to another until I found one that treated me decent, in a village a few miles outside the town. It was there I met Ben Granger. He worked as a gardener on a nearby estate and used to come in on a Friday evening. He started courting me and we were wed two years ago."

"Congratulations, Mrs Granger," Charles said gently. "But why did you not write and inform your parents of it?"

"At first, I was too busy surviving, and then the longer I left it, the harder it was to write. I missed them all so much that I blocked them out of my head. Then I had little Ben, and I thought it would be easier to explain in person. I've never been much of a hand at writing."

"I noticed," Charles said dryly, remembering her letter.

"Why did you think I was dead, sir?"

"We found a skull with a chipped tooth and the necklace I gave you in the lough."

It was almost dawn before Selena fell asleep; her heart was too full of happiness and she was reluctant to let go of the feeling. She lay with her eyes closed and a smile on her lips, reliving over and over again their waltz. Although Charles had uttered no words of love, she had seen it his in eyes, felt it in the tender, almost possessive way he had held her. She had not spoken of it to anyone, afraid to break the magical spell that bound her.

When she awoke the following morning, she did not feel quite as confident. Had she imagined the whole? But as the last wisps of sleep left her, she knew that she had not. She had waited so long for some sign that his feelings had changed, that she would be a prize idiot if she had missed the moment when it had finally happened. As her maid came into the room and topped up the water in her washstand, she stretched and yawned.

"What time is it?"

"Eleven o'clock, my lady."

Selena sat bolt upright. "So late? Why did you not wake me?"

"Lady Sheringham told me not to, my lady. She said she thought you might be tired this morning."

Selena pushed her covers back and jumped out of bed. Charles had said they would finish their conversation today. He might call at any moment, and she wished to speak with her papa first. Victoria's words about her father came back to her. *He is an extraordinary man like my dear papa, and would always put your happiness first, I am sure.* Selena knew in her heart she was right but was determined to leave her papa in no doubt as to her feelings on the matter before Charles spoke to him.

Her maid smiled indulgently as she laughed out loud. She suddenly realised that it had not been Lord Carteret the sisters had been suggesting she encourage but their brother. It was Charles who might need to be persuaded that she was not too far above him. What nonsense! It was she that hardly deserved him.

As she impatiently waited for her maid to twist her hair into the simple knot she had requested, she determined that neither of them would be sacrificed on the altar of his pride. The tactics which had so dismayed her when she thought she must use them on Lord Carteret, now seemed perfectly reasonable. If she was still convinced of Charles' regard when she saw him today, she would convince him by fair means or foul.

At last, she was ready. She raced down the stairs in a most unladylike fashion and made all haste to her father's study. She threw open the door, words tumbling from her lips.

"Papa, I must speak——"

She broke off as she realised he was not alone. She could see the top of a balding blond head peeking above one of the wing chairs set before the fire. She damped down her disappointment.

"Forgive me, Papa. I shall come back later."

Lord Bassington looked at her in some amusement. "Ah, I thought you might wish to speak with me this morning, my dear. Perhaps you should come back in half an hour. But before you go, let me introduce Viscount Rensley to you."

Albina and Selena had both been eager to see the man the Camberleys had hoped to foist on their granddaughter and had agreed to sit in the front parlour so that they would catch a glimpse of him when he arrived. Selena assumed a look of polite interest as he turned and bowed.

"Lord Rensley, my daughter, Lady Selena."

Selena froze and the blood drained from her face, the only splash of colour remaining, her wide eyes, fixed in an expression of fear and horror as they rested on the scar that ran across his cheek, the skin puckered on either side. She took a step backwards.

"Forgive my daughter," Lord Sheringham said, frowning slightly. "She has long had a fear of strangers."

The viscount's thin lips twisted, and he touched the fingers of one hand to his cheek in a gesture Selena found vaguely familiar.

"It is quite all right, sir," he said. "It is an old fencing injury I acquired at university when the button came off my opponent's blade. I am quite used to it upsetting the delicate sensibilities of young ladies."

Selena felt a hysterical laugh rise within her at this last comment but clenched her lips tightly shut so it would not escape. Her instinct was to flee but to do so would be to admit that he still had some power to influence her actions. He was not as she remembered him. He was painfully thin, his skin had an unhealthy yellow pallor, and the hand that still rested on his cheek trembled slightly. He must be about Gregory's age but looked much older.

She felt a mixture of anger and relief as she realised there was no sign of recognition in his eyes. Some perversity in her character prompted her to prick his memory.

She forced a smile to her lips. "It was not your scar, sir, that caused my momentary loss of composure, I have seen it before, after all, but surprise that you and Viscount Rensley were the same person."

A look of startled confusion crossed his face. "I know it is not gentlemanly of me to admit it, but I can't seem to remember…"

"It was some five years ago," Selena said. "We met at the Rowlands' house. I was visiting Cedric's sister Jane when you arrived with a party of friends."

The viscount gave an uneasy smile. "If it was that long ago, perhaps I may be forgiven my lapse of memory. You must only have been a child, after all."

"Some might think so. I was fifteen."

Lord Sheringham looked intently at his daughter. "As you are old acquaintances, come and join us, Selena."

As they sat down, Trinklow knocked on the open door.

"You were not at breakfast, Lady Selena, shall I bring you your coffee here?"

"Yes, I thank you." She had discovered that she was rather enjoying the viscount's discomfort.

"Bring a second cup," Lord Sheringham said, raising an eyebrow to his visitor. "You have not touched your wine, sir."

"No," the viscount said, a look of genuine shame crossing his face. "I have learned the error of my ways. *Wine is a mocker, strong drink is raging, and whosoever is deceived thereby is not wise.*"

"Ah, I see the influence of the Camberleys at play," Lord Sheringham murmured.

"I have much to thank them for," the viscount said earnestly, his gaze going inward. "I never prospered in India; everything I touched seemed to turn to dust. I drank to excess, did everything to excess if the truth be told. And then a distant relative I had never met wrote to tell me he was ill, and that I would inherit. The irony was, I was as ill by then as he. By the time I arrived at Rensley Manor, he was already dead, and I was not far from it.

"The Camberleys prayed for me and with me. Told me that my inheritance was a sign from God that I might be granted a second chance at life, that if I repented all my sins and begged His forgiveness, I would receive it."

Selena thought how very convenient that was. "What about the sins you could not remember?"

Lord Sheringham shot her a sharp look which the viscount took to be one of reproval. He held up his hand.

"Let her speak, sir. I will confess that this has troubled me greatly. I have woken up more than once in my life after a night of heavy drinking and not been able to remember what I have done. It is one of the reasons I am determined never to touch strong drink again; I believe it makes us vulnerable to the devil. But God knows and sees all, and I do not seek to hide anything from him."

"You are very frank, sir," Lord Sheringham said.

"I had intended to lay my past before you, sir. I would not have tried to deceive you or stepdaughter."

Trinklow entered with the coffee, but the viscount stood. "I believe Lady Selena had something of import to impart to you when she came into the room. I shall take my leave."

Lord Sheringham followed him to the door. "I shall see the viscount out, Selena. I shall not be many minutes."

Selena poured her coffee and sat back in her chair. She wrapped her hands around the warm cup, closed her eyes, and entered the place deep inside her mind where she had buried her memories of that night five years ago, taking them out and examining them anew.

It had been early April, a cold easterly wind had been blowing, and black rain clouds had threatened all day. When Cedric and his friends had turned up, Lady Rowland had suggested that the girls dine with her in her private parlour, but Sir Graham would not hear of it.

"We need to entertain our guests," he had said. "And the girls are almost sixteen, after all."

Selena had been quite happy to comply. She knew Cedric well and had treated his friends with the ease of habit she had always treated Gregory's. Viscount

Rensley had been Mr Tilton then. His scar had been quite fresh, still raw and red, and he had often put his hand up to it as if self-conscious. She had felt a little sorry for him and been at pains to put him at his ease, telling him that he must tell everyone he had acquired it in a duel.

When the young men had eventually joined the ladies in the drawing room after dinner, they had been a merry bunch, declining the offer of music and calling for a game of bullet pudding. Thankfully, it had been Cedric who had caused the bullet to slip from atop the mound of flour when he cut his slice and had had to bury his face in it until he found the bullet with his teeth. They had all laughed uproariously when he had raised his white face from the plate.

Lady Rowland had then insisted that the girls retire.

Selena took a sip of her coffee, surprised to discover she felt detached from the scenes revolving in her head. But she drew in a long, slow breath as the next one started to play.

As she got ready for bed the wind started to howl, and the storm broke. The windows rattled in their frames and cold fingers of air found their way into the room. No fire had been lit in the grate, and the maids had been too busy making up beds for the visitors to have warmed the sheets. She lay shivering, wincing a little as loud thunderclaps sounded overhead. She turned this way and that but could not settle. She decided to slip along to Jane's room. They had often shared a bed when they had been younger, and she would not mind.

She had taken only a few steps along the darkened

corridor when she saw a man walking unsteadily along it. She retreated into her room, her cheeks warm with embarrassment at the prospect of being caught in her nightgown and bare feet. But he followed and stood silhouetted in the doorway as a flash of lightning briefly illuminated his features.

It was Mr Tilton, and yet not Mr Tilton. The slash of red across his cheek looked sinister and was in stark contrast to the paleness of his skin, which glistened with a sheen of sweat. His eyes were bloodshot and his smile cold. Icy tendrils of fear wound their way down her spine, immobilising her.

"Go away," she said, her voice cracking as it forced its way past her dry throat.

"You don't mean that," he said, coming a little further into the room. "You have been throwing out lures to me all evening."

She began to take small steps backwards. "I have not!"

As another streak of lightning cut through the sky, anger flared in his eyes. She felt the small of her back press against the bed and edged around it. But again he followed until she found herself wedged between the bedside table and the corner of the wall.

"You are all such teases," he said, his low voice bitter. "Promising one thing with your eyes and saying another with your words."

"Mr Tilton," she said desperately as he came to a stop before her, "you are imagining things——"

He grasped the thick plait of hair which fell over one shoulder and yanked her forwards, covering her mouth with his own. She felt sick and terrified, but anger was beginning to seep through her fear. Her hands were flattened against his chest and she pushed with all her might, twisting her head away from him.

"Stop it," she cried. "You are disgusting and no gentleman!"

She had managed to create a foot of space between them and opened her mouth to scream, but he clamped his hand over it and began to pull up her nightgown with the other.

"It is your own fault. I will show you what happens to little girls who play with fire," he growled.

One frantic hand scrabbled for something, anything to use as a weapon against him. Her hand alighted on the leather-bound Bible that rested on the table and she simultaneously bit down on his hand and swung the heavy book with every ounce of strength she could muster. He stumbled away from her, but there was no room to run past him.

"I think, sir," she said, her voice as icy as she could make it, "that you have forgotten that I am the daughter of an earl and not without friends."

She frowned in confusion as he clutched his head and made a low keening sound, turning in circles. She began to think that not only was he drunk, but also mad.

He came to a standstill. "I am sorry. I am not myself."

"Get out of my room before I scream loud enough to bring everyone running."

He laughed rather wildly. "Scream away if you are in such a hurry to be wed. Everyone saw how friendly you were to me downstairs; I shall say you invited me in. Let this be a lesson to you. Never trust people you do not know."

With that, he staggered from the room.

She sank down against the wall and sat with her forehead resting against her drawn-up knees until the darkness outside her windows lightened to grey.

Selena put down her cup and let out a long, low sigh. Nothing had happened, apart from one deeply unpleasant kiss. It was the threat of what might have happened that had haunted her all these years, and the niggling doubt that it had somehow been her fault, that she had perhaps, unwittingly invited his attentions. She had felt too ashamed to confide in anyone, and by the time that shame had trickled away, her mama's health had started to decline, and she would not add to her burdens.

She had taken Mr Tilton's advice about not trusting strangers and made sure she never put herself in such a vulnerable position again. She was glad he had come to the court today. He had paid a heavy price for his debauched ways, and if she was not much mistaken would never recover his health fully. The monster she had created in her mind had been transformed into a creature to be pitied, who would probably be tortured by those memories he had lost until he finally met his maker. She could now look to the future without any regrets about the past. God had forgiven Viscount Rensley, and so would she.

Lord Sheringham came back into the room and stood in front of her, his eyes probing.

"Now, Selena, is there something you would like to tell me about the viscount? Perhaps something that he cannot recall?"

She leant forward and took his hand, holding it to her cheek for a moment. "No, Papa, I think I agree with Gregory that you cannot hold a man's youthful follies against him forever."

He turned his hand so that it cupped her cheek and gently tilted her head so that she must meet his gaze. Whatever he saw in her eyes seemed to satisfy him.

"I will not press you, although you looked like you had seen a ghost when I introduced him."

"Well, if I did, that ghost has now been laid to rest."

He smiled gently down at her. "I am pleased to hear it."

A discreet cough alerted them to the butler's presence.

"I did knock, sir. I would not have disturbed you, but Captain Bassington wishes to see you, and he seems a trifle impatient."

"Then you had better show him in, Trinklow."

Selena rose quickly to her feet, a swarm of butterflies suddenly fluttering in her stomach. She grasped her papa's arm. "It was about Charles that I came to see you, but I have had no opportunity——"

Charles must have been hovering near the door for he was just then shown in.

CHAPTER 20

Charles strode quickly into the room but came to an abrupt halt as he saw Selena clasping her father's arm as if in supplication. He suddenly felt as nervous as he had in the moments before a battle. Would Horton be enough to secure her? He pushed his doubt away as Lord Sheringham came forward to shake his hand.

"Good morning, Charles. It seems I am not to enjoy a moment's peace today."

His voice was friendly enough, but his expression gave nothing away.

"I hope I have not called at an inconvenient moment, sir."

Lord Sheringham raised a questioning brow. "Would you go away if I told you it was?"

Charles grinned. "No, sir."

The hint of a smile touched the earl's lips. "I didn't think so."

"I shall leave you," Selena said, looking searchingly at Charles.

He took her hand and squeezed it gently, his warm smile answering the question in her eyes. "Stay a moment. I have some news you will wish to hear."

"Then we had all better sit. Wine, Charles?" Lord Sheringham said.

"Thank you, no. I have just come from the Crake farm and am in no need of refreshment."

Lord Sheringham frowned. "That reminds me, I must go and see the vicar. He should have returned from his sister's by now. I'm hoping he will agree to bury Ellie's remains in the churchyard."

Charles smiled. "I am happy to be able to say without the shadow of a doubt that they are not Ellie's remains."

Selena gasped. "But how can you be so certain?"

"Because I have just left her happily ensconced in the kitchen of her former home."

"But the necklace," Selena said.

"Ellie left home an hour or so before dawn. She went cross country, intending to pick up the coaching road on the other side of Alnwick. Unless she wished to go miles out of her way, she had to pass by the lough. The sun was rising as she came to it and she sat down to rest. She began to idly play with the necklace and decided that it would be bad luck to go to James Rowe wearing another man's gift."

"So she did throw it in the lough," Lord Sheringham said. "And we have put two and two together and made five." He smiled gently. "It is a mistake I am happy to have made. As no one else has been reported missing we must assume that the skull has been there much longer than five years. There are many ancient burial sites scattered about these parts, after all."

Selena rose to her feet. "I shall go and find Albina. She will wish to know."

Lord Sheringham gave a low chuckle. "You may tell her that all of her reservations have been proven correct."

Charles went to open the door for her. As she passed close by him, he murmured, "Meet me at the old oak in half an hour."

She smiled her assent, the look in her beautiful eyes, almost shy. He took a deep breath as he closed the door behind her.

He came a few steps into the room and clasped his hands behind his back.

"Nervous, Charles?" Lord Sheringham enquired.

"A little—"

"Good," he said sternly. "After dancing with my daughter in so scandalous a fashion as you did last night, you deserve to feel a little apprehensive."

This comment completely threw Charles off his stride. He decided not to try to answer a charge he knew to be true but stick to the script he had memorised on the drive over.

"Sir, I have come to lay certain circumstances before you which I hope may make my desire to offer for Selena's hand not quite so contemptible as it might at first appear."

"That is quite a mouthful, Charles," Lord Sheringham said, "sounds like you might have practised it several times."

The rest of his carefully rehearsed speech deserted him.

The corner of Lord Sheringham's lip twitched. "Sit down, Charles, and let us have a plain talk."

Charles had barely complied with this request before he found himself under fire.

"Do you love my daughter?"

He easily dodged that bullet. "Yes, of course."

"How long have you loved her?"

This was a little more difficult to deflect. "It is hard to know the precise moment——"

"I shall rephrase the question. How long is it since you realised you loved her?"

That one found its target. He inwardly groaned, knowing his answer would sound weak. "Last night."

Lord Sheringham steepled his fingers and pursed his lips.

"What made you realise you loved her?"

"I was jealous," he admitted. "I have been ever since I came home and saw Carteret and then Ormsley buzzing about her. I found myself finding reasons as to why neither of them was suitable."

Lord Sheringham raised a brow. "Yet they are both titled, wealthy, and respectable gentlemen. However, I shall let that pass. I am more interested in why you think yourself suitable."

Here was an opportunity that might take him onto safer ground. "I began by mentioning my circumstances——"

"That is not what I mean, Charles. Prospects aside, why are you suitable?"

It seemed Horton was not to be the bargaining chip, after all. How could he sell himself without sounding like a coxcomb? He thought of how angry Selena had been with him in the church, how he had won from her a sweet smile afterwards, of all the things they had in common, and how he had not realised how much her presence in his life, even if it were at a distance, had always been important to him, how the sudden prospect of losing it, had left him empty. Words began to pour from his heart rather than his mind.

"I can make her smile even when she is unhappy or angry; I can protect her without curbing her natural spirit; I would not wish to change anything about her, and I would not have expectations that she could not or would not wish to fulfil. I care for the same things that she does; our families, our friends, our people, our land. I do not wish for a wife only to provide me with children or to warm my bed, as well as this I wish for a companion, a friend, someone to share my life. I would do everything in my power to make her happy."

A slow, wide, smile spread across Lord Shering-ham's face. "And that is why, Charles, I will give you my permission to approach my daughter."

"Thank you, sir," he said, jumping to his feet. "I shall go to her at once."

He crossed the room quickly and then pivoted and came back again, reaching into the inner pocket of his coat. He withdrew the sheaf of papers his father had given him and practically threw them at the man he very much hoped would be his future father-in-law.

"Horton will be mine when I marry. That is the proof that I can keep Selena in some comfort without her fortune."

He did not wait for a reply but strode hastily from the room. Trinklow was hovering nearby, and he grinned at him, murmuring, "Wish me luck," as he passed.

He felt buoyant, there was a spring in his step, and the anticipation rushing through every muscle and sinew of his body made him giddy. Lady Sheringham was in the hall, and he took her hand and bowed flamboyantly before whirling away. He almost collided with Gregory as he rushed out of the front door at the same moment Selena's brother was trying to come in.

"I say, Charlie, what's the hurry?"

He ran down the shallow steps calling over his shoulder, "Not now, Gregory. Not now."

He managed to run halfway to the oak before he had to slow to a walk. And then he saw her, leaning against the tree, watching him approach. She did not move to close the distance between them more quickly but waited for him, as she had waited for him for years. He felt a fierce surge of thankfulness that she had.

The success of his interview with her father must have been writ clear on his face, and he saw her shoulders relax as he drew closer; her eyes softened and began to glow with tenderness, and her lips curved into a smile that was somehow both inviting and innocent. His steps slowed, becoming languorous as the urgency to reach her left him. He didn't want to rush this moment; she deserved more.

He stopped an arm's length from her, his eyes drinking in every detail of her face, skimming over the smooth softness of her cheek, dwelling for a moment on the freckles scattered across the bridge of her nose and dropping to the sweet bow of her mouth, before rising to meet her liquid eyes, their brown centres rimmed with a band of green. It was so familiar and yet new somehow, shades of the child that had scampered up the tree remained but had been overlaid by the softened contours of the woman she had become. The combination slayed him.

He took the final step and pressed the palms of his hands against the rough bark of the trunk, resting his forehead gently against hers. He closed his eyes and breathed deeply, inhaling the delicate, sweet scent that was uniquely hers.

"Selena," he murmured, wondering how to tell her all that was in his heart. He opened his lips as soft words of love rose to them, but his throat closed as he felt the featherlight touch of hers whisper against them in a tentative kiss.

"Charles," she sighed, swaying against him.

He groaned softly and settled his mouth gently against hers, pressing his palms harder against the tree to keep his rising passion in check. But as her mouth opened beneath his, inviting him in, he took her head in his hands, holding it still as he gradually deepened the kiss. She pressed herself against him, wrapping her arms about his waist tightly. He gently grasped her shoulders and stepped away from her, his breathing ragged.

A lopsided grin crossed his face as she gave a mew of disappointment, her lambent eyes drenched with longing. His hands slid slowly down her slender arms, his palms tingling as her fine hairs stood on end. He took her hand and raised it to his lips.

"Selena, I love you. I adore you. I don't want ever to be without you. Will you live with me at Horton and raise a brood of impish children with me, in short, will you make me the happiest man alive and marry me?"

"Are you sure, Charlie?" she said softly.

"I have never been more sure of anything."

The uncertainty in her eyes was extinguished by a flicker of mischief.

"But I thought you wished me to marry Lord Carteret."

He growled and pulled her back into his arms. "I told you last night that I was ridiculous. I forbid you to ever again think of another man."

Her eyes widened. "But, Charlie, what about Papa, Gregory—"

He kissed her until she trembled deliciously.

"Selena."

"Mmm?"

"Are you going to give me an answer?"

"Yes," she murmured.

He resisted the urge to shake her.

"Yes, you are going to give me an answer, or yes you will marry me?"

She opened her eyes and smiled blissfully.

"Yes, I will marry you and live with you at Horton and help raise your rascally children."

He gave her one last, lingering kiss, and put his arm about her waist. As they turned to walk back to the house, he chuckled.

"It seems we have an audience."

A barouche, a curricle, and three horsemen had drawn up in front of the house. It appeared his family were eager for news. Selena's family had apparently found it necessary to come out and greet their visitors. By the time they reached the house, they had disappeared inside. They found them in the drawing room, glasses of sparkling champagne already in their hands.

Trinklow offered them a tray with two glasses of the beverage as they entered the room, murmuring, "Congratulations."

Lord Sheringham raised his glass. "May the light of friendship guide your paths together and the laughter of children grace the halls of your home."

"Here, here!" said Lord Bassington, putting one arm around his lady as she sniffled. "And to Adolphus and Caroline, who are going to present me with my seventh grandchild."

As the attention was deflected from them for a moment, Lord Sheringham approached. He kissed his daughter and took her hand. "I had thought you felt only childish adoration for Charles, but Carteret did not think so, and then I saw the way you looked at him when you came back from Eglingham, and I knew better." He turned to Charles. "I am glad you came to your senses, young man."

"What sense he has," Lord Carteret said dryly, coming up to him and shaking his hand.

As his intended was swept away by Judith and Victoria, Charles said, "I hope there are no hard feelings, old fellow. You never did make clear your feelings for Selena."

"None at all, Charles," he said. "I hoped that by concealing mine, I might bring yours to light."

Charles smiled wryly. "You certainly did that, and I thank you."

"I am glad you have found happiness," Lord Carteret said gently.

"Thank you. And I'm glad I have not found it at the expense of yours."

"Rest assured you have not. I esteem Lady Selena greatly, but have not yet met the lady who would complete me." A bittersweet smile crossed his lips. "I'm not sure she even exists."

ABOUT THE AUTHOR

I love history and the Regency period in particular. I grew up on a diet of Jane Austen, Charlotte and Emily Bronte, and Georgette Heyer. Later, I put my love of reading to good use and gained a 1st class honours degree in literature.

I have been a teacher and tennis coach. I now write traditional Regency romance novels. I like to think my characters, though flawed, are likeable, strong, and true to the period. Writing has always been my dream and I am fortunate enough to have been able to realise that dream.

I live by the sea in Plymouth, England, with my partner, Dave. I like reading, sailing, wine, getting up early to watch the sunrise in summer, and long quiet evenings by the wood burner in our cabin on the cliffs in Cornwall in winter.

ACKNOWLEDGMENTS

Thank you Melanie Underwood. It does not matter how many times I edit my latest opus, you always catch hundreds of things I have missed.

Thank you, Dave. Just thank you.

Printed in Great Britain
by Amazon